Woman's World

Woman's World

a novel

GRAHAM RAWLE

ATLANTIC BOOKS
LONDON

First published in hardback in Great Britain in 2005
by Atlantic Books, an imprint of Grove Atlantic Ltd

ISBN 1 84354 367 2

1 3 5 7 9 8 6 4 2

A CIP catalogue record for this book is available
from the British Library.

Printed by Bercker in Germany

Atlantic Books
An imprint of Grove Atlantic Ltd
Ormond House
26–27 Boswell Street
London WC1N 3JZ

For my Mum and Dad

Woman's World

No. 1

What

IS YOUR IDEA of a perfect home? Do you long for a gracious way of living that provides comfort without clutter and an atmosphere of charming elegance throughout the whole house?

I like things to be just so in my home. Mary, my housekeeper, never stops teasing me about it— though I'm sure that deep down she understands.

A richly coloured carpet that gathers the whole room together in a warm glow of friendliness. A cheerful kitchen warmed by a fire that never dreams of going out. *The* **brilliant shine on new furniture, in five lovely wipe-clean** ***DEEP GLOSS*** **colours** that invitingly wink the warmest of welcomes.

It's what any woman wants when she loves her HOME. And I'm really not much different from other women.

When, like today, my brother, *Roy*, is **'on vacation' (as the Americans call it),** my entire day is filled with womanly pursuits and the house is alive with feminine appeal. **NO** shirts tossed over the chair; no muddy brogues beside the bed; no ties strewn across the chest of drawers. Everything is clean and uncluttered with no trace of any dulling greyness to spoil the natural shine of the day.

One of the ways I fill my time at home is by designing my own blouses and accessories.

Sometimes I incorporate an idea or two from a magazine like *Woman's Own*. WOMAN'S OWN doesn't just give you the theory of a job—whether it's organising a supper party for Eddie Calvert, the world's greatest trumpet player, or refurbishing an old dress to look like a Paris model—it gets down to practice—to the details that really count. Mary's a wizard with a sewing machine so I often commandeer her for those easy-to-learn skills.

"I haven't got time for that sort of nonsense," she says. "I've enough to do around this house as it is." She's a real character! She's like some marvellous Tommy in the trenches—keeping everyone's pecker up —darning Richard Todd's socks and giving Bryan Forbes a drink from her water bottle.

In the MORNINGS, like most other women throughout the country, she sets about her daily chores, getting into the hidden crevices that ordinary cleaning methods fail to reach . She turns out cupboards and drawers, washes walls and woodwork, deals with flooring, cleans curtain tracks, and polishes painted surfaces. Then, when she's done that, she uses

Simply wonderful
BRILLO SOAP PADS
on the cooker, windows, sink, and draining board.
At the back of her mind . . . *cleanliness!*
And that's true of every woman.

Unlike our **CAT**, **COCOA** , who generally spends the morning asleep **in the airing cupboard**, I like to **help out where I can**. **H**ousekeeping is after all the most thrilling work in the world. **BUT** today, more than usual, I was in what **Mary calls one of my 'artistic' moods,** so that arranging a vase of artificial flowers on a what-not stand lasted the whole morning. **Yes,** my morning was very full indeed.

"I'm going upstairs for a little while. I shan't be long," I called out to Mary. She didn't answer. **Too busy, I suppose, Keeping** the **curtains** dust free by using the brush attachment on the vacuum cleaner.

To me, there is nothing more pleasant than to retire to my dressing-room for a feminine wallow among row upon delightful row of the *most elegant* evening clothes. Mary seems to resent the fact that I spend so many pleasant hours **there.** I try to explain to her that **the world's** best-dressed women sometimes have to change 15 times a day. As a woman, you must never look less than your loveliest.

THE FEMININE LOOK *appears, with becoming modesty, from the* wardrobe and the make-up box. To be a *Woman* today is no longer a disability but a challenge to be met with careful preparation and planning. I never leave charm to chance.

The make-up you put on first thing in the morning should, if it really suits your skin, last until midday, with possibly a quick touch-up during the course of the morning. When lunch time comes, you should clean your face with cleansing milk and renew your cosmetics right from scratch so that you are fresh and neat for the rest of the day. Everything depends upon using a hard-wearing and compatible foundation and a non-slip lipstick. **If you're anything like me,** you're head over heels in love with the new Cutex range.

NEXT

it's my old friend, mascara.

M*ascara* improves the fair splendour of

THE LOOK IN A WOMAN'S EYES

EYES ARE IRREPLACEABLE. Unlike our shoes, one pair must last us a lifetime. My eyes are like the windows of my house—nobody could ever guess what lies behind them.

Today's trends make no bones about it: FASHION WIGS **are the very latest thing.** Available in a variety of ready-to-wear styles they add luxurious fullness to limp or thin hair, curl to straight hair, length to short hair. I've worn one ever since my accident when I discovered how, with this **new crowning glory**, **I could make that** split-second change to a new personality. Bewitching, daring, **enchant-ing**, demure **—and all at the drop of a** headscarf.

The first **WIG** I ever had was one that ROY fashioned from the tail of our rocking horse. Mary was furious, but **I was delighted** with it and wore it for years. The one I have now is made of the finest Sarnel fibers that look and feel so much like real hair you'd mistake it for my own. And it can be washed, set or restyled **too.**

In the mirror my **natural loveliness** is quite breathtaking. But the mirror can never take the place of a real **PERSON.** I yearn to see my ***winsome*** charm reflected in the eyes of a real flesh-and-blood admirer. Not one admirer in particular, but any member of the public whose

HEAD might turn with an approving glance as I pass them on the street. **A dear old lady, refreshed by the sparkle of** my unassuming youth and beauty; **a teenage boy,** intoxicated by the heady perfume of ***feminine*** *Glamour*, compelled to lay down on a grass verge; or **an old man,** so entranced by my *sophisticated* yet **COQUETTISH** demeanour that he forgets his manners **and goes** to the toilet in his trousers.

that's the problem with being house-bound: if you never go out, you don't get *the* valuable appraisal of the casual onlooker. *Mary* occasionally makes some comment but it's usually to complain that my outfits are **TOO ALLURING.** Flaunting myself, as she calls it. "**THAT** dress is too short. Latest Paris fashion., **my foot.** Since when has it been fashionable to let your underskirt show?" She doesn't understand. ANYWAY, *how* **can a woman be TOO alluring?**

IT'S usually **Roy** who buys my clothes for me. Over the years he has learned which colours and styles flatter my figure and has become quite knowledgeable on the subject of *women*'s **FASHIONS**. *He's* fully *qualified* **to tell me when I'm looking my best, but it isn't always enough. A** *brother*'**S vote of confidence is all well and good, but** it's only natural for a Woman **to seek the approval of others.**

OCCASIONALLY, someone on the street will see me **through the window**, especially if I'm downstairs where it's easier for passers-by to look in. ***I often provoke a second glance.*** I might be at the window sill, polishing some ornaments with **LUX LIQUID** or be up on my FOLDING STEPS, giving the light bulbs a wipe with cotton wool soaked in milk. Each **viewer** receives **AN INTIMATE PORTRAIT OF A MODERN WOMAN** attending to her daily duties.

There were very few people on the street today though, and no one looking in my direction. I expect, like **millions of** families everywhere, **most people were** sitting down to a delicious Fray Bentos lunch. **The postman normally passes around this time, but there was no sign of him** either.

MRS. *Price* across the road had just finished red-bricking her doorstep and was **swinging** the doormat against the wall. Having **thundered** it into submission, she threw it down on the path and blew her nose. **She didn't know I was watching her** but she wouldn't have seen me anyway because

I was upstairs in my DRESSING room and not many people bother to LOOK UP. **THE** BLACK AND WHITE **dog** *from no.* **45** *was in the garden.* Dogs sometimes look up but they don't know what they're **looking at**.

THE **steady rumble of the traffic from the main road** gave way to the gay tinkling laughter of children's voices. I often see children from the local school on their way home for their lunch. A young boy and girl were racing against each other up Black Hill like a couple of Grand National favourites. I've seen them

many times before, the boy, perhaps only a year older, yet always strutting confidently ahead, **with** the filly **girl** struggling to catch up. Men are like that: they like to be masterful *and prove that women are the weaker sex.* My quarrel is with the convention itself but what can you do with a man who **barges in front** and insists on eating pork chops and suet pudding?

By the time they reached the **CORNER**, the girl **had fallen behind by several lengths** OF YARN. **Seeing this, the boy** dragged his heels just enough to let her gain some ground so that she wouldn't lose heart and give up the chase al**together**. **HE** took the usual short cut through VALENTINE'S garden— most of the **local CHILDREN** do, even though Mr. VALENTINE often comes out to shout at them.

Once inside the garden gate, THE BOY crouched down behind the fence. **It was a familiar old bread-and-butter routine—get her to** chase him, then hide somewhere and jump out at her. But, **to a hungry** boy, **bread and butter** *is* **the stuff of dreams.**

HE took a **PEEK-A-BOO-STYLE** peep over the fence TO CHECK HER PROGRESS, then, as she crossed the garden's threshold, lunged towards her, shoving her sideways with his outstretched arms. A boy's rough and tumble idea of fun. Jettisoned off course she seemed to go off at a tangent, her thin legs scissoring their way across the lawn before dumping her into the springy depths of Mr. VALENTINE'S rhododendron bushes. The boy ran off, laughing, leaving her squirming among the foliage. There was no sign of Mr. VALENTINE, but, since he is rumoured locally to be foreign, the girl was doubtless anxious not to get caught alone in his garden. As she scrambled to her feet her cardigan caught on something, so she yanked it free. With her hair in a mess and her dress having taken on a number of those stubborn stains that defy ordinary cleaning, she set off again in pursuit. She called the boy's NAME, telling him to wait for her, but he was long gone and had already chosen his next ambush position: the tree outside their Home. HE crouched on the big first branch, lying in wait for her to pass underneath. The tree's EASY- CLIMB branches make it a particular favourite with boys in the neighbourhood, local ROBIN HOODs, jumping down on to the Sheriff of Nottingham's men.

IT'S hard to say exactly how events unfolded. These things happen so quickly. At least, that's what they always say in the magazines.

- **"I'm afraid I didn't get a good look at him, officer. It all happened so quickly."**
- Nurse Goodall looked down to see that she was still holding her sandwich. It had all happened so quickly.
- **Marion's head was spinning in a whirlwind of confusion; everything had happened so quickly.**

SO, you see, there's no reason why I should be expected to remember.

A **fferton Road** doesn't normally get much traffic. Although it feeds off the main road, because it's a dead end only a handful of cars drive down it. **The van must have been coming down BLACK Hill and turning right INTO Afferton. It was a HōVIS Van.** *Hovis*— **give us this day our daily bread.** Perhaps the reason it was going **so fast** was because it was trying to cut quickly across a gap in the oncoming traffic, anxious to deliver **the whole-taste goodness of a freshly baked loaf** to someone further down the street. (We never have our **BREAD** delivered. Mary gets ours from the **cake** shop.)

How old should a child be before starting to learn road safety? **No child is ever too young**

to learn. I have seen some gaily coloured, well-illustrated pamphlets on road safety rules for little boys and girls that say an older brother or sister can help to teach the correct way to cross the road by pointing out **HIS or HER** own good example.

YES, YOUNG MAN, I'M TALKING ABOUT YOU.

Or is it possible that **the driver** was in the wrong?"

The experienced motorist takes necessary precautions whenever the road curves away to left or right. **Lorry drivers** are often thought to have the edge on other motorists because from their high cabs they can see over hedges at bends. **THE Hovis** driver must have **been mad not to make use of this advantage.** Perhaps he *was* a little bit mad.

GOING round the bend has a special meaning for the motorist. He is certainly out of his senses if he underestimates the potential danger each time he drives his car round a bend in the road.

Even a blind man could see he was

driving much too fast, **and a modern** bread van **is only a cup of tea slower than a car.**

The front of the van HIT the GIRL side-on, hammering her head hard on to the road. Her legs seemed to float up and the vehicle caught her again and pushed her along, folding her body into the TARMAC. By the time the VAN managed to stop the GIRL was lying on her back, but she didn't look right at all. Her LEFT leg was bent under her so that she was lying on it, and her foot was up by her face but with THE toes pointing the wrong way. Her HEAD had gone flat at the back like a burst football.

IT was the first time I'd seen anyone get run over. It wasn't what I thought it was going to be at all. Mary once saw a man get hit by a car on Cooper's Road. She said he went right up in the air and BOTH HIS SHOES landed in the tree outside the post office. For some reason, I always imagined they found them with their laces tied together. I don't know what made me think that; it made no sense.

THE GIRL still had her shiny red SandalS ON, firmly buckled. Perhaps it wasn't as bad as it looked.

Somebody came out of Mrs. PRICE's house, but it wasn't Mrs. Price. It did look like her but this was a much younger woman, her daughter possibly. She stood some distance away, rooted to the spot like a roast potato stuck to the pan. She put her hand to her mouth and began to shake uncontrollably before running back into the house. A MAN got out of the passenger side of the van and leaned on the fence looking winded and shaky, as if he'd been running in a RACE himself. He began to wander off down the lane, using the fence to steady himself.

THE BOY in the tree knew he was in serious TROUBLE. The *Highway Code* clearly states that he should have been holding her hand.

AFTER a minute or two, people began to appear. They seemed to come from nowhere, ***JUST LIKE IN THE FILMS!*** Extras showing up to express general concern.

" *PEAS AND CARROTS, PEAS AND CARROTS.*"

Actually, nobody said anything much. They just wanted to get a good look, yet nobody ventured near ENOUGH to see properly. It was as if she had been cordoned off by some invisible barrier. So instead, they winced and folded THEIR arms tight across their chests. Some of them I knew. Poor Miss Vine with her sad, scribbly face. And Mr. Ingram *from* the community CENTRE, peering over someone's shoulder, then, in what I took to be an unrelated gesture, poking his fingers deep into the seat of his trousers to alleviate some haemorrhoid-related discomfort.

THE van driver had fetched a blanket from somewhere and was telling EVERYONE it wasn't his fault—that the girl had just run straight out in front of him. He draped the blanket over her, as if to cover up what he had done.

"She'll be all right," he was saying. "I'm sure she'll be all right."

Nobody believed him. How could she be all right?

I once read about A WOMAN who had had asthma since she was three who cured it by eating twelve sticks of blackboard chalk a day. But this was different.

Somebody should have gone over to her, put a kind and reassuring hand on her forehead, cradled her limp body— it's what any child wants, whether they're AWAKE or not.

I knew what you were supposed to do but that was her MOTHER'S job. Anyway, if you get too involved in these things you end up going in the ambulance. I didn't want to go in the AMBULANCE.

Our little **ROBIN HOOD** continued to watch from the tree, undetected, and as yet unblamed

by the gathered throng. **He sat with his slim hands knotted between his knees, his boyish** complexion pale and sickly, like ***WALL'S ICE CREAM***. **Unlike the others, he had kept his distance because** he didn't **WANT TO** see the entire programme. He wished now he hadn't seen any of it. For him, **THE BLANKET** had come too late, and now the PIN-SHARP PICTURE would not leave him. **HE** stared down at the pavement below, but it was no use. His ice-cream face melted.

"What are you doing up there?"

"What ?"

"What are you doing up there?" It was Mary, calling from downstairs.

"Oh, nothing. I was just looking out of the window."

"Well get down here. Lunch is on the table."

Actually, Mary doesn't say 'lunch', she says 'dinner'. I've tried telling her. Dinner's what **we have in** the evening. And tea —what Mary calls 'dinner'— **is a refreshing afternoon** pick-me-up served in a delicate china cup and saucer. But for all the good it does, I might as well be reciting the alphabet.

MARY may not be familiar with all the nuances of Refinement, but she takes her housekeeping very seriously, and lunch is at one o'clock on the dot.

SHE SERVES FINE MEALS

like cold meat with Batchelors wonderful baked beans, salad, fruit, a simple meal—'but simply scrumptious!'

Well, I'm afraid that delicious Batchelors meal was just going to have to wait till I finished dressing. All the fuss and commotion out on the street had put me behind in my routine. LUNCHTIME already, and there I was, still in my slip.

NOW! What to wear?

I fancied something really romantic and "floaty" and was on the verge of settling into a filmy chiffon creation when I found a striking peacock-blue dress with a motif embroidered in white beads on the bodice and skirt. It looked lovely—something I could feel both glamorous and *comfortable* in.

I had scarcely finished DRESSING before

there was a ring at the front door, and a knock, authoritative and loud.

"The POST!" I sang out. "Perhaps there's something for me."

At one time, when the postman delivered letters, he put them through the letter box, but nowadays, he gives a smart rat-tat on the knocker, hoping, I expect, to glance at the warm, tender beauty of my natural complexion. PostMEN FIND FRAGRANT SKIN SO ALLURING! THAT'S WHY I BATHE WITH THIS LOVELY PERFUMED SOAP.

Mary prefers to be the one to answer the door to callers, but she must have stepped out into the back garden for a moment, so I decided to deal with it myself. With a graceful flourish, I opened the door to reveal a POSTMAN who stood on the threshold with a dominant nose on his face and, dare I say it, Postman's knock on his mind.

my eyes wandered past him and OUT on to the road. I half expected to see the *girl* still lying there, but in the time it had taken me to complete my toilette the ambulance had been and gone, REMOVING ALL TRACE OF the accident. The Hovis VAN had driven off too. Mrs. Price was back out in her garden, staring across. She always has to know business. I'd a good mind to stare back at her in defiance, but The Postman was vying for my attention.

"A parcel for the gentleman of the house," he announced, eyeing my neat but generously proportioned figure with sharp, BLACKCURRANT eyes.

"My Brother, Roy, isn't here. He's in the Himalayas, daring to pit human courage and skill against Nature." I wasn't quite sure why I'd said it; it wasn't strictly true.

The POSTman's goggling eyes were the deep blue of two enamel pans in the sink, and in his eyes there was frank admiration, cleverly masked by a keen look of indifference.

He leaned down and picked up a parcel from his Postbag. "I'll need you to sign for it," he said, holding out a fountain pen. "But first give me your name."

We continued to stand and stare at each other, until he said again: "What's your name?"

"If you want to know you can guess," I retorted playfully.

"Quite the little spitfire, aren't you?" The

a m u s e
m e n t
in his
tone stung
like
wasps on a

baby's bottom. I made an unconscious, protective movement as if to ward them off. "If you must know, it's a name that symbolises Larger than Life loveliness that has inflamed the dreams of many men. My middle name is Glamour!"

"Thank you," he said, with a tinge of sarcasm, "that is very helpful. Now, have you anything you can show me in order to prove your identity?"

I was momentarily distracted by Cocoa brushing against my legs and had to shoo him back into the house.

"Prove my identity? Well, not actually on my person. Anyway, it's hardly necessary," I explained. "This is my house; I live here with my housekeeper."

"I have never seen you before. How long have you been here? Has Mr. Little moved?"

"No."

Do you live in the basement flat here?

I was being interrogated. By a **Postman**!

"No. Nobody lives in the basement. There isn't a basement."

I caught him looking intently at me, as if weighing me up in his own mind.

JUST then, MARY appeared. She must have HEARD our voices FROM the garden.

"What's the trouble?" she said stiffly, squaring up to the POST man. "Who is it you want?"

I took a step back. WATCHING the postman closely, I saw that he wore a look of astonishment, as if he'd been struck by lightning. Already his face was flushed and the skin on his nose peeling. She almost snatched the Parcel from him. "I'll take that, thank you." Without a word, he turned and set off down the path. It seemed he didn't need a signature after all.

MARY banged the door shut behind her and turned to me with A REAL COAL FIRE burning in her eyes.

"What do you think you're doing? You agreed, not to open the door to strangers."

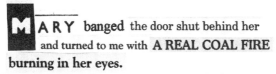

The words slammed in the teeth of my NERVOUS smile.

"What did you say to him?"

"Nothing of importance." It was Sheer Innocence by Lenthric.

"How much does he know about you?"

"Nothing. I've told you."

"I want your word about this," she said, her stiff finger pinning me like a cheap brooch.

"I don't want any more trouble from you. Do you understand?"

AFTER lunch I took the Parcel upstairs to my Dressing room. It was addressed to Roy but I sensed there might be something in it for me. With my heart jumping like a little boy in a sack race, I cut into the wrapping with a stainless-steel knife.

I gave a little amazed gasp when I saw what was inside. A pair of raucous red Boulevard court shoes with daintily styled Baby Doll Toes and mid-way 2¼-in. heels for up-to-the-minute elegance. "Ooh, lovely," I thought. I hadn't had shoes so vibrant and so shiny since I was a girl.

ROY must have ordered them in Secret. without my knowledge, wanting to give me a surprise present that would gladden my heart. Something I could be vain about. A Gift to treasure throughout the year. And what a remarkably clever brother to have ORDERED the correct size. It's NORMally so unlike a man to know about such things.

●

TWO

ON WEDNESDAYS and FRIDAYS Mary toddles off to Milford Grammar where she works part-time serving school dinners. *MORE DELICIOUS MEALS TO CONJURE OUT OF THIN AIR, BUT* MARY *TAKES IT IN HER STRIDE.*

I could hear her upstairs busying herself with the HOOVER before it was time to leave. There are always a hundred and one jobs to do in any busy household and, like **a contestant on one of television's popular game shows**, MARY accomplishes what she can in the given time. I generally feel it's better if there's just one **woman** wearing the apron. This morning, though, I'd felt a sudden urge to dust the pelmets, **SO** I got the little stepladder from under the stairs and stood it in front of the window.

We'd had a minor altercation earlier in the

WEEK, which I suppose was largely my fault. A slight error of judgement on my part as to the effectiveness of Dylon cold water fabric dyes on materials other than those recommended on the label. I'd first had a go at my old *Diana* SLING BACKS, hoping to GIVE THEM A NEW LEASE OF LIFE, but even after two coats of cardinal red, applied with a soft brush, no change in hue was apparent. I might have had more success had the SHOES been a light colour to begin with: a dark brown to bright red transformation is a tall order for any colouring agent.

There was still a lot of **dye** left over – ONE TIN MAKES A FULL GALLON – and I'd recently been impressed with a magazine feature on the auburn-haired beauty, Rhonda Fleming. As with the **SHOES**, the **DYE** had not really taken, and despite an hour-long soak in the KITCHEN *Sink*, earlier in the week, I was disappointed to find that I was still a brunette. **The cleaning power of Vim** and a vigorous elbow had **the sink spick and span** before MARY got the chance to see it.

Mary's PIFCO HAIRDRYER had accelerated the drying time, but it seems the wig's fabric lining, the only part to have changed colour, must still HAVE BEEN a touch damp when I put it back on. So it's no wonder that when I was reclining on my daybed (which is actually THE SAME AS MY night bed) some of the colour had soaked into the pillow where I had laid my head.

I turned the pillow over, of course, in the hope of it remaining undiscovered, but Mary is like a bloodhound when it comes to sniffing out stains, and She'd uncovered the unfortunate blemish before I'd had a chance to LET NEW DAZ WORK ITS BIOLOGICAL MAGIC.

She'd been very cross indeed and said that the pillow case was permanently ruined, and that I had no more sense than a monkey in a zoo. Which is not really fair, although monkeys are very intelli-gent and can peel bananas with their feet.

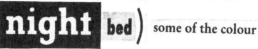

SO of course I'd BEEN anxious to make amends, helping out with the

29th

household chores, and saw the PELMET in the front room as the ideal opportunity to prove my self.

LIKE a spring lamb taking its first confident steps, with a hop and two skips *I was on top of the world*, armed with my feather duster, looking down on all creation. **Dusting.** As any housewife will tell you, the **art** of dusting is to remove the particles of dust completely, and not simply to disturb them and leave them to settle elsewhere. All dusting should therefore be done methodically, working from top to the bottom of the area being dusted. **I knew this, of course, but** it was difficult to concentrate on the job at hand, being all too aware that anyone passing by on the street would probably catch sight of my ***LEGS*** perfectly framed in the **window**. I couldn't be sure, with my head right up against the ceiling, but I judged I was at about the right height **to create the image of a stylish young woman, as seen** from the waist down, LIKE

an advert for a **SKIRT** in a MAIL ORDER catalogue.

IN stretching to reach the far end of the Pelmet, I found I was all of a totter and had to RAISE ONE LEG to balance myself. My carefully pointed toe and a gently rising hemline emphasised how *tone deeper* stocking seams fine down the shape of your legs, and the Boulevard court shoe's slender 2¼ in. heel flatters the ankle to a new slimness.

Just then, Mary came in. She had her hat and coat on and was in a **FRUMP** as usual.

"What are you doing?"

"Doing? I'm dusting, of course, like I always do."

"It's the first I've heard of it. Come away from the window."

"It's all right. I've finished now," I said, stepping down carefully. "I was just doing the Pelmets."

"We haven't got any pelmets."

"Oh. Haven't we?" I looked up at where I'd been dusting. "That's a shame. A well-designed and neatly made pelmet adds greatly to the appearance of a window."

"Does it really?" she said FLAtly. Her sarcastic tone is not one of her most attractive features.

She was fiddling with something in her handbag. "Right, I'm off up to the School. Don't forget you've got your interview at TWO. You'd better get yourself ready."

She snapped her bag shut.
"Ready? I am ready." I'd been up since dawn trying on outfits.
"Don't talk so daft," she said, with the familiarity born of years of faithful service.
"You're not going like that. Dressed like a common trollop. Your blue suit's hanging up in the bathroom. And don't forget to polish your shoes."
"They don't need polishing, they're new."
I instantly regretted having mentioned them, and went and stood behind the SETTEE, hoping she wouldn't notice.
"Where did they come from?" she said, leaning in to get a better look.
"The POSTMAN brought them yesterday."
"Oh, so that's what the parcel was. They're not from my CATALOGUE, I hope."
"I really couldn't say." I was plumping a cushion.
"Because if they are, they can go straight back. I've told you before about ordering stuff. You can't expect me to be paying for your 'DRESSING UP' clothes."
"Nobody asked you to pay for them, MARY."
She gave me a look. It always irks her when I call her Mary, though why it should, I don't know. It is her name.
"So, where's the money coming from?" she said.
Life being a hard economic business, money for the majority of us is an important

consideration, and the whole approach to money and the management of the household finances needs careful forethought. This time, however, the **solution was** as SIMPLE AS A-B-C.

"My new job," I said. "We'll be able to afford lovely things when I'm working."

"Well, you haven't got it yet." she warned. "You'd better get upstairs and take that muck off your **FACE**: make yourself look presentable. And when you get home, you can do the potatoes. I'll be back about five."

She looked at her watch and went out.

IT can be hurtful when a person makes an unkind personal remark. No woman wants to be thought of as looking like a common trollop. At times, Mary can be quite **CRUEL**. Part of the problem, I think, is that she misses ***Roy***. She always gets a bit tetchy when he's away for too long. I thought I looked lovely and just to spite her, decided I wasn't going to wear my **boring** blue two- piece suit at all. **Deep in her heart every woman knows** the importance of choosing the right outfit for the occasion, and I had chosen mine. Perhaps my neckline could have been considered more suitable for evening wear, and perhaps my **DRESS** was just a fraction shorter than recommended by the latest fashion guidelines, but I felt determined to present myself as an intelligent woman who is quite capable of doing a full-time job without making a sacrifice to glamour. Besides, I'd exhausted all the possibilities and I WAS CONVINCED this was the perfect ensemble to head me down the road to a successful career.

●

3

ONE HOUR

and several changes of outfit later, I was on my way to WHITE's LAUNDRY ON CROSS Street for the job interview. A fully fledged young woman going out to face what I was sure would be a happy world.

IN the end I had chosen a powder blue, STUD-FASTENED SKIRT by Alexon, pencil-slim for figure flattery, and fully lined with rayon taffeta—which, I decided, set off my new shoes more perfectly than the dress I had been wearing earlier. I teamed this with a matching BLOUSE with Peter Pan collar, three-quarter-length sleeves and button-through back. It wouldn't have been MARY's *First choice* for THE occasion, but I felt it lent me an air of sophistication. To complete the outfit, I wore my red pixie jacket and topped it off with my favourite handbag and satin evening gloves, BLACK and SHINY against the RED like raven's wings holding secrets to the past. How vital I looked. I could already hear Mr. White's voice in my head. "That cherry-coloured coat with the hood effect certainly makes you look terrific. Sit down while I tell you about the job."

I HAD taken special care with my make-up. My lips were velvety roses scattered profusely on the white satin background of my face, and my eyes were deep, dark pools of mystery. To ensure that all matters of feminine hygiene had been properly addressed, I had pouffed my naturally shining and glorious hair with some of Mary's

Evening in Paris.

It felt strange to leave the house LOOKING SO PERFECTLY COIFFURED IN the *daytime*. But this was an important interview and I was determined it should be a rip-roaring success. I wanted that job—as much for Mary as for myself. I knew how happy she'd be if I were to get it. But I aimed to do it my own way, *combining professional competence with* my *own particular brand of feminine charm.*

I was nervous—yes, even apprehensive—but there was a giddy knot in my stomach and *my* heart was skipping madly to the beat of Jack Costanzo's *Cha Cha Bongo.* It was such a thrill just to be outdoors, an ordinary woman going about her daily business, that I felt at any moment I might have to clutch at a lamp-post to save my self from succumbing to a dizzy sensation. My head was held high, but I found it difficult not to keep glancing down at my NEW SHOES as they confidently conveyed me to what I hoped would soon be my place of employment. All I had to remember, at the interview, was to create an impression, as suggested by *Woman's Realm*, of calm, ruthless efficiency and eagerness to devote my **DELIVERY**- driving skills single-mindedly to the interests of WHITE's LAUNDRY. Then I was sure the job would be mine.

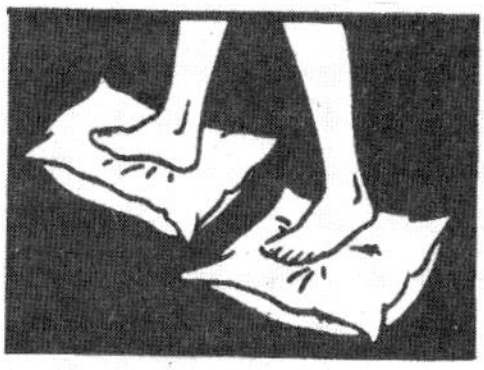

All the way there, I felt the heady excitement that SPRINGS from being young and confident and beautifully dressed. There was a lightness in my step as if I were

Walking on Pillows.

I felt everyone's eyes were upon me, and many of them were. Several people turned to stare, and outside the chip shop, a man looked at me with an interest that had nothing to do with **bongo music**. From across the street, a group of older children laughed and threw stones. I smiled good-naturedly. Their playful taunts could never shake my poise. One look from me, and they melt like ***Maltesers*** on the hearth.

THE HOUSES on the other side of the main road do not have the same **homely charm** as the ones on our street. Most of them have been turned into **FLATS.** Flat-dwellers who have no garden can sometimes contrive a miniature clothes line outside the window, or even on the roof, though this is apt to be a sooty eyesore.

20 YEARS ago, all those four-storeyed houses would have been lived in by proud families, keen to maintain the look of their HOME with DULUX GLOSS and pretty window boxes. Now a trail of rubbish litters the broken flights of steps leading to scabby pillars and groups of dirty milk bottles, their occupants oblivious to the niceties of HOME DECOR.

An old woman in a pinafore stared out from an upstairs window. She wore a look of defeat, as if a golden nugget or a great pearl had fallen into her hand and slipped through her thin fingers to the FAMILY LIVING downstairs, like the lost years falling silently away. She observed *me* with SEMI-DETACHED interest, faintly amused at how my unspoiled natural beauty contrasted delightfully with the old gas cooker that had been used to plug a hole in her garden hedge.

ON the other side of the common, the hard slate edges of the BUTTON factory were softened by a clinging FOG. It was not the prettiest of days. The colourless clouds above the broken chimney-pots and television aerials misted the air with a drizzle of cold rain, so that by the time I reached WHITE's LAUNDRY I was wetter than A SAILOR'S bath mat and bitterly regretting not having carried an umbrella.

The WOMAN at the reception desk was middle-aged AND, LIKE SO MANY OTHER WOMEN OF ADVANCING YEARS, HAD FAILED TO MAKE THE BEST OF HER APPEARANCE. Her fine brown hair was dragged into a slide and flopping to her shoulders. She hadn't chosen the style—it just 'happened' after a succession of mistakes, then two years of 'letting it go' She wore not a scrap of make-up, and her dress looked **cheap** and **ITCHY** like a dog's blanket. ***SHE*** had paired this with a *shape-less* beige cardigan buttoned tight across her burgeoning frontage. I would have suggested **a glowing raspberry red, slub-woven dress and jacket with pure silk shantung printed bodice** to complement her naturally rosy cheeks. But nobody asked **ME**.

There was a sign on her desk: 'Miss P. Harrow, Secretary to Mr. White'. The lettering was done in a not-quite-professional hand that suggested MISS Harrow might have painted it herself at **home**.

"Good morning," I began, my voice *a light and airy soufflé, straight from the oven.* "I've come about the vacancy."
She wore a look of puzzled surprise, as if I had told her I had come to feed the horses.
"The DELIVERY man job?" she said.
"Well, I was thinking more 'DELIVERY **WOMAN**'," I laughed.

"Oh, well. Yes, of course," she said, admiring my gloves discreetly. "What's your name?"

"NORMA. MISS Norma *Fontaine*."

In fact, my real name is **LITTLE**, but by the time I'd got myself all dressed up and ready to go, I'd convinced myself that Norma *Fontaine* was perhaps a better candidate for a professional career than NORMA LITTLE. It's a name I've always liked, *Fontaine*, ever since I saw Joan Fontaine in *September Affair*.

PROFESSIONAL, elegant and well-heeled. 'Little' tends to suggest a lack of ambition and diminished abilities.

"I don't have you down, Miss *Fontaine*," she said, wiping her nose on A TINY BALL of KLEENEX TISSUE. "Are you sure it's for the driving job? Did you send us a JOB APPLICATION?"

It was, in fact, *Roy* who had sent the letter, signing *his* name AT THE BOTTOM instead of mine, and there arose the confusion.

It was down to me to explain.

"Not exactly. You see, I'd heard that Mr. White was interviewing for the post of DELIVERY DRIVER today and thought I'd just take pot luck. Isn't there any way Mr. WHITE could squeeze me in somewhere?"

I gave her the lower-lip pout *I'd been practising*.

"Well, I suppose so, as long as you don't mind waiting. He's got some other people to see first. MOSTLY MEN, of course." She made some alteration to her LIST. "As a matter of fact, you're the only woman to apply."

"I hope this

Mr. WHITE

is broad-minded enough to appreciate the value of women in the workplace," I said.

"Yes, of course," she said. "He's an excellent employer."

I raised my eyebrows. "I hope he is. It is good when a man knows how to work with a woman who knows how to work with him. I expect, as his secretary, you have learned to anticipate his needs, but it's important to remember that men like being looked after— and loathe being fussed. Men will never discuss a quest-ion such as toilet tissue . . . yet they expect you to know exactly how they feel about it! All they want really is a firm, clean-handling toilet tissue they can use with confidence."

I had strayed off the point slightly.

"Yes, well, I wouldn't know about that," said MISS Harrow, swiftly changing the subject. "So you've got a DRIVING LICENCE and everything?"

"I'm afraid I haven't brought it with me," I said, almost helplessly. "Do I seem a dread-ful peagoose? I daresay I am!"

Miss Harrow made no comment.

"It's probably in the dresser at home. I'm sure I've seen it recently," I explained. "But there was really no point in my bringing it be-cause it's actually in my brother's name, though, since he's the one who taught me to drive, it amounts to the same thing. We sort of share it."

MISS Harrow seemed confused. She looked down at my clasped hands again. Is it poor etiquette to wear evening gloves during the day? If so, I was not aware of it.

"I *can* drive, you know. With remarkable aplomb, and just as well as ANY MAN. So I'm not sure having a licence is really so important. After all, it's just a piece of paper, isn't it? Like a page from a popular novel or the label off a soup tin."

"Well. I'll let Mr. White know," she said, looking a bit doubtful. "If you'd just like to wait."

She pointed towards the **waiting room** with her pen as she reached for the telephone.

The room was cold and dreary and lacked a feminine touch. I would have chosen to reflect its character in exquisite lacy curtains and satiny, flowered cotton draperies, bordered with pink ball fringe and tiny green tassels, then perhaps filled the cupboard with interesting ceramic pieces from Portugal. Instead, ***the cupboard was bare*** and a piece of grubby netting had been tacked to the window frame with drawing pins. Dining chairs lined the walls as if they were waiting for something to happen in the middle of the room. I sensed a long wait. I took off my scarf and my ***RED PIXIE*** jacket and hung them on the coat stand to dry before choosing a seat that gave me a good view of **MR. WHITE'S DOOR.**

Above it, fixed to the wall, was **a bare light bulb**

No. 44

PAINTED GREEN. MISS Harrow had not mentioned it, but I assumed that this was Mr. White's way of letting those that were waiting know WHEN he was ready to see them. They had a similar arrange ment at the clinic, so I knew the **Drill.** When the green light goes on, the doctor is ready to see you about your verruca or the boil on your neck. Until then, **you're supposed to** just wait patiently with the others, remembering whose turn it is to go next. There was no one else to see Mr. White, but I kept one eye on **THE LIGHT,** determined not to miss my cue.

SMOOTHING down my skirt, I felt a sudden chill. The PARAFFIN HEATER in the corner did little to dispel the damp. Its fumes hung in the air like wet washing. Over by the window, a grey **Filing Cabinet** stood on a square of ONCE-CHEERFUL carpet. I noted with interest that on top of it, next to a dying pot plant, was A PIECE OF CHEESE the size of a **boxing glove.**

BEing alone in the room gave me the perfect

opportunity to carry out a few running repairs to my ONCE carefully applied **MAKE-UP**.

IN reapplying my lipstick, I must have over-gilded the lily slightly because some of my ***SANGUINE SMILE*** somehow transferred itself to my **GLOVE** and I had the Charles Dickens of A JOB to get it off before it stained my blouse or my skirt.

I WAS just pressing my lips with a Kleenex when I was joined by a man **in a checked sports jacket**, who fussed and faffed a bit before finding a seat by the window. **HIS HEAD** was **PINK** and round like a balloon, and he had been clocking up BIRTHDAYS willy-nilly. He must have been nearly sixty. **IF** this was my only competitor, surely **THE JOB** was mine. Elderly people don't have the quickness of reaction, nor the keenness of faculties that younger people like me possess, and therefore DELIVERY driving by these people is much more dangerous. At this age, a large animal on wheels with a handlebar to push is a great joy and a much safer pastime.

IT began to dawn on me that this old-timer looked remarkably like Michael Miles from the popular quiz TAKE YOUR PICK.

No. 46

The resemblance made me wonder if he was after the key to my success. I was familiar with the routine from the television show. Contestants hold a key to one of the thirteen boxes, each of which contains a secret prize. And before they can say 'Open the box', the Miles-barrage starts. "I'll give you four pounds for that key, five, six, seven. Look, there might be a boiled egg in that box. I'll give you eight pounds, nine, ten." This technique of planned persuasion works on television, but here the bargaining was futile. I was determined to resist him. No thank you, Michael. I'll open the box.

THE OLD CROCK was staring unseeingly at a book about cars. Could he be blind? I wondered. Surely, that would narrow his chances.
"Have you noticed that quite a number of motor-car fronts look almost lifelike?" he said suddenly.
I straightened my back, slipping the Lipstick *kiss* into my handbag. "No, not really."
A moment later I was indignant to find that he was beside me with his car book.
"I say," he said, "excuse me."
I averted my face, tingling with annoyance.
"Please go away."
The sharpness of my words pierced his balloon. Deflated, he went back to his **chair**.

There *was* STILL

no hint of a GREEN light. I wondered if perhaps the bulb was no longer working, owing to some minor electrical fault, and if Mr. White was unaware that anyone was waiting outside. Seizing the moment, I leapt to my feet and made my way across the room to Mr. White's office, leaving my despondent opponent reeling in the wake of my fortitude. I gave a sharp knock on the door but did not WAIT FOR an answer.

My prospective employer was sitting at his desk. His attention was concentrated on me from the moment I opened the door. He was not disconcertingly handsome, nor did he have dark, crisp hair and piercing blue eyes. Though, despite that, I must admit that he had a special appeal. Here was a man of immense power who looked as though he could make kingdoms totter with nothing more than a propelling pencil and a pointy grey beard.

I paused in the doorway. I wanted him to see me just once in all my glory, with my soft blue SKIRT that does gratifying things to my eyes. My hair, thanks to the soaking that it had had, curled satisfyingly round my face in elegant waves. It really is a pity that I can't go around with my hair always slightly damp.

I was as nervous as an eighteen-month-old baby meeting Marlon Brando for the first time, but I was determined not to show it. I strode confidently into the room and sat down in the chair opposite him.

"I had to come at once or not at all. I've a frightfully busy day ahead."

"Just a moment, madam," he said. "I think there's been some mistake."

"My name is Miss *Norma Fontaine.* That's *Fontaine* with an 'e', like Joan."

"Joan?"

"Yes."

"Well, Miss *Fontaine*, I'm afraid I can't see you now. Didn't Miss HARROW tell you that you would have to wait? I'm expecting someone at two o'clock."

"Ah, would that be Mr. **Little?** I understand he is unable to keep his appointment."

"Is he?"

"Yes. So I wondered if you'd like to interview me instead."

"You wish to apply for the job?"

I nodded.

"No, I'm terribly sorry," he said with a dismissive snort. "The position advertised was for a DELIVERY MAN. I'm not looking for a **WOMAN**."

I was feeling suddenly breathless.

"Look, Mr. White, let's get a few things straight. I don't see why A *Woman* shouldn't be considered for this position. The archaic notion that driving is a man's job simply does not wash the dishes these days. And those hackneyed JOKES about women drivers being feather-brained and incompetent are as tired as old toast. What about Mrs. Kim Petre, winner of the Monaco Grand Prix and little Gwenda Stewart who has smashed countless championship records in her Lotus? Are either of them men? No, Mr. WHITE, they are women. And very fine drivers they are too. But men will always find an excuse not to employ them FOR DELIVERY WORK."

Mr. WHITE took off his glasses. "The problem isn't with your being a Woman, MISS Fontaine, it's with your not having a valid driving licence. It is one of the necessary qualifications for the job, and it's against the law to operate a motor vehicle without one." He made a gesture to indicate that his hands were tied. Typical male short-sightedness. Did anyone ask to see Gwenda Stewart's LICENCE as she crossed the finishing line at Brands Hatch?

"Just because a woman doesn't have A SAUCEPAN, it doesn't mean she can't cook, Mr. White. The real proof is in the pudding. And I think you'll find that eighty per cent of all motor accidents are caused by men. Or perhaps it's 100% —I'm afraid I don't have the exact figures to hand. Men have a much more slapdash approach to driving. You've only got to look at how meticulously a woman applies her lipstick to see how much care she's likely to take when she's BEHIND THE WHEEL."

MR. White shook his head, as if not knowing quite what to say. He put his elbows on the desk and made a church steeple with his fingers. The gesture was wasted on me because I'm not a religious person.

"Tell me," he said curiously, "with no driving licence, and, therefore, I assume no previous experience, what makes you think you'd be suitable for this job?"

"My dream is to be gainfully employed in a worthwhile career without having to surrender any of my innate womanliness. LIKE Mrs. Gwenda Stewart. A first-class driver who is not afraid to show her *femininity*. Last winter she cried real tears when she was runner-up in the Monte Carlo Rally."

Mr. White looked faintly taken aback. Suddenly, I realised that I was betraying my innermost thoughts to a man whom I scarcely knew. I laughed lightly. "I'm being awfully silly. I'm inclined to dramatise life, I'm afraid."

He leaned back in his chair AS IF TO distance himself from me. He was still shaking his head. "This is a delivery DRIVER'S job. It isn't about SPEED and RACING," he said.

"OH, I quite agree," I chimed. "I'm all too aware of road safety and the dangers of reckless driving. In fact, as a young girl I was knocked down by a motor vehicle driven by a man heedless to these dangers. My injuries were very serious. If it hadn't been for MY BROTHER, I wouldn't be here today. I still bear the scars, but don't ask me to show them to you, Mr. WHITE, because they are emotional scars which go a little deeper than ***SKIN DEEP***."

An impatient monosyllable burst from him. I decided to plough on regardless, determined to state my views on the subject.

"It seems to me that the very first thing required is the rigid enforcement of the speed limit, which at present is ignored by a very large percentage of motorists. Here's a bright idea I had a few weeks ago. As an amateur inventor, I Would be happy to make a loud-sounding siren to fit to **EVERY** delivery van which would operate once the vehicle exceeded a speed of 30 m.p.h."

"I couldn't possibly ask you to do a thing like that."

"You didn't ask me. I suggested it myself."

"I couldn't allow you to."

"Please, I'd like to help. I'd much rather do something constructive like this than potter about at HOME."

"No. We don't want sirens on our VANS. It's a ridiculous idea." The whole idea seemed to irritate him, so I decided to let it drop. I wondered how I had fared otherwise.

"Well, Mr. White, do I qualify?" I said, with a searching look in my eyes.

"Well, NO, MISS *Fontaine*. Frankly, you don't." He slid the letters of application into a file and closed it. ROY's, I noticed, was

On top.

"Why ever not?" I said, my voice faltering like a newborn foal.

"Quite apart from the question of the driving licence, there's a great deal of lifting involved in the job. Loading and unloading LAUNDRY ***BAGS*** of considerable weight. It would be too physically demanding for *a* *Woman*."

"I may appear as some frail and delicate flower **to you**, Mr. White, but I assure you I am stronger than I look."

I decided A PRACTICAL DEMONSTRATION

was called for.

"How much do you weigh, Mr. White?"

"Weigh? What's that got to do with it?"

"Would you stand up for a moment, please?"

"Stand up?"

"Yes, just STAND UP."

When he pulled himself up into a standing position, his legs, although strong and sturdy, looked slightly bowed. His face wore the quizzical look of a monkey with a LEMON SQUEEZER.

Before he knew what was happening, I had my arms around his thighs, and, with my hands clasped tightly under the seat of his trousers, I lifted him several inches off the ground. His hands touched my shoulders, trying to push himself away, while his DANCING LEGS struggled to make contact with the FLOOR. (OUR cat, Cocoa, often reacts in the same way when I try to pick him up.) I could sense his discomfort, so I let him down. Mr. White suffered the humiliation with what little dignity he could muster. His shirt had pulled out of his waistband and his trousers had ridden up to reveal a plump portion of uncooked turkey leg. He tucked himself in and tried to recover his composure. The goods were back in the larder, but I had proved my point.

Mr. WHITE checked his hair with the

flat of his hand. "Yes, well, thank you, Miss Fontaine, but I think this has gone far enough. I don't even know how you came to be here, but you might as well know now, we won't be hiring you for the position. I'm afraid you're simply not qualified. GOOD DAY."

I stood dumbfounded, momentarily glued to the LINOLEUM FLOORING.

Not qualified? 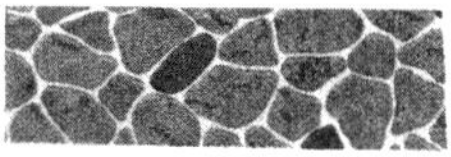

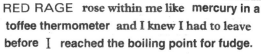

RED RAGE rose within me like mercury in a toffee thermometer and I knew I had to leave before I reached the boiling point for fudge.

I paused dramatically in the doorway, my hands firm on the reins of reason.

"I feel sorry for you, Mr. White," I said. "You recognise me as *the perfect woman*, yet you are unable to see me as THE PERFECT MAN FOR THE JOB. And if you think for one minute that I'd trade this lovely new BOULEVARD fashion footwear for the opportunity to step into a man's shoes, you'd be wrong. I'm proud to wear the badge of womanhood because personal dignity and feminine pride matter far more to me than a dangerous and useless career of this kind."

Mr. White WAS SPEECHLESS. IT WAS GOOD, BUT I NEEDED SOME-THING ELSE. The 'some-thing else,' that every film director hopes to find in his players and hardly ever does.

"And next time you decide to take this particular

stance, you might want to take a good look at your legs in a long mirror."

And with that as my closing bid, I stormed from *his* **OFFICE**, vowing never to darken his door again.

Mr. White's personal secretary was standing just outside the door, with a concerned look PINCHING her flat features.

"Get on to the employment agencies, Miss Harrow, and see if they have a RACING DRIVER who's prepared to double as a circus strong-man," I said, putting on my coat. "Better still, phone *Stirling Moss* and find out if he can bend an iron bar over his head."

She looked at me as if I were insane.

The balloon-faced old man was still there, but his attitude had changed. Perhaps he had overheard the hostilities. His assured expression had faded and now he seemed to wear the guarded, remote look of the puzzled physician. But he was also a very frightened, lonely old man. All alone . . . like a cake on a plate.

"Don't worry," I said, pressing the sleeve of his sports jacket with the flat of my hand. "I'm afraid you're simply not qualified EITHER, but your winning personality should open a few doors."

He was visibly touched by my gesture. **NO** man could expect a young woman to surrender

THE KEY TO HER OWN HAPPINESS. His eyes gleamed and any remaining

No. 56

fumes of vexation evaporated in the sunshine of my own loving kindness.

I didn't go straight home.

I knew I had to get back before Mary so that I'd have time to change, but she wouldn't be home until FIVE —plus, I'd decided to catch the bus instead of walking, so that gave me a bit more time. It had stopped raining, so I would have gone for a nice stroll over to Marcia Modes, but my NEW SHOES — made to *feel* blissful, even to the going-est, busiest feet — were beginning to pinch a bit on the heel. NOTHING SERIOUS: an *Elastoplast* and a couple of dabs of Germolene would soon sort that out!

Marcia Modes has always been a favourite because it stocks fashion items for the larger woman. Its owner, Mrs. Marcia, once told *Roy* that she has several male regulars who like to buy things for their wives or secretaries, so she's become quite an expert in the art of recommending colours and styles as well as guessing women's sizes. Inside, there are *dozens* of dresses to choose from: silks and wools and satins, and maybe even a lovely brocade. They often have shoes to match, too. High heels, flats, warm boots for dress-up and sport, though their shoe sizes only go up to a size eight.

In the end, I went and sat on the bench out side the library, though it was hardly the weather for it. It had turned decidedly nippy and I had to pull my collar up. In my hasty departure from WHITE'S LAUNDRY, I had inadvertently left my SCARF behind. It was a particularly festive one, with views of London buildings all over it in a newsworthy duet of lilac and sage green. It had always been a favourite. I'd realised what I'd done as soon as I stepped out on to the street and felt the cold air FINGERING my throat, but as I turned to go back inside, I saw Mr. White was now OUT OF his office and talking to the receptionist. I remem-bered reading somewhere that one should never mar the effectiveness of a dramatic exit by returning for some forgotten trifle, so I decided I'd go back tomorrow when the coast was clear, and my performance had been logged in Mr. White's THINK AND DO book.

●

4

Having just missed the QUARTER PAST, with another bus not due for eleven minutes, I did what nine hundred and ninety-nine other women would have done. I looked in a shop window to see what was on offer. Like most MODERN ladies, I have very strong ideas about shopping and think the women of this country, particularly the working-class women, need to be educated in the art of window-shopping. *It doesn't take a minute and it can be fun for* A WOMAN to gaze longingly at something she will never be able to afford.

NEXT to the shoe menders was a SHOP I had never noticed before. Perhaps it was new. Dowling's PHOTOGRAPHIC STUDIOS. The

name above it was picked out in BIRD'S CUSTARD YELLOW. In the window, there was a CAMERA on display with two smiling wax ladies (busts and heads only), who found themselves with smart little Parisian umbrellas leaning nonchalantly against their ears. A sign read: '**We photograph your face, not your feet — 4 WALLET-SIZE PRINTS, only 2/6d.**' There were FRAMED PICTURES of people, none of whom I recognised. One particular WOMAN, though not especially beautiful, had an air of charm about her. The photographer had caught 'that certain something'.

I have always regretted the fact that I have no photographs at all of myself looking young and pretty, which is why, in a bout of wishful thinking, I wondered if I dared venture into the lion's den.

It was then I became aware—consciously aware, that is —of a man STANDING directly behind me. He had been nattering away at my sub-conscious because I could see his reflection in the window. His face was obscured by a CAMERA. The camera clicked.
Clickety-click.

. . . . He came towards me, with his hand outstretched like a cheerful Girl Guide, his camera swinging on his chest. With him came a gust of vitality and enthusiasm that infected me long before he reached my side.
" I am so sorry to have bothered you. I could not resist it. It is the best picture I have made this afternoon. The light . . . the background . . . your beauty . . ."
He had some sort of foreign accent.
"Oh, no," I laughed.
"You English women do not like compliments, no?"
"We love them." I began blushing and threw up my hands with a little tinkling, knowledgeable laugh.

ThOUGH NOT **AN**
an impressively handsome man, his body was

broad and powerful, hinting at his tremendous capacity for work and life. HIS TEETH had that Continental look of yellowing stains that can cause bad breath, and he wore a little, brown, TYROLEAN-STYLE trilby with a GREASY brim.

"You were thinking about a PHOTO SESSION, no? I can offer you the same Professional SERVICE at a third of the price. A shilling, or sixpence, if you prefer."

He was clearly no mathematical wizard, but this was truly A MARVELLOUS BARGAIN.

"Permit me to introduce myself," he said. "My name is HANS." He gave a little bow and raised the jaunty hat. It had a feather in it, a red feather, I noticed.

"Is it a portrait you are seeking?" he asked.

"Well, yes, in a way, I suppose I am," I answered, guardedly. "Though not a portrait exactly. Being a woman, I do have a dream. I would love just once to model a glamorous evening gown, and have it on film to always look back on to prove that I *could* look feminine AND ALLURING."

"With you, proof is unnecessary," he said, with disarming sincerity. "Perhaps you will do me the honour of joining me at tea? I believe there is a small café just across the road. We can discuss how you should be PHOTO-GRAPHed *to bring out your radiant loveliness.*"

I thought it sounded exciting, like something out of a WOMEN'S magazine. I looked at my watch. "I'm afraid I've got to

catch a train at Charing Cross in twenty minutes."
"Then we have just time."

HE grasped my arm and propelled me at great speed to his small café with the ruthless technique of an experienced campaigner. I wasn't catching a train and CHARING CROSS, as far as I was aware, was over a hundred miles away IN LONDON, but I thought it sounded like the kind of thing a sophisticated woman like myself might say. The truth was I knew I had to leave in ten minutes to make sure of being back HOME before Mary, but I was still smarting from the interview and this was just the kind of pick-me-up I needed.

THE Excella was the sort of snack bar you knew, even from the doorway, would be patronised only by people who were broke. But it had a quaint charm that someone without my eye for stylish decoration might not recognise.

INSIDE

it was noisy and smoky, with clattering cups and hissing steam from the big urns on the counter. HANS went up to order our tea while I sat down near the window. I was hoping to check my reflection in it, but it was thick with condensation.

I experienced a sudden nervous qualm at the thought of being there alone with a man — a man I barely knew. A wave of trepidation washed over me and I was sorely tempted to pick up my skirts and run. The urge startled me, scared me. Don't panic, I exhorted myself. Think about something else. My eyes rested on a man at THE NEXT table who was eating a plateful of *pie and gravy* with a spoon.

I straightened my dress and refreshed my lipstick. ***HANS*** had called me *radiantly lovely* and I didn't want his opinion to change. I wondered if he'd noticed my *NEW* SHOES.

I stuck my legs out into the aisle and couldn't help admiring the way the shoe's slender heel-contouring flattered my shapely ankle. My legs are probably my best feature. I hitched my dress a little to reveal my knees and that delicious *'peep'* of petticoat — just to prove my point that flounced, beribboned petticoats have lost their coy, under-cover strategem.

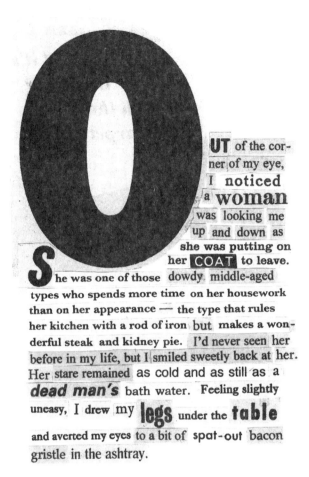

OUT of the corner of my eye, I noticed a woman was looking me up and down as she was putting on her COAT to leave.

She was one of those dowdy middle-aged types who spends more time on her housework than on her appearance — the type that rules her kitchen with a rod of iron but makes a wonderful steak and kidney pie. I'd never seen her before in my life, but I smiled sweetly back at her. Her stare remained as cold and as still as a *dead man's* bath water. Feeling slightly uneasy, I drew my **legs** under the **table** and averted my eyes to a bit of spat-out bacon gristle in the ashtray.

AS she passed my **table**, she bent her head to speak. She managed to mask her jealous admiration for me with a look of utter contempt.

"What do you think you look like, dressed up like that? You should be ashamed of yourself." Incredulous surprise held me motionless. Her wrinkled, flabby, sagging skin hovered over me.

"We don't want your sort round here," she said abruptly.

"What sort is that? *Women with glamour and poise*? Women who combine natural beauty with *fashion flair*? *Women whose* loveliness draws crowds of admiring glances? I suppose Miss Elizabeth Taylor and Miss **Jayne Mansfield** are not your sort either. **OR** Miss Kathy Kirby, who makes all her own lampshades and cushion covers."

THE WOMAN was clearly stumped. "There's something wrong with you," she suggested. "Very seriously wrong." She stomped out of the door, leaving me momentarily dazed by her outburst. The words had arrowed through the cotton wool layers of a false calm.

Why *are women like her* so **frightened of glamour?**

THEY CANNOT BEAR TO LOOK AT ME. **The reason, they say, is that I'm too glamorous.** Either women must go on disguising themselves, behaving as he-men and being treated as such, or admit that they are feminine after all and watch the miraculous return of that charming old-world courtesy we women have discouraged and made unfashionable.

Luckily, ***HANS*** was unaware of this little contretemps and by the time he returned with the tea only a fiery scratch remained on the cheek of tranquillity. **He had bought**

two CAKES, which, I subsequently discovered, were both for him. For me there was a SANDWICH. HOORAH!

I thought I had never enjoyed a cup of tea so much in my life. It tasted like pink champagne and seemed to have the same effect. Or perhaps it was just the way Hans looked at me.

"I hope you like meat paste," he said.

"**Don't say meat paste, say Shippam's**," I said, rather too loudly.

An awkward pause hung in the air. Hans started on his cakes while I tried to think of something to say. Help, I thought. I've frozen up inside and I'm sure he thinks that I'm a nose-in-the-air girl. At last, I cleared my throat and said in a feeble voice, "I believe that travel broadens the mind."

"Yes, so I believe," said Hans.

"I've never had tea with a foreign gentleman before. Where are you from exactly?"

"CARDIFF."

"Your English is remarkably good."

"Thank you," he said, dunking the ECLAIR into his tea with the quiet air of a man who knows what he wants and knows how to get it.

A LARGE, *soggy* chunk fell off on to **the table** before he could get it into his mouth. WHY is it that some men make such a mess when they try to feed themselves while others take to it so quickly and easily? Soon he will probably want to pick up a few lumps from his plate. I know it's horribly messy, but letting him do this will help him to manipulate a knife and fork later on.

To enjoy eating at the Excella you had to be hungry as well as broke. I wasn't very. I was too nervous, though I must say I wouldn't have refused a meal of salad and caviare with vodka, hors d'oeuvre, soup, fish, meat, poultry, fruit and coffee (choice of six kinds). Still, one had to eat something, so I nibbled at my meat-paste sandwich.

HANS took off his hat and laid it on the table. There was a ragged scar above his right eye, and his fizzy ginger beer hair was sticky with *perspiration*, dark against the pale dampness of his face.

"You look most becoming in that dress. Are you meeting someone special?"

"As a matter of fact I've just been for a job interview at WHITE'S LAUNDRY," I explained.

"**White's?** Yes, I think I know it. On CROSS *Street*."

I was about to tell him all about it, but **Hans** seemed keen to get down to the matter in hand.

"Now, when can you come to my studio? I'M QUITE ANXIOUS *to capture your feminine allure*."

These Continental men certainly have a way with them. I felt myself responding to his charms.

"Can you really make me look like one of the glamorous models from the women's magazines?"

He assured me he could and made a comparison

with **DIANA DORS,**

MAKING MY HEART *Travel* **'OUT INTO SPACE'**. I put my **SANDWICH** down before speaking.

" I'm prepared to bet that people who just know her on their television screens think of her simply as the living face off a chocolate box. Her true beauty is never even glimpsed by the public," I said. " This is surely because happiness in life has given her face something more than mere beauty."

Hans appeared not to have heard me. His eyes had a dreamy, faraway look. "Ah yes, dear Diana. I have several pictures of her in my private collection."

To take my mind off my nervousness and the taste of the sandwich, I concentrated on the idea of having my picture taken with DIANA DORS. Reason skimmed around in my mind, too big to be grasped, as I imagined Diana and myself sharing a dressing room while preparing for a **PHOTO** session. **ME wear**ing a dressing-robe, but such as I had never seen before, lined with satin and richly embroidered with intricate patterns of gold which formed a crest at one spot.

"What will you wear, ***NORMA***?" asks Miss Dors, envying my lack of freckles and unflustered air. "Your pale yellow organza with the intricately swathed strapless bodice and enormous crinoline skirt supported by a dozen layers of stiff tarlatan?"

"I'm not sure, Diana. It's true, I do **look** **wonderful** in it, but I saw myself in my Mattli's elegant white and gold, Sekers brocade evening gown, or my Digby Morton taffeta and lace cocktail dress."

"*Sensational!*"

DIANA, who not a moment before had been a statuesque vision in trailing green chiffon, steps into a clinging woollen dress with a wide, gold belt. STRAIGHT FROM DIOR in Paris – and with more than its share of chic. (Such a treasure should never be trusted to anything but Dreft – for Dreft takes care of wool as nothing else can.)

"Is the collar clean?" she adds practically, "Or do we take it off and substitute beads?"

"Beads, I think," I decide. "I think they look more sophisticated, anyway. A collar is too little-girlish."

"Here, let me help you with them, Diana darling."

I was just fastening the clasp at the nape of Diana's lovely neck when **Hans** coughed THICKLY and broke the spell.

"OF COURSE, the Continental magazines go for pictures of girls in thoughtful black corsets with white frills," he said, wiping his finger on the table.

"Yes, a good FOUNDATION moulds the

figure into perfect contour. I am wearing one of
them now," I said.

"Really?" His eyes widened and he edged forward
in his seat, folding his arms tight across his chest.

"It's like no other girdle, without a seam, stitch
or bone, invisible under the most clinging clothes.
Everywhere you go you hear about Playtex.
It's like stepping into another world to see how
this figure-flattering girdle slims and trims you
from waist to thigh."

"The more exotic the clothes you describe,
the better I shall be pleased," said Hans,
his eyes resting appreciatively on the tips of
my Peter Pan collar.

The odd thing was that his regard did not seem
so much admiring as curiously calculating. As
if he were wondering whether I would stand
up to some test he had in mind for me. I had a sudden impulse to beat a retreat, but pride held me
rooted to my chair. And gradually he teased
me, encouraged me, laughed with me, until I
came to realise that all his teasing was only
a cloak, a disguise for the admiration he had for
me. It was wonderful. For the more he admired
me, the more sure of myself I felt.

"ALL right," I said suddenly, "I'll
come a WEEK on Friday." The
coming Friday was too soon; I
needed time to plan my wardrobe.
"I could meet you there, about seven
or seven thirty."

"Around seven," he cut in. "*Excellent.*"

He took out his notebook. Please be kind enough

to let me give you my name and address."
He tore off the sheet of paper and pressed it into my hand.
I compared my watch with the clock on the wall opposite.

"Good heavens! I really must fly! I'm having dinner in a fashionable Piccadilly restaurant with **Petula Clark, who is kept busy** with radio and TV appearances as well as films." It wasn't true, of course, but I needed an excuse to leave. I was being too quickly swept off my feet and my head was spinning in an undisciplined but welcome whirlwind of excitement. **I needed some fresh air. I dashed** out of the café — **perhaps 'fled' would be a more fitting word** — hardly daring to breathe.

I clutched the **PAPER** with his address as if it were **a birthday telegram from the Queen.** Was I really going to be *immortalised as a* **glamorous** **woman?** **A REAL photographic studio with a professional photographer**? Would Diana Dors be there? Did **Hans** really know her? I wondered whereabouts **his studio was located** and whether it had a **NAME**.

IT was only when I looked at the piece of PAPER he had given me that I realised **his name was** HANDS, not **HANS.**

Mr. Hands. **THIRTY-ONE Egmont Street.**

FIVE

THE whoo-hoo of the factory siren always mystified me when I was young. I never knew what it was or where it came from, but to me it sounded like *a recently* smacked child bursting spontaneously into tears. Now the whoo-hoo reminded me that it was FIVE-THIRTY and I was late. I was not looking forward to this confrontation with MARY.

When I reached home, it was just getting dark. There were no lights on in the HOUSE and the CURTAINS hadn't been drawn, so for a minute I thought I was back BEFORE she was; but when I opened the door, I saw her sitting on the stairs, and all at once my spirits were plunged into the gloom. The stairs meant she was upset. And her being upset was much worse than her being angry.

"I was going to do the POTATOES, but I missed the bus," I said, gingerly setting my handbag down on the hall table.

She could hardly bear to look at me.

"I knew you'd gone dressed like that when I saw your SUIT STILL hanging up," she said.

I was ready to try and explain why I had CHOSEN THE PARTICULAR OUTFIT I had, but she seemed reluctant to listen, and, besides, I suddenly felt horribly conspicuous in it.

"So that's another job down the SWANEE," she said resignedly. I'd imagined she'd be mad and start shouting like she usually did, but this time she seemed defeated, like a BOXER leaning against the ropes, too weak to fight any more. Seemingly, I'd got off lightly, but this reluctance to fight signalled that we'd moved to a different level of seriousness. I was keen to get some sort of conversation going but she seemed in no mood for THE KIND OF lively debate that would usually clear the air. I paused on the hall mat, unsure what to say. Finally she spoke; her tone was dismissive.

"There's a pie in the oven. *You can get it yourself.*"

"Thanks." I said, sheepishly. "Are you having some?"

"No."

"Shall I make a pot of tea?"

"Do WHAT YOU LIKE."

With that, the door to the debating room slammed shut so I went into the kitchen and took out the CASSEROLE DISH using the big oven mitts, listening out in case she changed her mind and decided to engage in combat. But it was **All Quiet on the Western Front** and I knew that this time I was not going to be forgiven. I had thrown away the chance of a good job for the sake of my own selfish vanity.

Silence fell between us. It seemed to sit inside me, that bruised silence. I spooned some cottage pie on to a plate, wondering if I should change out of my clothes. My appearance was clearly aggravating the situation, but I didn't want to have to try and pass Mary on the stairs.

THE fullness of my petticoats brushing against her WOULD rub *like* SANDPAPER on an open sore. So, instead, I sat alone at the **KITCHEN** table eating quietly. It was far too early for dinner but I felt it was the wrong time to broach the subject of ***FASHIONABLE DINING ETIQUETTE.*** "It's marvellous, it really is!" I said it loud enough that she might hear, thinking that perhaps a compliment about her COOKING might break the deadlock, but ***THERE WAS NO RESPONSE.*** I wasn't actually very hungry. Mr. Hands's MEAT PASTE SANDWICH had taken the edge off my appetite but I continued eating because I didn't know what else to do.

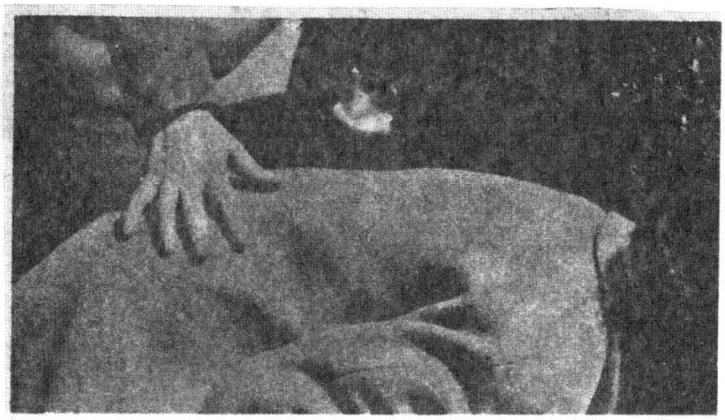

WHEN ***I FIRST HEARD*** the noise, so unfamiliar was it to me that I thought **MARY** was having a **COUGHING** FIT. But she wasn't. When I put down my knife and fork and stood **in the door-way** I saw that she was sobbing quietly into her hands. I wanted to go and comfort her, sit next to her on the stairs with my arm around her shoulder like they do in the MAGAZINEs. I wanted to say: DON'T RISK A NERVOUS BREAKDOWN. If you're growing irritable and easily depressed, and your nerves are suffering from strain, try taking Phillips Tonic Yeast with your meals. I wanted to say I was sorry too, but I couldn't find the words.

THOUGH I never hear her CRYING I sometimes think she privately mourns the loss of her little *NORMA*. However Lovely a *woman* I am NOW, it must be hard for her to see me as her little girl.

So I sat back down to my lonely supper, and with each forkful I could feel Mary being swept further away from me in a sea of her own tears. Outside, now that it was getting darker, the sickly ORANGE glow from the street lamps was becoming more distinct. In the fading light of *the kitchen*, I felt pressure building in the empty cavity *behind my* FACE and, despite the disastrous effect I knew it would have on my carefully applied make-up, I found that I, too, was crying. WHOO-HOO.

●

SIX

ROY *is* HOME.

HE got back unexpectedly this morning, while Mary was still asleep. He'd been away for more than a WEEK, this time, and I knew she would be anxious to see him, but so far I was the only one who knew of his **return** and I was keeping it to myself. There'd be time enough for *MARY* later.

SO there I was at half-past seven, watching in the bathroom mirror as **ROY** got himself ready for the day — dabbing **BRYLCREEM** on to the palm of his hand, running it through his thick, dark hair with stiff fingertips before combing it into a lustrous BLACK LACQUER shine. His hairline is so crisp and even that one would be forgiven for thinking that a long-playing record had melted on his head. I watched as he shaved stubborn bristles from the rugged squareness of his jaw, his forceful chin emerging

No. 83

clean and pink from beneath the creamy WHITE soap. WITH his suit sponged and pressed, and his shirt collar fastened, he picked out a tie that suggested *infor-mality* but really meant business.

When she did get up, Mary heard the usual sounds of someone moving around upstairs but naturally assumed it was me, not Roy. I've always been an early riser so she's used to hearing me pottering about. It often takes me so long to get ready in the morning — getting my look just right — that by the time I appear downstairs it's gone *ten* and the breakfast things have long been cleared away. I usually make do with a bowl of cereal. NO COOKING – JUST ADD COLD MILK AND SUGAR. *IT'S ALL A WOMAN NEEDS*, and it's so munchably, crunchably different. Besides, it's all Mary is prepared to dish up. It would have been a different story if she'd known it was *Roy* who was doing the pottering. She would have cheerfully rustled up a hearty feast of Wall's plump pork sausages, eggs, and **Heinz baked beans in a rich tomato sauce. WONDERFUL!** But there was no time for that today; *Roy* had a busy morning ahead of him.

He slipped out of the house without so much as a word of hello, good-bye, or how are you? to MARY. Probably unsure, like I was, what to say. There had been nothing since then to suggest any change in Mary's mood. AFTER spending most of the evening on the stairs, she had opted for an early night. No COTTAGE PIE; no Ovaltine at bedtime. She didn't even WATCH EMERGENCY—WARD 10 and she's never been known to miss an appoint-ment with Dr. Forrester.

MARY WOULD HAVE heard the gate slam and footsteps on the path but, assuming it was the milkman, thought nothing of it until later in the morning when she found Roy's comb on the side of the washbasin, along with his LITTLE selection of men's grooming products. Like most men, *Roy* doesn't fuss about his appearance — faultless grooming with as little effort as possible — so he requires only the basics to make himself clean and present-able. Still, for a wily old sleuth like Mary, these items were evidence enough, and with the lingering smell of NAIL VARNISH REMOVER in the air as a further clue, she quickly put two and two together and realised he was back. There was no real need to feel so jaunty, but a sudden lightening of the heart robbed her face, for the moment, of its usual severity, and she afforded herself the faintest flash of her old smile. And when she smiled it was like the sun coming out in November.

Roy was not smiling. He was on his way

to **WHITE'S**
LAUNDRY

wearing a look of white-boned determination. His plan, primarily, was to PICK UP the *Scarf* I had left there yesterday, but at the same time to give that Mr. **WHITE** a piece of his mind about how unfairly he thought I had been treated. Roy's argument was as strong and as solid as a dining chair made by **UNIFLEX**. He had all the answers and the questions to go with them. **MR.** White **would be more inclined to listen to a man— men are far better than women at this sort of thing—** and Roy aimed to give him a few pointers on equality for women. *Roy* and I have always seen eye to eye on this and I knew he would make his point emphatically, unequivocally, and without mincing his adjectives.

IN contrast to yesterday's greyness, today had a brighter, fresher outlook. The colours more real than paint, more vivid than the hues of everyday life. THE FRONT OFFICE, from which I had **FLOUNCED** not twenty-four hours before, seemed gay with flowers and polish, the sun slanting through the windows, throwing cheery squares of light on to the **RED LINOLEUM**

FLOOR.

No MISS Harrow to cast her dark shadow this time; in fact, no one ABOUT at all — the perfect opportunity for Roy to check the waiting room to see if my SCARF was still there. It was. Splendid. Looking a little like A MAGICIAN PERFORMING A VANISHING TRICK he deftly slid it off the hook and had just begun feeding it into his inside pocket, when he heard a voice behind him.

"Are you here about the job?"

It was a young woman of about twenty.

"Well, yes. I suppose I am," said Roy, turning to face her. "My name's LITTLE."

"Is it?"

"Yes."

"**How little**?"

"I'm sorry?"

"How LITTLE is it? Is it like . . . **ED**, or something?"

ROY looked confused. Was she teasing him?

"No, it's not **ED**, it's *Roy*," he said.

"Roy? Well, I suppose that is quite little."

"No, you don't understand. My surname is **LITTLE**. I'm Roy Little."

Roy felt a trifle foolish, suspecting she might have **UNDERSTOOD** all along. During their exchange, he had noticed her glance at the SCARF protruding from inside his jacket. She probably thought he was **PLANNING**

TO STEAL IT.

"I found it hanging up here," he explained, removing it from his pocket. "I was just feeling it. SILK, isn't it? My sister has one just like it."

She took it from him, inspecting the label.

"One hundred per cent RAYON SATIN."

He noticed how pretty her hands were—pale and delicate like the ones in the MAGAZINE advertisements. DON'T IMAGINE that women with exquisite hands always have maids to do their work. Nowadays it's *much* more likely that they're cooking and washing dishes themselves. But they give their hands a very inexpensive, marvellous kind of beauty care . . . they wash their dishes with Lux!

"SOME woman left it yesterday, app-arently," she said, holding the SCARF up in front of her.

"You weren't here yesterday," said Roy. It was meant to sound like a question but it came out as a statement.

SHE slipped the scarf round her neck, bunching it at her throat. "I'm not sure about this PATTERN, but the COLOURS are quite nice. What do you think?"

Roy was quite taken with her loveliness. Her pale skin was slightly flushed, her lips red. Her hair was pushed into shallow waves LIKE MOONBEAMS ON A LAKE and her eyes were very green, and clear. She looked appealingly carefree, pliant as a young willow.

"It suits you," he said.

"Really?" She seemed pleased. "Well, we'll just

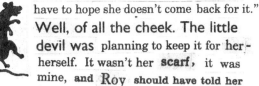

have to hope she doesn't come back for it." Well, of all the cheek. The little devil was planning to keep it for her-herself. It wasn't her scarf, it was mine, and Roy should have told her so. I don't know why he didn't. He should have said, 'Excuse me, miss, but that scarf belongs to my sister. She left it here yesterday when she was BEING DISCRIMINATED AGAINST by your boss.' Roy knew what he should have said, but he didn't say anything. He just stood there staring at her.

Meeting corner with corner, she folded the scarf neatly, into a square. "Well, you'd better go in, if you're here about the job," she said, turning to leave.

"Don't I have to get the green light first?" said Roy.

"I'll give you the GREEN light when I'm good and ready, MR. Little." Her voice was suddenly firm and unyielding. It seemed his remark had been misinterpreted as some gauche piece of philandering dalliance. The reaction was understandable. A YOUNG WOMAN LIKE HER — perfect, or as near perfect as any dream can get to realisation — must be used to dealing with the unwelcome advances of THE UNSCRUPULOUS CHARMER. Roy wanted to make it clear that he was referring to the light above Mr. White's door, but she was already walking away. Suddenly she turned. A tiny teasing smile danced a cha-cha across her lips. "Just knock and go straight in," she said.

When it came down to it, Roy's AUDIENCE with Mr. WHITE was a much more civilised affair.

MAN TO MAN.

No nonsense.

Roy had taken off his coat and was holding it over his shoulder. He looked like some strikingly handsome young architect or a **dashing British diplomat** on his way to a conference in Zurich. He opened the door and took a few steps into the office.

"Good morning. I hope I'm not intruding," he said. "My name is Little, Roy Little. I've come about the delivery job."

MR. White was caught off his guard. He had been reading a ***HOBBIES MAGAZINE*** whilst warming **the seat of his trousers** against the radiator and gnawing at a particularly troublesome hangnail ON HIS INDEX FINGER. **HE** sat down at his desk in a bid to establish himself in the driving seat.

"Ah, yes. Mr. **LITTLE**. We had you down for YESTERDAY. You're rather late."

"Yes, I'm terribly sorry. I'm afraid I was otherwise detained. **A FAMILY EMERGENCY**."

"Oh dear. Nothing too serious I hope."

"My sister has special needs."

"Ah yes," said Mr. WHITE knowingly, although Roy sensed he didn't know at all. "Something like that can be quite a burden."

"I don't consider it a burden," said ROY, a touch icily.

"No, no, quite." Mr. WHITE found himself in reverse gear. "Nevertheless, she's very fortunate to have you to take care of her."

"I

CALLED

three times from the telephone box. The number was busy, busy."

"I see. Well. You might as well sit down. I think I still have your application here somewhere."

ROY wondered if his apology had seemed inadequate.

"I hope I didn't inconvenience you too much," he offered, " —— missing my appointment."

"We'll say no more about it," said Mr. WHITE in a grim little voice. He began sifting through a manila folder of letters on his desk. "As it turned out," he said, brightening, " a strange **WOMAN** turned up in your PLACE."

"Really?" said Roy forcing a smile. *'Strange'? What did he mean, 'strange'?*

"I don't know where she came from — ***outer space*** possibly — but she was most peculiar, ranting on about this, that and the other. I think she might have been a bit mad."

NOW was Roy's chance to give him what for. Really lay into him.

"Oh, dear," he said, **lamely**.

And that was it. He **just sat there quietly** while Mr. WHITE reviewed his application. A tactical move, perhaps.

"Ah, yes," said Mr. White. "You spent eighteen months as a **DRIVER** at

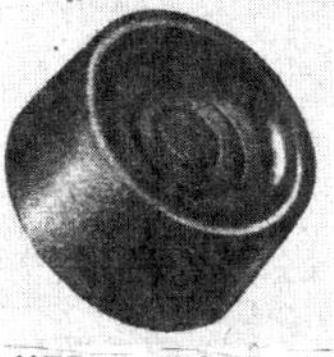

Mackintosh's

THE

CONFECTIONERY PEOPLE."

"Yes, Sir. Delivering to local retailers from their central warehouse."

"I see. Sounds perfect. Ever get any ***FREE SAMPLES***?"

"Sometimes, sir. If they had a new product they wanted to test."

"One of the perks of the job, eh?"

"Well, you get a bit sick of it after a while."

"Really? I can't imagine getting sick of Macintosh's ROLO S. They're my favourites."

"Yes, they're very good."

Mr. White savoured the idea of FREE CHOCOLATE for a moment before moving on.

"And you left there in . . ." he paused to refer to the application again, ". . . FEBRUARY this year. What have you been up to since then?"

" ODD JOBS mostly. Casual employment. But now I'm keen to get back to DELIVERY DRIVING full-time. I enjoy the work and I think I'm good at it."

"I see." He picked up a pencil and tapped it lightly on the desk, then looked down at the application again. Setting the papers aside, he sat back in his chair clutching the pencil in both hands.

"Well, the job here's pretty straightforward — probably the kind of thing you're used to. We provide a collection and delivery service to our private customers as well as our business clients. It's nearly all in this area. Are you local?"

"Yes, sir. I've lived here all my life — with my MOTHER AND SISTER"

"Not married?"

"No, sir."

"Well, there's plenty of time for that," was *Mr. White*'s response. "Sooner or later, love will knock at the door of your heart —no other qualifications being necessary!"

HE *started to* outline the business. He was not an engaging man and the monotonous drone of his description failed to hold Roy's attention.

THERE was a side door , which, Roy imagined, led out into the passage. Through the pane of *'winter-frosted', semi-obscure glass* IN IT, Roy caught sight of the young woman he'd just met. He couldn't see her face but he recognised the *Delphinium Blue* OF HER DRESS refracted **blearily** through the window's crazed surface.

He forced his glance back to Mr. White, who was still talking. "... bed linen and towels from small hotels ... overalls ... uniforms ... private homes ..." *Roy* nodded encouragingly, though his concentration **had drifted out to sea in a small dinghy.** What was she doing out there? he wondered. She was standing perfectly still. Perhaps she was eavesdropping. Mr. White brought him back with a direct question. "So you know your way around?"

"Pretty well, I think," said Roy modestly.

"Good. Well, we'll give you a **MAP**, obviously. I'll see the road maps are in the DOOR pocket. Otherwise, I think that's everything. DRIVING LICENCE?"

Roy handed it to him across the desk.

"I'll need to take details for the **INSURANCE**, but I think I have everything else."

He opened up the little **red** BOOK and copied some numbers on to the bottom of Roy's **job application.**

"Any questions?" he said, without looking up.

"No, I don't think so."

"The wage is as OUTLINED IN THE ADVERTISEMENT. If that's agreeable, I can't see any reason why you shouldn't start straight away. How about MONDAY?"

"Yes! MONDAY would be fine. Thank you very much."

Mr. White remained seated while they shook hands.

"See Miss Harrow on Monday for the keys. She'll let you know what's what."

"Is that the young lady I saw JUST NOW?" He knew it wasn't.

Mr. WHITE was momentarily dazed by the question.

"In the blue dress," prompted Roy.

"Oh, no, that's EVE. Miss Harrow won't be in until Monday."

Out in the front office, *Roy* was delighted to find the young woman was STILL THERE. Her back was to him as she leant over the desk where Miss Harrow had sat the previous day. She was flicking through one of the monthly glossies. Her featherweight, special all-day dress in gossamer linen, all over embroidered and belted with a small, slit sleeve, hugged her figure like a long-lost cousin. This is what a DRESS should do for a woman, thought Roy. And though she wouldn't have been out of place on the cover of the VERY fashion magazine she was reading (once she'd turned round, obviously), she looked like what she was—a live, intelligent, sky's-the-limit working girl. Not a rich man's caprice.

"Are you EVE?" His voice was gentle.

"Yes."

"So your name's little as well."

"Yes. It is." She smiled to acknowledge his joke and ROY felt pleased with himself.

"Quite a coincidence," he said.

"Yes, isn't it?" she said. "Imagine!" And they both laughed.

"**How did it go**?" she said, indicating Mr. White's office with a little jerk of her head.

"Got THE GREEN LIGHT."

"Well. Congratulations, Mr. Little."

There was a pleasantly satiric gleam in her green eyes., the pleasantest he had ever known, and the eyes and the arms and the ways of this pleasant woman were stamping themselves on his nerves with a John Bull printing set.

"Look, why don't you call me Roy?" he said, ringing with conviction. It's a bit silly, our being formal, now that we're going to be working so much together."

There was a second when their looks met intently, a second when he thought he saw in her eyes that questioning, awakened, surprised warmth that every man wants more than anything else. Then the lashes dropped, guardedly, and she answered with a slow, dimpling smile that made a little joke of the new intimacy. "Of course, Roy. Except . . ."

"Except what?"

"Except I don't WORK here."

7

MARY is like a song of sunshine! Since Roy got the job, she's been humming tunes off the radio and going about her housework looking as mild and happy as a pink baby. And if she is ever serious, it is with the seriousness of an April morning, when the sun briefly retires, to shine the more brightly the moment the cloud is dispersed.

But if Mary is like a song of sunshine, Roy is like the whole LP, if there is such a record. And it's All About Eve, the pretty girl he met at the interview. When she told him she wasn't a White's employee, his heart had slipped deep into the lining of his overcoat. He had been looking forward to working alongside her, getting to know her better. To be away from her now., to know she was inaccessible, that was something he did not want to think about. He had been too shy to ask her where she lived, or how he might contact her, and now she was gone. What had she been doing there that day? Who was she if she didn't work at the laundry ? And how did Mr. White know her name? Every-thing had become exquisitely clear on that first Monday morning.

ROY was early. Miss Harrow gave him the keys to the VAN and told him that Mr. WHITE would be in shortly to explain everything and to give him his route for the day. Roy stood about for a while, TWIRLING the keys on his finger and whistling under his breath as he watched the ironmonger across the road setting his wares out in front of his shop.

Miss Harrow seemed irritated by Roy's presence, so he left her to it and wandered out to the yard at the back where the TWO delivery vans were parked. They were both PAINTED WHITE and had 'White's Sanitary Laundry' written on the side in flowing script. The first van looked dauntingly big, bigger than anything he'd driven before, but, next to it, its baby brother looked something similar to the van he used to drive when he was at Mackintosh's. Roy hoped this would be his.

By eight fifteen, there was still no sign of Mr. White, so Roy decided to pop across the road for some cigarettes.

Cross Street POST OFFICE was much like any other, abundantly stocked with sweets and tobacco, magazines and newspapers. There were a few children's toys (paintbrushes on cards, colouring books, jigsaw puzzles, that sort of thing), as well as birthday cards and odds and ends of stationery. Every surface displayed something colourful and appealing. HE was cold and slightly on edge as he came in from the street, but suddenly there were these good things, cheerful and comforting, and he was quickly enchanted by the little shop's charm. The shop counter ran in an L-shape. In the back corner was the POST OFFICE bit, which which was caged in with brass-coloured wire mesh. An oldish woman in a cardigan stood glumly inside as if she'd been put in prison. She had forms and rubber stamps and postal orders to play with, but it seemed she was only biding her time while awaiting her parole.

The assistant in the shop **part** was busy with other customers, so Roy took a look around. At the front of the counter there were magazines standing in a thin wooden rack, **held in place by a length of curtain wire**. The ones near the middle were grubby and their corners were curling where customers had rubbed up against them. The variety of titles and all their colourful covers made Roy's head swim. He knows how much I love my MAGAZINES. He was particularly taken with the latest issue of **WOMAN**, which featured an article on entertaining at home — something HE KNEW would be of particular interest to *me*. Practical hints on topics such as the etiquette of invitations and acceptances, party conversation, (how to make a joke sound funny when you tell it, how to think up three conversation pieces in advance; how to use Persian proverbs as icebreakers). Essential reading for the modern woman. He decided to get it for **me** on his way home rather than having to take it with him to work. Then he noticed that **WOMAN'S JOURNAL** had a ★Look marvellous beauty pull-out as well as a complete new romance story by Rosamond Chace. He picked it up and was **skimming** through a SPECIAL FEATURE on Princess Anne's First Year as a Brownie when the young lady behind the counter spoke.

"Hallo," she said.

Roy looked up.

It was Eve. Her morning-fresh face was smiling at him from under the row of magazines hanging on a string above her head, and her eyes were alight with that excitement he had seen in them before. To-day she wore a pink cardigan —a soft pink it was, the colour of hedge-roses in June, very becoming indeed to Eve's fair skin, to her soft ringed hair that held the warmth of chestnut in its brown. To complete the outfit, she wore a gemstone brooch and the scenes of London scarf I had left in the waiting room. It was the perfect colour combination and I have to admit, even though it was really my scarf that added the finishing touch, that this young woman had an enviable sense of style.

Hello," said Roy, slipping the magazine magazine back in the rack. "What are you doing here?"

"I work here."

"Oh, I see. When I saw you the other day, I just assumed you worked at White's. You seemed to know your way around."

"My friend works in the sorting room, so when it's not busy here, I sometimes pop across for a chat or a cup of tea."

ROY knew that as delivery man he was unlikely to be spending much time in the laundry building itself, and was languishing at the thought of the missed opportunities to meet up with her during these visits.

A man behind him slapped twopence halfpenny on the counter and took a newspaper. She scooped up the coins without looking and put them in a drawer.

"Did you want something?" she said. Her voice was pleasant but he was suddenly aware of other customers jostling to be served.

"Oh, yes, I did. Sorry. *Ten* PLAYER'S."

She turned to the little piles of Cigarettes behind her.

"PLAIN OR FILTER?"

"FILTER, please."

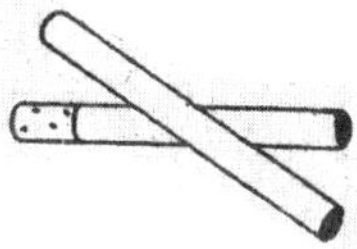

Roy always buys filter in case I want one in the evening. Eve placed them on top of the magazines on the counter.

"TWO and a penny." When ROY was slow to respond, she added, "Anything else?"

"Yes. I'll have, er . . . a quarter of Everton mints."

He hadn't planned to buy sweets but he wanted to prolong the exchange. If he'd had enough money, he might have bought the entire shop. Anyway, Everton mints *are good for concentration* and he was probably going to need it on his first day. She tipped up the jar and shook the sweets into the weighing tray and they both watched as the needle rose towards the four ounce mark. When it was just on the line, she put her hand into the JAR and added a few extra, tipping the balance in Roy's favour.

She flashed her eyes at him conspiratorially. "Tenpence. Two and eleven altogether," she said. She shook a paper bag open and up-ended the weighing tray's contents into it. Grabbing its top corners between each thumb and forefinger, she flipped the bag over in a double somersault, sealing it shut. Roy had seen this done with practically every bag of boiled sweets he'd ever BOUGHT, but when Eve did it he wanted to rush out to the local calligrapher and have a diploma made. Instead, he handed her the money. He would have said something else, but another customer was waiting to pay so he had to cut it short.

"Don't eat them all at once," she said as he was going out of the door. And then she turned to someone else, saying, "Yes, Ted, what can I get you?"

Roy stood outside the shop. He unwrapped one of **the toothsome sweets** and popped it in his mouth. The reflection from the window made it difficult to see in, but it was comforting to know **EVE** was there and that he could call on her at any time he liked on the pretext of buying something. Theirs was only a transitory meeting, but one does not need to spend a month with people to learn their quality. **The mint was creamy and good.** He looked at his watch. Twenty past eight. He wondered if **Mr. White** was in yet.

Just a few yards away, a man in a shabby brown suit stood reading the **postcards on the board in the window**. He was tugging hard on the stubby end of a ***cigarette***. Roy knew him at once; he recognised the Continental-style **hat with the little red feather in it**, just as I had described it. It was Mr. **HANDS**. Roy half expected him to say something, but when Mr. Hands glanced in his direction there wasn't the faintest flicker of recognition. But then, why should there have been? He had never met Roy. Still you'd have thought that a **PORTRAIT ARTIST** like Mr. Hands —one so attuned to the characteristics of the visage —might have spotted a family likeness. Maybe there isn't one. My brother is very unlike me really, so unlike me that you wouldn't believe it. It seemed odd not to say something. Perhaps I should introduce myself, thought Roy. But it was too late. Mr Hands threw down his CIGARETTE and headed off. HE strutted, with rather apart legs, like a robin in a shrunk red cardigan. As he passed within a few feet of Roy, his glazed expression confirmed that, if there was a family resemblance, Mr. Hands had failed to spot it.

IN a few days, I would be there at his studio, and I was already counting the moments to the time when I could see myself captured by the camera's lens. We do have a CAMERA at home but

Mary has always refused to take my picture. I loop the strap around her neck and strike a pose but she just stands there with her arms by her sides, letting the CAMERA dangle on her BUST like an Olympic medallist who feels unworthy of the decoration. "I'm no good at taking PHOTOGRAPHS," she says. I tell her it doesn't matter, but she just won't. I've even tried getting in on the SHOT when I've caught her taking a picture of *Cocoa*, pressing my face close up against his fur, but somehow she always manages to cut me out of the shot. When Roy's saved up enough money from his wages, I'm pretty sure he'll be getting one of those cameras that has a self-timer on it. Then I can take as many pictures of myself in as many outfits as I like. There's one in Mary's catalogue but it's 20 weeks at 6s 9d. Perhaps he can find one SECOND-HAND •

There are plenty of pictures of Roy dotted about the house, on the sideboard and the mantelpiece —Roy in his new suit, which he had taken at Mackintosh's Christmas do; ROY by the wishing well at Bude; Roy eating an ice cream at Caernarvon Castle — but not one single picture of me. For so long I have yearned— yes, yearned, I don't think that's too strong a word for it— to have my picture taken so I can see myself all dressed up and feminine-looking. Perhaps sitting demurely in an armchair with my legs crossed, or engaged in some womanly domestic pursuit – sweeping the hearthrug or mopping the kitchen floor. Well, I'll have to leave all that to Mr. Hands. He's the professional.

As ROY waited to cross the road, he noticed the cigarette stub lying on the pavement, its end nicotine-stained and wet where it had been between Mr. Hands's lips. It lay there, still smoking for a moment, until a gust of wind caught it and rolled it away into the gutter.

8

Using boldness of invention and the lion courage that had distinguished his social career, Roy had embraced the laundry delivery business with the single-minded concentration of a professional footballer chewing Wrigley's spearmint gum. *Mary* was, of course, delighted. He'd been there nearly a week and seemed to be getting along splendidly. I really ought to have been cross with him for not standing up to Mr. White on my behalf at his interview, but I had to admit that things were a lot happier in the Little household now that Roy was working again. Besides, on his way home from the interview he managed to find me an amusing cotton print blouse with miniature wheelbarrow, harp, and flower motif, in strawberry pink. And though it was clearly a peace-offering to make up for failing to retrieve my SCARF, it was difficult to feel too hard done by. The BLOUSE is only from the rag market—Roy doesn't get paid till next week— but once Mary has given it the Daz treatment, it should look quite smart. PINK, almost a basic nowadays, goes with nearly everything. It's perfect with my new shoes —a highly personalised creation that could best be described as 'spirited'. I'm planning to wear it for my session at Mr. *HANDS*'s studio on FRIDAY.

The DELIVERY work itself is straightforward There is a predetermined daily route, each day covering a different area of town. Roy does mostly private houses, though much of the LAUNDRY comes from hotels, nursing homes, and restaurants. This contract work is generally handled by a bigger VAN, driven by someone called Mike, whom Roy has never met.

THE dirty laundry is bundled in bed sheets and left on the customer's front doorstep, ready for collection. Roy's job is to pick it up, tag it, and throw it in the back of the van. Mr. White was right about one thing: the work certainly is physically taxing. The bundles are heavy and cumbersome. Very smelly, too. He didn't mention that. The smell gets gradually worse as the day wears on and more and more bundles are collected, his customers seemingly oblivious to the existence of 24-hour protection against perspiration break-through even in the hottest, most humid weather. At the end of the day, the laundry is dropped off at WHITE'S where everything is washed, ironed, and starched to each individual's requirements, and parcelled up ready to be returned to the customer a few days later. On DELIVERY days, as if as a reward, the pungent smell of soiled linen is replaced by the heady aroma of fresh, clean laundry as the VAN is stacked high with neatly wrapped brown-paper parcels tied with string. At each drop-off, Roy has to collect payment, if the customer is at home, or, if not, issue a bill that can be paid in person at WHITE's. At present the job is taking ROY a lot longer than the previous driver, but he has been assured that he will speed up when he gets to know the ROUTE. HE gets to take the van home at night too, which is a bonus, and Mr. White seems pleased with his performance, *so it's smiles all round.*

The change in Mary has been remarkable. Not only does she look after Roy, making him sandwiches to take to work and cooking special dinners for when he gets home, but she also has much more time for me. Her attitude towards me has improved immeasurably. She's much more tolerant of my ways and habits than she has been in the past.

I stay in my room while Roy's at work, anxiously waiting for the end of the day when he comes home. I'm really only starting my day when his key turns in the front door. And while he's at work, Mary gets on with the housework, benevolent and happy, as though she'd flipped over to the last page of a depressing book and found a happy ending. **I find her doing little things for me, things she never used to do.** She washes and irons my clothes, and has even taken to **laying particular outfits out on the bed so that I can change into something glamorous when** Roy **gets home.**

On MONDAY, Mary and I were sitting together watching the television. It was Inspector Maigret **and we're both fans.** Earlier in the evening I had been **WEARING** *a graceful shirtwaister, buttoned to the hip and cleverly panelled to give a smooth line, and carefree movement*, but for the sleuthing Frenchman I had chosen to relax in *a light-hearted, yet versatile cotton* dress *with a full, semi-circular skirt in an inexpensive navy blue and white scribble print*, worn with a jaunty *jacket in salty blue and white checks.* The perfect outfit *for an informal evening* at home. To make myself snug, I had slipped off my shoes and tucked my legs under me, comforted by the feel of **my suspenders pressing into** the soles of my stockinged feet.

114th,

Just as the programme was getting started, someone rang the doorbell, so I had to dash back up to my room again until the coast was clear. It was **ONLY** a lady with a collection box for Oxfam. Luckily, she was collecting money, not clothes. I have to keep an eye on Mary. She's a fervent supporter of charities, selflessly giving so that refugee children in faraway lands — where they grow the tropical fruit goodness that goes into **KIA-ORA** — might benefit. That's *Mary*, always keen to donate whatever she can to them – any clothes that she feels **we** no longer need. At times, though, her dedication to the cause could be construed as overzealous. There was one occasion when **ROY** and I were small when she took it upon herself to pack up all my clothes, instructing Roy to take them down to the Salvation Army. Heaven knows what she was thinking. It was just after my accident, so I didn't have any say in it, but even Roy could see something was wrong because **these weren't just** clothes I'd grown out of but my best and newest things too. *Mary* was going through a bit of a funny period at that time and things were rather getting on top of her. Any doctor would have told her: behind all your troubles there's likely to be one basic reason—nervous tension. And "nerves" are something you need help to overcome. But instead of turning to Sanatogen for that help, she chose to occupy herself by throwing herself into her charity work — sadly at the expense of some of my favourite clothing items. I'm all for giving to the needy, but the pendulum had swung too far. In British Honduras, Fiji, and other parts of the world, beautifully turned-out REFUGEES were parading around in PASTEL WOOL-KNITS AND PRETTY, FLORAL-PRINT DRESSES while I was stuck at home in my room with barely a stitch to wear. Now that I'm a fully grown young woman at the height of my loveliness, it's no wonder I'm keen to wear nice things and have a range of gorgeous wow-the-men fashion items hanging in my wardrobe. And who could blame me? Haven't I earned the right to look chic?

I could hear Mary downstairs, trying to find her purse, and could feel the draught coming up the stairs. I *thought I might have had time to change* again, but then I heard the front door close and in two shakes of a lamb's tail we were back to Maigret. We'd only missed the titles. It was quite cosy really: Mary in her usual chair; a shilling bar of Cadbury's Dairy Milk, broken into squares, on a saucer resting on the sofa arm between us; the fire burning brightly in the grate, with the curtains drawn tightly against the night chill. All very nice, but it can get a bit much, spending night after night cooped up at home. I just sometimes wish we could see **OUT**. I'd like to be able to observe the night sky – Ursa Major and the Plough —and see the rain on the windows; it would make it all the more cosy inside. But that doesn't happen. The minute I switch the light on in our living-room, Mary tells me to draw the curtains for fear people should see in. We never agree on this point, I simply can't stand spending so many hours shut in a room like a rabbit in a hat-box. I feel smothered. Everybody here lives behind shut curtains after dark, as if it were a crime to be seen having a cup of tea or trying on a new blouse. Some evenings I feel so stifled that I have to rush upstairs to my dressing room and fling open the CURTAINS, even though the lights are blazing. Mary would be furious if she knew, but for me it's like a breath of fresh air.

During the day, they always remain open. That's the rule. The only time you draw the curtains during the day is to announce that someone has died. This is done as a mark of respect, and often neighbouring houses will follow suit. It's always been done this way, though it's never really made sense to me. The flaw in the system becomes evident when a family member is called to meet their maker after the hours of darkness. What happens then? The curtains are already drawn as a matter of course, so none of the

NEIGHBOURS

are going to know anything about it until morning. And what if the ***fatality*** OCCURS **just as it's getting dark ? How can anyone tell the difference?** Are the CURTAINS being drawn in accordance with **twilight** etiquette, or to **BROADCAST** a visit from the grim reaper? That's just the way it is. When the daylight has faded enough to warrant switching on the lights indoors, the curtains are drawn IMMEDIATELY. It's a single action — lights on, curtains drawn. The law of the land states that NOT ONE RAY OF ELECTRIC LIGHT SHALL LEAK OUT OF THE HOME. It's **as if it** were **wartime again.**

MARY had been flicking through my **WOMAN'S OWN** during one of the commercial breaks and had spotted a dressmaking pattern for a simple daytime frock you can make yourself at home.

"Do you think this would look nice in brown?" she said, showing me the **magazine**.

Golden Brown

"Lovely," I said. Brown's not really my colour —**I tend to go for something a bit more feminine**— but Mary always looks nice in it, in her ***OWN*** matronly way. Her question had caught me somewhat off my guard; I was surprised she'd asked my opinion. She generally avoids the topic of WOMEN'S CLOTHING altogether, claiming that I tend to 'go on about it', which is possibly true, but perfectly natural for any woman famished, as I am, for someone with whom to discuss her favourite subject – haute couture.

"It only takes three and a half yards of material," she said. "I've got some remnants under the stairs. Would you like me to make it up for you?"

"For me?" I was shocked.

"Yes, we could get some ribbon to trim the collar and cuffs."

" Oh, Mary, do you really mean it?" I said excitedly. I'm not supposed to call her Mary; it just slipped out, but she didn't say anything. I took the MAGAZINE and re-examined the lady in the photo who was modelling it. She was tall and glamorous like me, with a slight look of Kay Kendall about her. Dressmaking at home gives you the FASHION wardrobe you want without tugging too hard on the FAMILY purse strings. Vera Lynn, of the silver voice and golden bank balance, makes lots of her own clothes and everything for her five-year-old daughter, Virginia. The dress itself was simple — bordering on the plain, really — but it was quite a becoming shape. Perhaps with white collars and cuffs, a belt of coloured ribbon, a flower on my shoulder? I couldn't help thinking it would have suited me better in gay daffodil yellow with a smart ocean blue for contrast, but I didn't want to make waves.

It was the first time Mary had ever offered to make anything for me. Most of the time, the subject of my wardrobe is an irritation to her. Once or twice she has passed on a few items of her own, things she no longer WEARS (that's if Oxfam doesn't get there first), but it's always done in a slightly offhand manner, taking little or no interest in how the things might look on me. These GARMENTS are always donated with the strict understanding, naturally, that they should be FOR HOME USE ONLY and never worn out of doors. She needn't have mentioned it. I certainly wasn't going to be seen out in any of Mary's old hand-me-downs. What would the neighbours think?

"We'll have a go at it tomorrow night, if you like," she said.

"Tomorrow's FRIDAY. You'll be going to THE PICTURES."

"I'm not going this week. Betty's got flu."

"Oh."

"So we'll get the MACHINE out."

"Oh. OK."

I could see that Mary had detected the note of uncertainty in my voice, so I quickly masked it with a gracious smile. The truth is I was rather banking on Mary being out tomorrow so I could keep my rendezvous with Mr. Hands without her knowing anything about it. I knew she wouldn't approve, especially after all those promises, but I'd figured I could leave after she'd gone out and be back home again before her with no harm done. *Of all the luck.* She's been going to the pictures with BETTY every Friday since I can remember, and here she was, offering to make me a DRESS on the very night I was to have myself captured on film— with Diana Dors, possibly. *It was all too much.*

9

PERHAPS YOU ALREADY know Mrs. PRICE, or someone very like her. In every neighbourhood one meets the woman who is always "popping in". Her visits always occur at the most awkward times—just when you've decided that the stair carpet needs moving to even out the tread, or you've settled down for a quiet read, or you are enjoying sticking seashells on to a favourite heirloom. Marjorie Mullins in WOMAN'S DAY says that the only way to deal with the persistent "popper in" is to be firm with her.

Renie PRICE is a thin worry of a woman. Always busy with one thing or another and never sits down. COOKING, cleaning, queueing from morning till night: like all housewives, Mrs. PRICE works a seven-day week and mostly loves it. There she goes, spring-cleaning every corner, getting every nook and cranny absolutely, positively, perfectly clean — Parozone-clean. She could **Brighten your FRONT PORCH** with red-brick polish before you could shout "Cardinal!"

The **PRICES** have three children. They've all left home now, but when **Roy** was young he spent quite a lot of time over at their house playing with Michael, who was the same age. There was Dianne in the middle, and Maureen, the eldest, who **had a funny eye that looked** SOMEWHERE ELSE. **THE house** always smelled of CABBAGE, yet the only thing they ever seemed to eat was ***JAM TARTS***. After my accident, *Roy* had to go over to the ***Prices***' for his tea while MARY was up at the hospital, but there was no proper

FOOD,

just those big horrible things with **CHEAP SYNTHETIC** jam and dank, stale pastry. When Mary came home, he'd walk back across ***THE ROAD*** feeling sick. The **TART**s came in two charming varieties: **RASPBERRY**

JAM, CLOYING and strange with seeds that lodged themselves between your teeth; and LEMON CURD, dirty yellow AND SWEET *enough to give you a headache.* Heaven knows where she got them — BULK-BUY from the market, probably. Michael used to eat dozens of them; IT'S A WONDER he was never *fat.* (This was before the war, so there was no rationing either.) There were stale BISCUITS, too, no doubt from the same source. Unlike Roy, Michael had free access to the BISCUIT TIN at all times of the day, yet never offered ONE to Roy unless his *MOTHER* told him to. He'd stand there with a fistful of spares, humming greedily to himself as he ate. NYOmm–NYOmm-NYOmm.

When she wasn't tackling the housework or popping in on somebody, Mrs. PRICE could be found sitting at the dining table in their back room 'doing her chains' to make a bit of extra money. The chains were thin, gold (or at least gold-coloured) NECKLACES-to-be, AND Mrs. Price's JOB WAS TO undo the last link with two pairs of pliers and attach a jump ring to one end and a clasp fastener to the other. The chains always occupied the dining-room table, laid out in thick straight piles with little brown envelopes of clasps and rings all shiny under the LAMP. She'd wear her 'OTHER' glasses when she was doing her chains, and her fingers would TURN BLACK FROM the metal.

For many housewives, RUG-MAKING is one of the most enjoyable pastimes because it needs no previous experience and is so delightfully simple to follow. Once you start you find the work so fascinating that you don't want to put it down for a second. Yet there is the joy of knowing that you can stop in the middle for a cup of tea and a CHARLOTTE RUSSE. FOR Mrs. PRICE there was no CHARLOTTE RUSSE, just more chains.

THE ongoing chain set-up was a permanent fixture on the dining table, so the family always ate in the KITCHEN at a tiny *table* Mr. PRICE had made, which folded down from the back door. Have you ever thought about using the back of your door in this way? No, neither have I. Mrs. *PRICE* was paid a certain amount for every batch of chains she did, but Mary said it wasn't very much, just a few shillings. Even with all those clasps and rings in place, she was still unable to make ends meet. There was something symbolic about that, if one took time to look closely. Renie didn't see it, but she was probably wearing her

other

glasses.

EVERY WEEK a man came to collect the chains she'd done and left her WITH *new* ones to do. It was an ***endless task she*** could ***never hope to complete, with no fairy god-mother or magic elves to help her out.*** And to this day, her tired face is a **frank admission of all the** sacrifices she has **made, and the** less than **kaleidoscopic experiences** this part-time work has given her.

20-**ODD** years later, Mr. and Mrs. ***PRICE*** are still there and nothing much seems to have changed. She's still doing the **chains**. ***They own a car now,*** passed on to them by Renie's BROTHER, but Mr. **PRICE** is a bit **SPAM**-handed and can't drive it. It took him **YEARS** to pass his test, and when he finally did **he was** still **too nervous** to really do it. **His biggest problem seems to be** getting the car into the drive, experiencing great difficulty in negotiating the space between the gateposts. Every day when he gets home from work, he pips his horn and Mrs. ***PRICE*** comes out to open the gate and try to guide him in. Since she can't **DRIVE** either, for all the good it does, she might as well be Tommy Steele's mother performing an African war dance. Consequently, this manoeuvre will sometimes take ten or fifteen minutes, with her **WINDING** and waving her arms, and him going **BACKWARDS AND FORWARDS** until it's in. He'll often end up too close to the

GARDEN

wall and have to get out of the passenger door. I think he'd prefer to SELL IT and go to work on the bus, but Mrs. PRICE thinks having a car in the drive makes them look posh.

What has kept Mrs. PRICE light of step and buoyant of mind through her ENDLESS years of CHAIN LINKing is a jolly good **GOSSIP** with the neighbours. Ever since we were little, she's always found some excuse to POP OVER TO trade little snippets of news. Whether she is buying or selling, the commodity is always tittle-tattle. No, Roy is not ' ODDLY SECRETIVE ABOUT HIS MOVEMENTS ' ; he simply prefers to *STAY OUT OF IT*, believing everyone should mind their own business. So, on WEDNESDAY as he was getting home from work, when he saw Mrs. *PRICE* making a beeline for the **HOUSE** he tried to get inside quick before she caught him. She was holding something inside a paper bag on the flat of her hand. Perhaps he had it wrong; perhaps she was going next door to see Mrs. Gordon. The *Gordons* are our neighbours TO THE LEFT. We don't have very much to do with them. **BECAUSE** they use their **BACK** room instead of the front, they're not so involved in the street's GOINGS-ON. **THE** couple are in their mid-forties, **no children,** and are particularly fond of SCOTTISH COUNTRY DANCE Music. We also have to endure the **RASPING** yap-yap of their little Pekinese when they let it out in the garden. ***We never complain,*** though. Mrs. **GORDON** worships him. **APPARENTLY,** she treats her PRECIOUS POOCH better than she treats her HUSBAND. She once told ROY: "His vocabulary consists of six words: ballie, drinkie, walkie, meatie, kitty, and naughty" —— but it wasn't clear if she was talking about Mr. **Gordon** or **the dog**.

"Cooee!" trilled Mrs. PRICE. *Roy* pretended he hadn't seen her, but it was too late. She caught up with him as he was fumbling for **the front door key under the mat.**
"I was just coming to see your mum with this," she said, looking down at the **paper bag**.
"Oh. Shall I give it to her? I don't think she's back yet."
"She is. I've just seen her **come home**."
She was standing too close and ROY was forced to scrutinise the face before him. Beauty lies hidden in every woman's skin, but hers was buried *pretty* deep. He was hoping to take whatever it was in the bag and leave her there on the doorstep, but Mrs. **PRICE** clearly wasn't going to part **with her offering** so easily. This was a trade, and she wanted INFORMATION in return.

Resignedly, ROY slid his key in the lock and opened the front door, CALLING into the HOUSE: "Mum! It's MRS. Price!"

There was no answer.

"It's just a few JAM *TARTS*," explained Mrs. Price. BOB gets them from WORK. I know you like them, Roy."

ROY nodded.

"I thought you might like some CAKEs, what with you having a guest staying."

"Guest?" said Roy.

"Yes, THE YOUNG LADY."

"What *young lady*?" said Roy guardedly. He knew this was trouble.

"Oh, haven't you got staying with you? I SOMEONE thought I saw someone yesterday. A young woman in a RED COAT."

"Staying here? No, I don't think so." Roy stepped inside the HOUSE, hoping to terminate the conversation, but Mrs. PRICE was like a terrier tugging at a bit of rope. How would Marjorie in *WOMAN'S DAY* have suggested he handle it? "What a pity I can't invite you in," you must say regretfully. "As you see, I'm just tackling the stair carpet. But you must come one day when I've made some of my special chocolate cakes. What about tea next Friday at four?" No, he couldn't make CAKES and he didn't want her there on FRIDAY. He didn't want her there at all.

Mrs. Price was still going at it.

"Well, whoever it was, she let her self in the front door so she must have had a key."

"Really?" said Roy, pretending to look puzzled. "Well, I can't think who that could have been. Must have been Mum."

"No, it wasn't your mum. She was only young, in her twenties. Quite tall."

Roy shrugged his shoulders, not knowing what else to say.

"Well, that's odd. I just assumed she was staying with you."

"No. There's nobody staying here."

Mrs. PRICE wouldn't let go. Roy imagined her at a police training display in Earl's Court with her jaws clamped on to a make-believe villain's heavily padded forearm.

"Well, who was that WOMAN who answered the door to the postman the other day?" she said.

"I don't know. I've been away for a few days. Mum, I should think." Roy's irritation was beginning to show, but Mrs. Price was impervious to it.

"No, I'm sure it wasn't. I'm sure it was the same young Woman. She was in your HOUSE."

ROY HEARD the toilet flush and Mary coming down the stairs. Gratefully, he stood aside.

"Oh, hello, Mary," said Mrs. PRICE. "I was just saying to ROY, I thought you might like a few JAM TARTS — with you having a GUEST."

"Oh, that's very good of you, Renie," said Mary, playing it cautiously. Mrs. PRICE slid the plate out of the bag and handed it to Mary. There were THREE of the *much-loved tarts,* ALL WITH *raspberry jam filling.*

"There's one each."

"How lovely," said MARY politely.

Mrs. PRICE could see that Mary wasn't going to volunteer *anything in return,* so she dug deeper.

" Roy doesn't seem to know anything about **the young woman** you've got staying with you."

"THE WOMAN?" Mary knew at once that Mrs. Price was referring to me but ADOPTED Roy's puzzled look.

"Yes, the one I saw letting herself in the other day. Around five it was. **RED COAT.** A relative, was it?"

"Oh, yes," said MARY, changing tack. "My SISTER's daughter came to stay for a few days. She's gone home now."

Mary's mind was like a rapier in the hands of a *frenzied* swashbuckler. Mrs. PRICE cogitated on this NEW INFORMATION for a moment.

"Oh. So you didn't get to see her, Roy?" she said.

"No. I've been away."

"Yes, ROY. I forgot to tell you your cousin had been." Mary sounded as if she were acting in a play. Roy felt too embarrassed to look her in the eyes. He knew she hated being put in a position where she was forced to take part in amateur dramatics. Mary's sister doesn't even have a DAUGHTER, but Mrs. Price seemed to be buying it. GOOD OLD MARY.

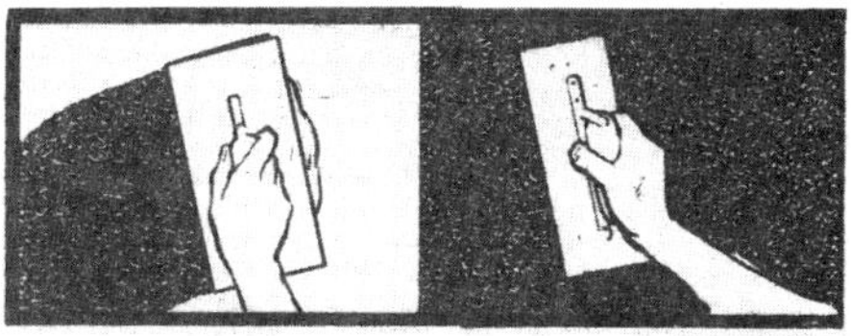

Her brilliantly ad-libbed UNTRUTH appeared to have PLASTERED OVER THE CRACKS in their defence.

" *Roy*'s been so busy with his new job I haven't had time to tell him all the news," she explained with a WEAK laugh.

"Yes. That's right," said Roy, treading carefully, still unsure whether Mary's flimsily constructed story would withstand his weight.

"Oh, have you got a new job, Roy ? ***That's nice.*** Where are you working now?" She would, of course, have already worked that out for herself, having seen the van parked on the drive.

"I'm DELIVERY MAN at **white'S** LAUNDRY on CROSS *Street*," said *Roy*.

"Oh, well that's good because you've been out of work a long time, haven't you?"

"Hmm."

"Do you get a discount, Roy ?"

The question took him by surprise.

"I don't know."

"Ooh, you should ask, shouldn't he, MARY? ***Save your*** mum ***a*** BIT ***of hard work."*** There was a pause, everyone smiled and nodded.

MRS. Price looked down at the plate and said, "Well, you probably won't need THREE, then, if there's only the two of you." She took one of the TARTS off the plate and put it BACK in the paper bag, which she folded round it. Roy was amused at this and, glancing at Mary, thought he saw the shadow of a smile float across her face. "Don't worry about the plate, Mary, I'll fetch it another time. It's only an old one." Once it was clear that Mrs. Price was leaving, MARY felt safe to offer her hospitality. "Do you want to come in for a cup of tea, Renie?" "No thanks, love. I've got to get back. BOB will be home in a minute and I'll have to open the GATE."

And with that, she was off, scuttling back across the road with her paper bag.

ROY and MARY stepped back into the house, shutting the door behind them with thank-goodness-for-that relief. They had triumphed most beautifully and Roy chuckled in celebration at such an easy victory. Mary's expression, though, had become serious. "It isn't funny, Roy. She's bound to find out. You know what she's like when she gets wind of something."

"She won't 'get wind' of anything. I'll make sure."

"HOW?"

"I'll make sure Norma stays indoors. Permanently."

"How many times have I heard that before?"

"I mean it this time."

"And no answering the door ?"

"And no ANSWERING THE DOOR," he assured her.

"Or standing in the window."

"Or standing in the window."

"Promise?"

"Promise."

IT WAS a game of ping-pong and ROY had won the point. Mary took his hand. "Oh, Roy. You've got a real chance now with your NEW JOB. Don't spoil it."

"I know. I won't. I promise." Roy squeezed her hand reassuringly. For the moment, Mary seemed satisfied. The nagging doubt had been temporarily quelled by Roy's happy-go-lucky charm. He seized the opportunity to capitalise on it. "Right. Let's start on those delicious jam tarts." Mary smiled a guilty smile. "Oh dear. These blessed tarts. What do we do with them?" she said. "I couldn't eat anything that's come out of that HOUSE."

When I came downstairs later in my radiant garnet-red dress with Spanish airs, its slim skirt knee-length, its overblouse lavished with jewel-trimmed sleeves, I saw that MARY had crumbled up Mrs. PRICE'S TARTS and thrown the bits out on to the back lawn. Some sparrows were pecking at the crumbs, quickly adapting, as birds do, TO THE IDEA OF having their natural diet supplemented by RASPBERRY JAM.

So I'm CONFINED TO QUARTERS —which is fair enough, I dare say. *It is how it was always supposed to be.* And it's a small price to pay to keep MARY HAPPY. Besides, with Roy earning a regular wage now, I'm sure he'll be bringing home **the occasional item of evening wear** — a sleek and elegant full-skirted charmer, or an oh-so-smooth, sophisticated jersey cocktail dress — things that up until now he has been unable to afford to buy me. *Evening Wear* seems to be my thing these days. Since Roy started his job, my other **Frocks** HAVE BARELY SEEN *the* light *of* **day.**

10

IN any perfect week there are bound to be one or two hiccups. It's only natural. I have learned to be philosophical about it. If it isn't one thing, I often assure myself, it's two. Mrs. PRICE was number one. The second hiccup was a little more serious. It happened on FRIDAY and it shook *Roy* up like sauce in a ketchup bottle.

It was the hour of the midday meal, and since Roy had already done most of the day's deliveries, he decided to park up in the leafy lane that leads to the ***LIBRARY*** and the church hall. *Roy* is perfectly entitled to take a lunch break, though, like many hard-working men, he often eats his meals on the go. The sandwiches on Mary's menu today were **BACON**. Delicious, satisfying, easily digested. **A quick meal of bacon is just the job for people in a hurry.** That's why active people need bacon regularly. It keeps them going. Mary had added a spoonful of delicious Branston Pickle to give the sandwich that special, luscious flavour that's packed with honest-to-goodness goodness.

When he had finished, **Roy** carefully folded the *waxed paper wrapping* and put it in his pocket. Like me, *Roy* abhors thoughtless littering, and besides, Mary LIKES HIM TO save the paper so it can be used for next day's SANDWICHES. He would never dream of simply throwing it down like so many other young men would do. I WONDER if motorists realise how dangerous it is to throw objects from car windows?

The other day, on a busy road, Roy saw a motorist throw a banana skin away, and drive on, unaware that it had hit a girl cyclist in the face.

She completely lost control of her bicycle and skidded right across the road, falling heavily a few feet from the kerb.

Only swift action by a following driver averted a nasty accident.

AFTER lunch, when **ROY** opened *up* the back of the van to check his delivery sheet against the number of ***PARCELS***,

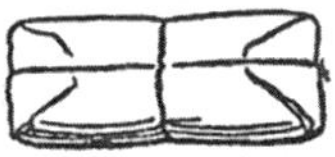

he noticed that the string securing one of them had slipped its knot so that the brown-paper wrapping had become loose. The parcel was destined ***for a*** Mrs. Wintergarden on

West Close, which overlooks a park in one of the more salubrious areas of town. He had not met Mrs. Wintergarden but she sounded like the kind of woman who might send her DRESSes to WHITE'S to be cleaned. She wasn't —not this week, anyway. The INTRIGUING-LOOKING FLORAL FABRIC peeping out from beneath the paper turned out to be nothing more interesting than a set of cushion covers. Having secured the WRAPPING, Roy returned the parcel to the rack.

HE lit a cool, smooth Kensitas and strolled a little way along the cinder path to stretch his legs. His footsteps, by no volition of their own, slowly wandered along with him, crunching the cinders underfoot. The cinders are some kind of industrial waste, from coke smelting possibly, that have been laid down over what would otherwise be thick mud. THE PATH isn't really meant for MOTOR VEHICLES, but who was going to know? There was no one about.

Glancing at his watch, he thought of Eve and tried to imagine what she would be doing at this moment. Weighing out Dolly Mixtures or rubbing the price off a birthday card? Was she thinking of him at all? Was she counting the hours as he was? Perhaps he'd stop by the shop later to buy WOMAN'S JOURNAL.

ON one side of him were the walled grounds of the church, where tramps go to **DRINK** **PALE** Ale and **CREAM SHERRY**; on the other, a row of postage stamp gardens belonging to the terraced houses that backed on to the path. The extent of these gardens is

defined by inexpensive creosoted **FENCING PANELS** which run the length of the lane and is bordered by straggling weeds and shrubs. **Wild and garden flowers can be combined so charmingly—something that very few people seem to realise.**

BY standing on a log, *Roy* was able to see over the **FENCE** and survey the backs of the houses on Greenwood Avenue **and** their **modest gardens.** Some have little lawns with flowers growing in borders; others have gone for the '**CONCRET**ing it over' option. Each garden is separated from its neighbour by a low fence or hedge. I always say, if **you are going to have a hedge, have a good one and look after it. That means cutting it at least twice a year to keep it trim and encourage growth. There is no need for hedge trimming to be a dull and laborious job. You can do it in a quarter of the time with very little effort, if you use a Tarpentrimmer.**

There was no evidence of any truly green

fingers at work there, no wonderful things like bougainvillaea and purple and scarlet and magenta-coloured blossoms, oleanders, and fig trees, cypresses, and olives. **Roy** hadn't expected anything like that, **but, then he has always been more down to earth than I am.** I had envisaged **great wide** orange groves with all the trees weighed down with oranges. There was no sign of any oranges. (Nor was there any sign of the yacht, *La Fortunella* —**but that was no surprise to anyone.) Instead there were**

SHEDS & LEAN-TOS

of various sizes, garden swings for the kiddies, and, in one,

an enthusiastic gardener had contrived a little home-made **POND**. **Each** **GARDEN** **reflected the individual needs, aspirations and accomplishments of its owners.** Discarded **FURNITURE**, **a home-made rabbit hutch. In one,** a pram with its hood up; **in another, a** dog chained up to a rusty mangle. **Each different from the next yet, in its own way,** **typical of the traditional** *ENGLISH* **country** *GARDEN*.

AND, of course, on MONDAYs there would be **washing** there. Most housewives find it convenient to do a big wash once a week.

If possible, do **it** early in the week, so that the ironing and mending can be completed in good time. Though Monday is the traditional washday—**it certainly is in our home— one of the houses that backed on to the lane had broken with tradition and** had **their washing out to dry** on a FRIDAY instead. Perhaps the happy housewife responsible was taking advantage of good outdoor-drying weather, or maybe **celebrating the arrival of one of the brand new** Bendix Automatic Washers **and couldn't resist getting the first load in to test how it coped with her weekday whites.** All she'd have to do is set the machine, add the soap and leave the rest to the Bendix while she relaxed and got dinner ready.

Everything was pegged neatly to the washing line, the wooden clothes prop **thrusting** the line **high into the autumn breeze.** Billowing **white shirts and** towels**, baby's bibs and nappies, sheets, pillowcases, and various ladies' underthings** including, **Roy** noticed, a SHORTIE NIGHTDRESS with a floating on air feeling, highly trimmed all down the front with scalloped lace, lurex and ribbon, plus ruching round the hem.

All **SHINING *SHINING* WHITE!**

How pleased the little woman would be. "**I've never seen a wash come out like this before,**" she'd be saying to herself, "**never in all my** born days. Don't talk to me about white! These things boiled in Omo are better than just white—they're bright. If that's what Omo does, I'm all for Omo from now on." She's right too!

Hanging at the end of the LINE nearest the fence there was a selection of other ladies' undergarments: a girdle (which looked like it might have been from the FIRM 'N' FLATTER range by *Silhouette*); two pairs of NYLON BRIEFS daintily trimmed with White lace; and a brassiere. The **bra**, unless I'm much mistaken, was from *Exquisite Form* — Delicately pretty, White Nylon lace, with wide set straps and unique inner cup construction to provide special uplift. Undies are now following the mainstream of fashion so conscientiously, there's virtually no difference as far as styling and finish go between top clothes and underclothes. **My dream is to one day own a** 'MADAMOISELLE' LIGHT 'N' LOVELY BRA by CONTRABAND. Roy has seen them in Marcia Modes on Great Colmore Street. They have all manner of head-spinningly gorgeous things in the window. But as **Bras** go, the one hanging just a few feet away on the washing line was really rather pretty and, seeing it was on the **large** size, *Roy* fancied it would fit **ME** perfectly.

HE was really only going to take a closer look at it —to see if it would be something I might want to put on my shopping list, something I could look for in Mary's catalogue. All quite innocent. There was a convenient little door in the fence with a drop-lever latch to it. What harm could it do to take a peek?

There were no signs of life from the **HOUSE.** **Edmund Hockridge was singing** on the wireless **somewhere,** but that seemed further along. Roy naturally assumed that **this particular housewife, having pegged out her wash,** was probably **out at the shops or taking baby up to the welfare.**

With the stealth of A CARTOON MOUSE, he tiptoed up to the line and gave the ***BRA*** a squeeze, just as he had seen Mary do **ON A HUNDRED WASHDAYS.** **It felt perfectly dry. The *pants* were dry too.** This washing had a fresher, more outdoor smell than the laundry parcels in the van. It was probably the '**Sanitary**' bit that gave **White**'s laundry its whiff of carbolic. Roy **bunched the** nightdress to his face to **breathe it in.** This was definitely different from our **WASHING** at home. Perhaps it was

or *Fairy Snow.*

He'd always enjoyed Washing DAY. As a boy, he would run in and out of *THE CLOTHES* on the washing line, letting the cold, wet things drape across HIS FACE. He was momentarily lost in reverie. Memories came unbidden, as did **the sudden slam of the back door,** which brought him to attention. **Someone was coming.**

THE peg that had been holding the **bra** somehow pinged off and Roy was left with the garment in his hand. Though billowing SHEETS obscured his view, beneath them he could see some LADY LEGS AND A PAIR OF SLIPPERS approaching. Same SLIPPERS as Mary's, he noticed.

"Oi, what do you think you're doing? Get out of our **GARDEN**," came the voice.

Instinctively, ROY started to run. He was still holding the *intimate apparel*.

"Hey! Put that back," she said, advancing towards him with stiff-legged gait. "That's our Sarah's."

WITHin seconds Roy was back through the GATE and sitting in his van, fumbling with the keys. His heart was racing like a greyhound chasing a sausage on a string, his mind in tumult because of the agonising conflict within him. What have I done? he thought. Why did I run out like this? What am I running away from? He threw the BRA on to the passenger seat as if to dissociate himself from it. It wasn't his. He didn't want it. It had all happened by accident. "The blessed thing just came off in my hand," he would say. "Then what is it doing sitting next to you in the van?" What would be his answer to that? The BRA had been hitch-hiking and he was innocently offering it a lift.

It was an incredible, impossible thought. But it was the only explanation that would fit the circumstances.

The engine roared into life just as the WOMAN appeared at his side window. "Give us it back. You b*****." I am afraid she lost her temper and forgot her manners. She slapped the window with the flat of her hand as Roy jerked the gear stick into first. The WOMAN stepped away as the VAN leapt forward and sped off down the path towards THE MAIN ROAD, sending a cloud of black cinders into the air as the tyres span to get their grip. He could see her in his rear-view mirror, standing in the middle of the path. Now he was in trouble. *SHE* would have seen the name on the side of the van and was probably planning to turn up at WHITE'S to make a complaint. She might even tell the police. Either way he'd get the sack and *Mary* would somehow get to hear of the incident. EVE too, probably.

The best thing, he decided, would be to throw the bra out of the window WHILE the WOMAN was still watching. It would get all dirty from the cinders on the path but at least she might not pursue her complaint if the item was returned. A quick going over in the Bendix and it would look like new again. But, glancing down, he saw that the BRA was no longer next to him on the passenger seat; it must have slid off on to the floor when he swung the VAN round. He didn't want to stop the van to look for it, yet he knew he'd have to make sure the WOMAN saw him throw it out before he turned left into Greenwood Avenue. Staring straight ahead and with his right hand still on the wheel, Roy leaned over to the passenger seat and fish ed around in the foot-well, but came up with nothing. In fact, the BRA had slipped sideways into the gap between the seat and the passenger door. A tiny portion was peeping out. He only took his eyes off the road for a SECOND while he reached over to make a grab for it, but when he looked up again he saw a little girl stepping out in front of the VAN. I can't remember the rules about stopping distances, but this was much too short and *Roy* was going much too fast. HE slammed on his brakes and gripped the wheel tight as the VAN skidded across the black dust.

Over 150

There was a voice, surprisingly powerful for a woman, shouting "Wait!" and a MOTHERLY hand reaching out to snatch *the girl* back to safety. Intelligent use of the brake-pedal becomes increasingly important in these situations, but even the most careful driver can find himself in a skid caused by treacherous ROAD conditions. The back end of the VAN swung round, grazing the FENCE, before coming to a halt a few feet short of the need to summon an ambulance. ROY froze at the WHEEL. In that one moment it seemed inevitable that *the girl* would be tossed aside and strewn like spilled paint on the pavement. The engine had stalled and it was suddenly strangely quiet. A cloud of black dust drifted silently towards the WOMAN AND CHILD, completely enveloping them for a brief moment before passing by.

THE GIRL'S MOTHER —he assumed it was her mother—gave him a look that suggested she felt no one was at fault, but, seeing an opportunity for a valuable lesson to be learned, she decided to reprimand **her daughter** anyway, yanking her backwards by the shoulder of her coat and saying: "What have I told you?" The WOMAN glanced

No. 152

up at ROY as if seeking approval for her PARENTING SKILLS. She had assumed an 'US AGAINST THEM' —parents versus kids— coalition, to which ROY felt no allegiance. The little girl started to cry, which seemed to be the cue for HER MOTHER to take further action. Spinning her round against her knee, she smacked THE GIRL hard on the back of the leg. Roy hid his guilty look in the folds of his coat. He knew he was the one who should have been SMACKED. As the woman nudged her wailing daughter out of his way and headed off down the avenue, she gave *Roy* a silent nod of acknowledgement. It had been a near thing— just a banana skin away — but no damage done. They were moving on.

But ROY couldn't move on. He sat there alone, with brakes jammed on, his knee so stiff he could not take his foot off the brake, his hands like vices on the steeringwheel. After a minute his hands AND knees relaxed and trembled uncontrollably before he could calm them. He opened the glove compartment and stuffed the bra into it before slamming it shut — as if by throwing the culprit in jail he could close the door on the whole INCIDENT.

HE checked his rear-view mirror again, fearful that *the Bendix* washerwoman would have caught up with him. His view was skewed by the slantwise angle of the VAN, but there was no sign of her. Tossing undergarments willy-nilly on to THE PATH OF ABSOLUTION would have been a pointless exercise with no one there to witness it.

He started the engine and the VAN TRUNDLED gently out on to the road, but now he felt as if he had no control over his speed or direction, as if he was sitting in a car on a fairground ride where the steering wheel was just for show. This was no big-dipper thriller; it was just a kiddie ride—yet, *as always*, *Roy* felt sick and wanted to get *off*.

●

THE ELEVENTH

ROY was supposed to go over to Sutton delivering but he found himself driving back to **CROSS** Street.

He didn't know why.

He began to feel increasingly unsure of his driving skills, dithering over the simplest action. Every time he had to release the clutch, his KNEE shook. He knew he was driving too slowly; other motorists were getting annoyed.

"The too-slow drivers. The ones that dither and dawdle. They are the dangerous ones, the really wicked ones, too." says top racing driver, Stirling Moss.

When he came to turn into the YARD at **WHITE**'s, he suddenly felt unable to gauge the distance between the concrete gate pillars. Another motorist had stopped to let him through, but Roy couldn't bring himself to make the turn. He felt as though everyone was watching him. Eventually he opted out of the manoeuvre, canceling his indicator and pulling into the side of the road outside **The Post Office**, bowing his head in shame as an embittered motorist taunted him with his spiteful horn.

ROY could not get out of the van. Perhaps he should have gone home. He seemed plunged in some listless, heavy stodge. Suddenly he felt very cold. He lit a cigarette and sat looking out. A lady with a pram stood outside the POST OFFICE and he noticed that Eve had come out to talk to her. The two women peered into the pram and EVE showed *appropriate* feminine interest in its CONTENTS, something that neither ROY nor I had ever been able to do convincingly. NEVERTHELESS, WITH the mother's continuous care, in a few weeks this little chap will soon manage a tricycle and can be entrusted with a pair of blunt-edged scissors.

THEY chatted animatedly for a few minutes with the WOMAN rocking the pram idly back and forth before she said goodbye and set off up towards the bakery. Eve waved her own goodbye INTO THE PRAM and as she turned to go back into the shop, she caught sight of the van and went over. She must have seen at once that something was wrong.

"What's happened?" There was alarm in her voice. "Are you all right?" Her voice was muffled against the GLASS.

Roy shakily rolled down the window and all the sounds of the outside world flooded in. His face looked white and strained like ***sauerkraut***.

"Hello," he said, trying to sound cheery. As a matter of fact, he was feeling wretched.

"What's wrong?" she asked with sudden anxiety.

"I'm—I'm all right," he stammered. "I was driving the van and a little girl stepped out in front of me."

"Oh my God," said EVE. "Did you hit her?"

"No. I managed to stop in time but it's shaken me a up a bit."

"You look dreadful. Come into the SHOP. I'll make you a cup of tea."

"I'm all right really. Just a bit shaken. I've got deliveries to do."

"You can do them later. Come and sit in the back till you feel better. You're as white as a sheet."

WITH the irony, of her remark floating overhead like SCOTCH MIST, she opened the driver's door, and Roy found himself out of the van, being led into the post office. Taking his arm, EVE steered him behind the counter and through to the door at the back of the shop. His footsteps felt loose and sloppy. It reminded him of the time he had to have gas when they took out his back teeth. Even in his unstable condition, Roy felt a thrill at the touch of her hand on his arm.

"I'm just making this man some tea, Auntie. He's had a nasty shock." She was talking to the woman in the cage.

"What is it? What's happened?" said Auntie.

"I'm all right really," repeated Roy, offering a feeble smile. "Just a bit shaken."

"Put his head between his knees," suggested Auntie.

"I'll be in the back if it gets busy," said Eve.

THEY WENT through a hallway that led to a KITCHEN at the back.

"You just sit down. I'll put the kettle on," said Eve. "What were you doing sitting outside?

Were you on your way back to whites?"

"No." Roy shook his head. "I don't know where I was going. I couldn't stop thinking about the little girl and what might have happened. I suppose I really came to see you.."

She reached out impulsively and touched his shoulder. "I'm going to give you a nice cup of tea, and make sure you're all right. Don't you worry."

She took his hands and drew him to a chair near the fireplace. She lit the fire, and flames crawled slowly along the paper and wood. She stood then, and looked down at him like a duty nurse at a busy hospital deciding what should be done next. The full fresh muslin of her pink skirt brushed against ROY's knees as she turned to the STOVE, and he caught a whiff of some fresh delicate fragrance.

ROY watched her as she busied herself with the tea things, fiddling with clattering cups and jugs. The band on the Radio was playing that old favourite, "The Blue Danube". It had never before been Roy's favourite, but it was now.

He was only vaguely aware of the surrounding KITCHEN; it was all merely a painted backdrop to provide a setting for Eve's loveliness. She used little make-up, but what there was gave her a subtly exotic look. The most amazing thing was that she seemed hardly conscious of it. She stood there in the old-fashioned kitchen, looking what she was—someone special, someone important, a woman beloved. The kettle began to sing its own praises and in less than a

"JIFFY"

Eve was bringing the teapot to the table. Roy noticed for the first time that there were three cups and saucers laid there.

"How are you feeling?"

"I'm all right," Roy said. He stood up, in an effort to help.

"Just you lie still, cowboy. You've had a rough passage."

She was very close for a moment. Her nearness held him motionless, and for that long moment he did not breathe. His hands felt heavy at the ends of his arms. Ten pounds each. He was looking at her and she at him, and all of a sudden he was panic-stricken to realise that he did not know what came next. The play he had been rehearsing all his life was about to begin and there was a danger of him forgetting his lines. As if sensing this, Eve smiled warmly and put out her hand. In eager response, he gripped it tightly. Her heart was no doubt beating in a strange way as she felt the warm, envelop-ing grasp of his strong masculine hand. Looking up at him, she could see that his rugged features had softened like margarine in the growing, rosy light of the fire. They stood without speaking. The Scotch mist had turned to a light rain that whispered against the windows.

BEING there with Eve, so close in the dusky room, her silky hair outlined against the kitchen cupboard, unsteadied Roy still more. He stood caressing her hand, trying to muster words. Finally, he spoke. "I have never known anyone like you," he said.

A bit of firewood snapped and flared; the rain was louder.

"That was a very nice thing to say," she said gently. Her hand was still in his. If she had left her hand there another second he would have leaned forward and kissed her, in spite of those faltering footsteps, but for the time being, Madame Fate had other plans.

EVE sighed, and withdrew her hand as a silvery tinkle sounded from the hall. At first, Roy thought it was a cat's collar, but when the door opened, it turned out to be a charm bracelet on the arm of Eve's Auntie. She bustled in, unaware that her arrival had broken the tremulous spell between them. Eve leaned back against the sink. ROY sat down and stood up again as if PLAYING A PARTY GAME. Auntie peered at Roy, squinting through her glasses.

"IS HE ALL RIGHT?"

She said it as if he were deaf or in a coma.

"Yes, he's fine," said Eve. "He was nearly involved in a road accident but everything's all right now. He's just a bit jittery A thing like that can shake you up."

"He does look a bit washed out. Does he want an ASPRO ?" She rattled the little packet she was holding as if to test Roy 's response to stimulus.

Eve deferred to Roy for the answer.

"No, I'm fine thank you, Mrs . . ." He paused, but nobody supplied the name.

"Is there sugar in this, Eve?"

"No."

Auntie spooned sugar into her teacup and gave it a stir. "The man from Benson's has just been. He's left the stuff on the counter."

"All right, Auntie. I'll be through in a minute," said Eve.

Auntie set the ASPRO bottle on the table and headed back to the shop with a couple of biscuits tucked on to her saucer.

Roy and Eve were alone again but the mood had changed and they were back to square one.

Eve offered him a biscuit. Rich Tea or bourbon cream.

He shook his head. "Do you mind if I smoke?" He took out his cigarettes and offered her the pack. She slid one out and put it to her lips.

He was glad he'd bought filters. It was just s just right for her — cool clear and refreshing. As he held the lighter to it, he saw with amazement that his hand was shaking. Feeling embarrassed, he LIT HIS OWN CIGARETTE and drew hard on it till the tip glowed red, as if that would stop it.

Roy glanced at his wrist watch. "I should be getting back to my DELIVERIES. I've been away longer than I intended."

"Are you going to be all right to drive?"

"Yes. I'll be fine."

"Do you want me to come with you?"

"In the van?"

"Yes. I can help with the DELIVERIES."

"Haven't you got to be here in the shop?"

"Auntie can manage. As long as I'm back in time to do the EVENING PAPERS."

The idea appealed to him but he was having trouble rearranging his travel plans.

"Well, I don't know. Do you thing it's all right? I'm probably not supposed to take PASSENGERS. What if Mr. WHITE sees you?"

"He won't. Anyway, I can explain things."

When they were in the van and the engine was running, Roy rested his hand on the gear lever and took a deep breath. If it weren't for EVE, he might not be doing this. He still didn't feel quite up to it. As if sensing this, she patted the back of his hand reassuringly.

"You'll be OK. It's best to get straight back on the horse."

Although it belonged to WHITE's, even in the few days he had been driving it, Roy had begun to think of the DELIVERY VAN as his own. Prior to the little girl incident, at least, he had felt very comfortable behind the wheel, whether he was driving it or just parked somewhere, looking out. The thrill of having Eve there, sitting next to him was in part because he felt she was now on his territory. THE *van* was his domain and by being there, it was as though she had agreed to become part of his

WORLD.

Waiting at a traffic light, she caught his sideways glance. "You're doing very well," she said, with an encouraging smile. She had a comfortable, protective manner, as if she were keeping an eye on EVERY Jockey Jack who fell down and broke his crown.

She was so lovely, sitting there, with her nice legs and smart skirt. Everything sweet and fresh, and all perfectly shaped. He wanted to scoop her up and hold her fiercely to him like the men in the soppier women's magazines. He wanted to gaze into her eyes and say romantic things. "My darling, my darling! Your hair is like honey-coloured silk and your lips are sweet as grapes. I want to strew your path with flowers and beauty. I want you with me always, my darling. I love you."
What would she do if he did say these things?
What would she say?
"And I love you too, Roy. Oh, my dear, dear love!" I could not go on living without

you. You know it. I know it. I want you always, for all eternity. My dear, sweet darling!"

THE AFTERNOON DELIVERIES took them to a part of town that Roy knew well, so there was no need to look at the map—just follow the list of addresses on his delivery sheet. As promised, Eve rolled up her sleeves to help, but because it simply wouldn't do for any CUSTOMERS to have seen her making the deliveries, in case it got back to Mr. WHITE, they decided to forgo collecting payment in favour of leaving the laundry packages on the doorsteps and *STUFFING* the customers' bills through their letterboxes. **It saved time and it** was **FUN TOO.** Their giddy laughter wore the SHORT TROUSERS of youthful exuberance as they dashed backwards and forwards to the van like contestants on Beat the Clock, hoping not to run into any customers for fear it would slow them down and lose them points. And beat the clock they did. By 3.45 all the parcels had been delivered. They were back in the VAN just as it started to rain again.

Eve didn't seem overly anxious to get back to **work.**

"I'm all right for ten minutes," she said. "Let's just sit here. It's nice."

They looked out on the tracery of blackened roofs, watching the ordinary people of Sutton hurry home through the rain. Housewife 'stocking-splashers', whose legs, after two steps on a wet pavement, are a complete beauty let-down. Housewives with shopping, housewives with kids, kids with pets, and husbands with families to keep.

THEY WERE parked at the top of Lee Hill Road, looking down towards the railway bridge over Union Street, and a clock tower in the middle of nothing. A few hundred yards further on is Stonehouse Street, where you can get a fish supper, or a stolen radio, or a hangover—or a girl friend who plays the banjo and laughs nearly all the time. Perhaps adding something to the *character* of the place.

Much of this area was bombed out in the war. *The rubble is still piled high, and no* shops have been rebuilt. Most of the locals have moved out to the new estates on the fringe of the city, but there are a few older folks still haunting the once picturesque streets, people who have lived in these parts too long to 'LIVE THE MODERN WAY'. They don't care so much for the new bathroom as they do for the old memories. At George Street *market,* you could buy anything, from a pork pie to a wedding dress.

AS it is, most people would say that the area has as much cosiness and charm as a prison cell. It offers no invitation to linger. They would as soon think of dallying on an airstrip as on the bleak pavements of Lee Hill Road. Yet to Roy this was the most glorious spot in the city ; **there was nowhere on earth he would rather** have been .

A splash of wind-driven rain stung the windscreen, blurring the picture before them. Eve snuggled into her seat. Turning to Roy, she said: "Would you like to have dinner with Auntie and me tonight?" Her eyes searched his for an answer, and then, as if as an added inducement, she said: "We're having chops."
He didn't answer right away, not because he was stupid or bad- mannered but because the unexpected often threw him off his balance. He couldn't find words to express his feelings. He didn't quite know what his feelings were, but he was deeply touched. After a while he said the only concrete thing that came into his head. "I like chops."

Her eyes met his own eyes, and there she read his sincerity. A gentle flush stole gradually up her cheeks. She felt oddly moved. A tiny glow warmed her heart.

"I'm glad," she said. "I'd like it if you could come."

"Thank you," he managed. "I–I'd be delighted." Their hands reached out, knuckles brushed against knuckles before the clasp was made. But from that point on, there was no hesitation. Everything came at once like THE CHRISTMAS MAIL. Overwhelmed by their feelings, They practically fell into each other's arms. *This* was *the genuine article. 100% pure.* He put his hand under her chin, lifted her face, looked into her eyes, with a very serious, direct question in his own gaze, and then, as if she'd replied to him, kissed her, and kissed her again as if for all his life, and all that life held for either of them.

"Oh, Eve."

She leaned towards him. "Yes. Oh, yes." Her great eyes were eloquent with appeal. She moved her face against his shoulder, pushing it down into the warmth and roughness of his jacket, feeling his shallow breath against her cheek as she nuzzled up against him. With the back of his index finger, he stroked her temples, the line of her jaw, the smooth skin of her neck. This is what is meant by the term 'the art of love', which married men find themselves called upon to perform. He was too close to really see her face IN FOCUS, but nevertheless able to form a blurry perception of its delicate features. No one, ROY thought, had ever looked quite so beautiful. Eve was a NATIONAL monument to beauty. He was reminded of the film 'North by Northwest', where Cary Grant and Eva-Marie Saint are

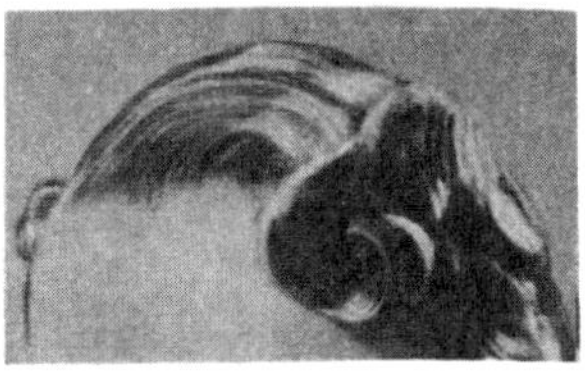

Standing alone

on top of Mount Rushmore, looking down at the faces of the American presidents carved into the rock, just as he was now., looking down at Eve's face. Her kiss had put him there, on top of the world. She might not have been a world leader, but Eve beat George Washington hands down in the looks department.

Eve seemed contented too. She smiled dreamily in the cocoon of warmth they had created in the small enclosed space of the delivery van. ROY kissed her hand, swept by the desire to draw her to him and hold her close, never to let her go.

"I'm glad I found you," he said. "You'll always take care of me, won't you?"

"Always," she promised, with an attempt at lightness.

His hands gripped her tightly for a moment, then relaxed.

"And then I'll be back on top of my game so I will be there always to take care of you.

I'm going to work hard every day and make enough money so that I can buy all the sweets in your shop."

"Then all your teeth will fall out, and you'll look like Old Mother Riley."

He covered his TEETH with his lips and made a gummy chomping motion.

They laughed at themselves; everything seemed delightful.

Roy was very happy, with a throbbing happiness that turned the whole world into a glamorous fairyland. GRADUALLY, he had been able to obliterate the cinder path incident, and his confidence seemed fully restored. Eve's unique double tonic action had revived him back to health. If Stirling Moss himself had knocked on the window and asked Roy to stand in for him at Le Mans, he would have happily agreed. As long as he could have EVE there with him. With Eve by his side, nothing bad could happen. Was that permissible in Grand Prix Racing, he wondered?

Roy began mentally preparing for his date with EVE AND HER Auntie. He decided he would go home, shampoo his hair with Vosene and take a long bath. After that, he would comb his hair for ten minutes, eyeing himself in the bathroom mirror with concentrated criticism. He would polish his shoes and try on three shirts before he acquired the correct air of casual concern.

THEN IT HAPPENED. As if he had suddenly spotted me, his neglected sister, *IN THE* mirror's reflection, looking wistfully at him over his shoulder, he remembered. And all at once, he was slapping him**SELF** in the face with A FAMILY SIZED LEMON MERINGUE PIE.

Lord knows why it took him so long. It was the first thing that came to my mind as soon as she suggested it. Dinner with Auntie indeed. What was he thinking of? Weren't there other, more pressing engagements on this evening s agenda? "Oh, wait. Tonight's **FRIDAY**,'' he said. "I can't come over tonight."

"Oh." Eve's face fell. The champagne fizz of excitement in her tummy had turned into a BEDTIME DRINK of wet concrete.

"I've already promised to spend time with my sister," he said.

"Tonight?"

"Yes. I'm sorry. She's housebound. I have to be there."

"But tonight?" she reasoned.

"Our housekeeper goes to the **PICTURES** on Friday," he explained. ''My **MOTHER**, I mean. We don't have a housekeeper."

But of course Mary wasn't going to the **PICTURES**; she was staying in to **make a dress** for me. And I wasn't supposed to be going out either. She would expect me to be there, to try the dress on.

Aaargh! Tonight of all nights. **ROY** squirmed at finding himself facing this tortuous trichotomy of options. He was going to mention the dressmaking but it would only have complicated everything further, and

Eve already seemed confused.
"What's wrong with your SISTER, Roy? What's her name?"

"NORMA. Nothing's wrong with her," he said, a little huffily. And then: "I'm sorry. It was stupid of me. I forgot all about it. She has an important engagement this evening."

"I thought you said she was housebound."

"She is—usually. It's difficult to explain. She had an accident when she was little. She does go out sometimes but MARY—that's our mother—prefers her to stay indoors. She worries about Norma getting herself into trouble."

He sensed Eve was still looking for a way round it.

"I have to be there. I'm sorry." There was firmness in his tone.

Eve looked down at her hands.

"You know — if it could be avoided . . ." he said, trying to round off the edges.

"It's okay," she said.

"I'm glad you understand, and don't mind . . ."

He had perhaps too quickly assumed her acceptance of the situation.

"I mind of course," she interrupted. "I mind very much. But I know —I have always known— that SISTERS come *first*."

He shrugged his shoulders. "I'm terribly, *terribly* sorry, my dear."

He turned towards her, his hand resting gently on her shoulder.

She stared at him in silence for some moments. It seemed a long time, then slowly she placed her hand over his on her shoulder.

"You must not be sorry," she said very tenderly.

"Of course you must go. I do understand."
What a dear, sweet angel she was. Yet she was just a girl, a poem written by God.
"What about tomorrow? I suppose it's too much to hope that you're free."
"As it happens, I am," she said. "Isn't that nice for you?"
"Very." The voice was warm, with a chuckle in it.
"We could take the **VAN** and go somewhere for the day," she said, excitedly. Maybe have a picnic."
He didn't have any money but that didn't matter. You do not—yet, anyway—have to pay anything to swing your legs in the country; there is no charge for breathing purer air than you can inhale in the best hotels.
"Think how pleasant it would be, to be able to go away by ourselves," she said. "For the day, I mean—especially if it's fine."
"Good weather is no longer as necessary as it was," said Roy tenderly.
"Oh, shall we, Roy? *I'd love it!"*

Roy had his doubts about RECREATIONAL use of the works van but Eve's spirits seemed so lifted by the idea that he could not refuse.
"All Right. I'll pick you up about half past eight."
"Half past eight?" she spluttered. "You are keen. All right, I'll be ready. I'll do some hard-boiled eggs and make some sandwiches. What shall I put on them?"
"I don't mind."
"Well, what do you like?"

"Chops," he said. "I like chops."

The rain had stopped now but for a few heavy drops that were bouncing intermittently off the VAN's roof like CHOCOLATE-COVERED PAYNE'S POPPETS thrown from the branches above them by playful confectioners. A good deal of condensation had formed on the inside of the windows, and Roy felt almost embarrassed, imagining that he alone was responsible, that his steamy thoughts about her had caused it.

Eve looked at her watch. " Lord, look at the time! I must go. I've got to MARK up the evening papers. Are you okay to drop me back at the shop, Roy?"

"Yes, of course."

The spell of romantic langour was being superseded by the practical. He jiggled the gearstick and prepared to turn the key in the ignition. Eve rubbed a small area of the WINDSCREEN with her fingertips and asked: "Have you got a cloth?"

Roy felt around in the pocket in the driver's side door but found nothing suitable. Then, for the first time, a premonition thrust itself like a thin, steel shaft into his thoughts. But before he had time to act on it, the damage had been done. EVE had opened the glove compartment and taken out the BRASSIERE.

She held it out in front of her by the SHOULDER straps. The TWIN CUPS stuck out impertinently.

"Whose is this?" she said.

"Nobody's. It's just . . . it's just a rag."

"It looks brand new!"

"No, it's just a rag. Put it back." It seemed to him that his voice was unnaturally rough and unfriendly.

"Well, can't we use it for the window?" she said.

"Yes. Yes. Use it," he said tetchily.

Roy knew he was making a poor attempt at establishing his innocence. He could feel her looking at him, *reassessing, re-evaluating.* He stared straight ahead and tried to act casual. He drummed his fingers lightly on the STEERING WHEEL, COUGHED, and then touched the knot of his tie. He looked demented. It was absurd for a man of twenty-nine to be so self-conscious. All he needed, he told himself, was a nonchalant opening remark to get him over the hump. He considered 'That's a lovely dress you have on' or 'My mother sometimes wears wellingtons in the house', but when he tried them out in his mind, they sounded too stiff, too obviously rehearsed. He toyed with a couple of other possibilities. The thing was not to mention the BRA, not to draw attention to it.

"It's not mine," he blurted out, defensively. "It was already in the *VAN*."

EVE said nothing. She had scrunched the bra up into a ball and clutching it in her fist, she was leaning forward to wipe the WINDSCREEN.

"The previous delivery man must have put it there. It must have fallen out of one of the LAUNDRY BAGS when he was collecting. Of course. He probably put it in there intending to take it back to work and then forgot all about it."

Roy felt like an eighteen-month-old baby trying to climb out of his cot. His explanation hovered unsteadily in the air.

When all that she could REACH was done, Eve passed the makeshift Chamois over to ROY who did the same on his side of the glass. He rubbed hurriedly and then discarded the bra ON THE FLOOR TO DEMONSTRATE HIS lack of interest in it. He wiped the side window with his SLEEVE.

Eve picked the BRA up again, inspecting the damage. It was stained with dark brown dirt but was still white in the creases where it had not made contact with the Window. It looked like a dirty big footprint.

"It seems a shame to have marked it,' she said. "It'll never come clean."

" It will – with OMO said *Roy*, agitatedly.

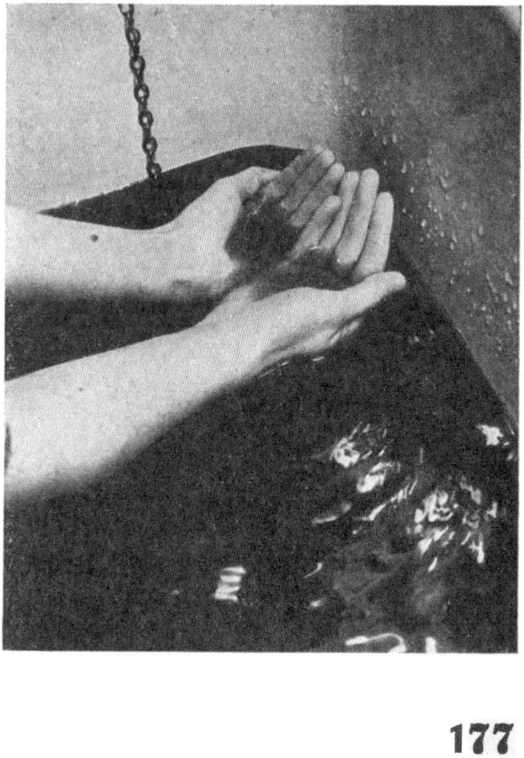

"It's the Blue-Whitener in **OMO** that makes the difference. It's an active whitening ingredient that can actually get your clothes whiter than the day they were bought."

"Roy?" She laughed uneasily, unsure if he was making a joke. His face was tense. "You sound like one of those adverts off the television."

"Do I?" said Roy. He laughed nervously and then he **sang**.

"Opal Fruits! Made to make your mouth water!"

She smiled but it wasn't very funny. He knew he sounded crazed but didn't know how to be normal now. Everything he said seemed to make it worse. He tried another one: *"YOU'LL WONDER WHERE THE YELLOW WENT WHEN YOU BRUSH YOUR TEETH WITH PEPSODENT."*

The silence lay there between them like a stain on the carpet. Perhaps he'd got the tune wrong.

"I've got to get back," was all she said.

"Yes, sorry."

He started the engine and drove steadily back towards THE POST OFFICE. Neither of them spoke. The ***BRA*** hung over them. A big rude bra *barging its way in.* It was as if he had rubbed the damp, dirty thing in her face, just like Mary used to do with a wet flannel when he was a boy. It always seemed that no matter how much he wriggled, the rancid-smelling cloth remained clamped to his features. And now it was Eve who was trying to get away.

He pulled up in the same place outside the shop WHERE he had parked before.

She was sitting there, staring in front of her,

clasping the **BRA** in her lap.

"ANYTHING wrong?" he asked, nonchalantly.

"No. **Nothing,"** s**he replied.**

"Well, why are you sitting there like that if there's nothing wrong?

"Like what?"

"So quiet."

"I'm sorry," she said. "I'm not feeling very chatty.

"I know there is something. Won't you tell me, my darling?"

"Nothing," s**he repeated.**

Why was he pressing her? He knew very well what was wrong. She'd found a *bra* in the **glove compartment.** That's what the 'something' was. He had to try and explain.

"Listen, if you're worried about..."

" Roy," she said abruptly. "Be fore you begin, I've something to ask you." Her voice sounded sud denly sharp, nervous. He couldn't look her in the eye. "Are you . . . are you married?"

"**MARRIED** ? *No.*" **He hoped his voice carried conviction. She looked at him narrowly as though she did not feel it did.**

"I won't have anything to do with you if you have a wife or a fiancée," she said.

"No, I've nothing like that. I don't want you to think you're out with a man who's living at home with his wife, or anything." He shook his head decisively. "I'm not that kind of man."

"**So, you really are going out with your sister** tonight?"

"Yes." He glanced at Eve with a hint of shyness.

"You don't sound very sure," she said.

There was another pause. **It was too difficult for** ROY to explain.

Eve said: "I hope you're serious, *Roy*, and

you're not just playing games with me."
"Games?" he said innocently. "Who wants to play games?" But in a way, he was playing games. In a way it was as if he had gone upstairs and had brought down Monopoly, and set it up on a card-table between them.

She started to get out.
"Well, goodbye," she said, tossing the BRA behind her on to the SEAT. "Hope your sister enjoys herself. See you in the morning." Her voice had A HINT OF DARK CHOCOLATE BITTERNESS to it.
"Eve."
She paused, halfway out the door.
Before she knew what he was about he had pulled her back inside and kissed her once, hard, on the mouth. For an instant she yielded, the barrier she had built between them going down before the wild sweetness that clamoured in her heart. She turned and looked at him, meeting his gaze steadily, and behind the grave and questioning eyes was the same hint of pleading.
"You still want to meet tomorrow?" he said.
"Yes. I've got to go though. The papers are in."

On his way home, Roy stopped on Wyvern Avenue and threw the BRA in someone's dustbin. It was just a BRA; it was nothing to get sentimental about

12

THERE are no two ways about it: the best

formula for acquiring the wardrobe you want at the price you can happily pay is to sew it yourself. Being your own dressmaker automatically entitles you to all the custom-made extras. You can indulge your fondest

COLOUR

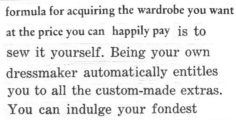

whims, you can select your very favorite fabrics, and you can always achieve a fit that's flawless even if your figure isn't.

FROM **my dressing room,** I could hear Mary rooting around in the cupboard under the stairs for **remnants of material. I think she was rather** looking forward to our spending a cosy evening together, working away at the **DRESS**. The truth is, at any other time I would have liked nothing more, but tonight Mr. HANDS's ***CAMERA*** awaited and it was too much to expect me to forgo the chance to be **immortalised** on film. I couldn't tell her I was going ***OUT***, not after all the promises. The problem was: how was I going give her the slip **and keep my appointment —tonight of all nights, when** she'd **expect me to** be there? I decided to get myself ready and then go **down** and try out my brilliantly conceived

COVER STORY.

ROY was hovering several feet above the BEDROOM FURNITURE, but the giddy knot of excitement in his stomach, the result of his afternoon with EVE, occasionally gave way to a twinge of sinking uncertainty about how things had been left between them. In matters of the heart, this is a common ailment, and though not a doctor or nurse myself I quickly came up with the perfect remedy. It works every time! All Roy's worries and concerns quickly dissolved into a sparkling Alka-Seltzer fizz of effervescence as soon as I began dressing for my SESSION with Mr. Hands.

I sang to myself from sheer happiness—tra-la-la — and from the pleasantly extravagant feeling as I slipped on my softest, most elegant chiffon undies, my sheer silk stockings. These are the essential foundations on top of which all the other stages to becoming a woman are built.

I'LL never forget my first time in stockings. I was dressing for a party at HOME —actually, it was just Mary and me— when I realised Mary was wearing real nylon stockings with garters!. It was just after the war and nylons were virtually impossible to come by. Mary had somehow procured several pairs through her friend, Betty, who had a cousin in America. I was sore with envy and was thinking of discarding my socks and going bare-legged when Mary came into my BEDROOM.

IT WAS CHRISTMAS and I remember noticing the gentle hum of SHERRY on her breath. She laughed, then took me into her room and gave me one of her very own suspender belts and a pair of the precious pale stockings to wear. **Well, I hardly need tell you how thrilling that was. It was the best** Christmas present **I'd ever had.** My legs floated me about all evening. I slipped my hand up and down over the silky nylon, feeling like an adult of seventeen instead of an ungainly thirteen. I went through the evening in a glow of satisfaction, feeling just this once like a raving beauty. I wanted to rush out and tell all the girls in our street that I had on Loretta Young's underwear.

I had already decided to wear the blouse Roy found at the RAG market last week. It had shrunk ever so slightly in the wash, where 'kind-to-colours' Oxydol had reneged on its promise and dulled a little of its vibrancy. Nevertheless, it was still my first choice and, teamed with the right **skirt**, would make an intoxicating contemporary cocktail of casual silhouette and rich, resplendent fabric. Just the thing for a PHOTO SESSION. Yesterday I had been considering a simple black dinner frock, classic and elegant, but to-night the sombre hue did not match my mood and I longed for

COLOUR.

Perhaps Mr. HANDS would have flowers for me — a great spray of orchids, tawny and gold and mauve. They would lend a touch of vibrancy to my toilette.

THE canary yellow street-length cotton skirt is an eased bell shape with figure-flattering durable box pleats which stay in through countless washings. Its faint criss-cross pattern is overprinted in a subtle new colour called 'nugget'. I was planning to wear a petticoat under it, but for some reason Mary had chosen today, of all rainy days, to wash every single one of my slips and underskirts so nothing was dry. Fortunately, cotton is a non-static fabric so not wearing a slip isn't the disaster it might be with something in, say, rayon or nylon, which clings to the legs LIKE a rock climber in a gale. I decided I could go without one for once. Who was going to know?

WHEN

I came downstairs, Mary had already cleared the table in the FRONT room and the Singer

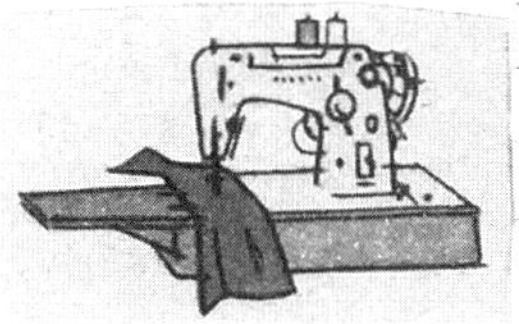

Sewing Machine was set UP. Its foot pedal was plugged in and the little work light was switched on, ready for action.

THERE was the free illustrated booklet, 'The Pounds, Shillings and *Sense* of Owning a New Singer' which Mary had never looked at. The DRESSMAKING PATTERN she had out was one of those from Butterick, and it must have been used on another occasion because the pattern pieces no longer fitted into the bulging envelope. On the front was a sketchily drawn picture of A WOMAN, elongated and mannequin-like, wearing the finished article. It was similar to, but not quite as nice as, the DRESS we had seen in the magazine. The artist had ATTEMPTED TO make it look stylish and modern, but I sensed that in real life it was going to look frumpy and old-fashioned, like something Mary would wear. In the drawing, it was depicted in a gay lemon hue, but I noticed with a tinge of disappointment that, having talked her out of the BROWN she had previously suggested, the material Mary had chosen (originally earmarked for some bathroom curtains) had pictures of tropical fish on it. This is what in fashion circles would be called an 'amusing' print, but I wondered if this time the joke was going too far.

MARY looked up for the first time since I had entered the room. She had been reading the instructions and had her glasses on. "Oh, you're all dressed are you?" she said. "I wondered what you were doing."
She sounded surprised, probably because tonight *Roy* hadn't rushed straight up to my room the minute he had got home, as he is wont to do. His emotions were still all of a flutter and I think he was bursting his LUNGS to tell someone about the recent developments in his romantic circumstances.
"She's a wonderful girl, Mum. You'd like her."
Mary had been all ears. All questions too. "How old is she? What's her name? Have you asked her OUT yet?"
"We're meeting tomorrow for a picnic, she's called EVE, and she's twenty-one," said Roy excitedly, answering the questions in reverse order, like a contestant on *Double Your Money*. Yet there was that nagging moment of doubt again, wondering if the incident with the BRASSIERE would make Eve change her mind about their date. Mary snapped him out of it.

"Well, come on, then, tell us all about her."

"Well . . ." Roy began, " like Petula Clark, she's English in background and upbringing, is simple and natural, with the unaffected enthusiasm of a schoolgirl. Although she has a gay vivacity, you get a sense of calm, almost of repose, while you're with her. There's not the slightest hint of restlessness or fluster. The first thing I noticed was that she was very well-dressed. She has a stunning figure — and such an air—so aristocratic yet down to earth."

"That's wonderful, Roy. It's about time you met a pretty girl with a lovely smile, a firm handshake and a wonderful sense of humour. She sounds deliciously normal, too. I'd like to meet her."

"You will, Mum. If things go according to plan."

"Whose plan? Yours or hers?" A wry, MOTHER-KNOWS-BEST smile came with it.

"Mine, mostly, though I think she's keen," he said with unassuming modesty.

"And how much does she know about . . . you know . . . ?" She FLICKED her eyes to the ceiling, indicating my dressing room above them.

"Nothing," said Roy firmly. "And she's not going to either."

Mary smiled, and went on smiling. "Well, I'm delighted for you, Roy. I really am."

She really was too. I THINK she felt that she'd finally got ROY on the straight and narrow, and that consequently I would be less bothersome. I'm sure that's why she was GIVING UP her time to MAKE THE DRESS. Landing a new job and a new girlfriend in the same week! *Roy* had **'HIT THE JACKPOT'**. So now she was prepared to make certain concessions and I was the lucky one who was going to reap the reward.

"Right, let's get you measured," said Mary. "I bought this **PATTERN** to fit me, so we're going to have to try it on a few times, I expect."

It's not that I'm fat. **There really is no need to be burdened with fat** these days, with **Energen Rolls** to **solve the problem**. I'm just a bigger build than Mary is, and I suppose I am quite tall for a woman. **Think** Rosalind Russell in *Auntie Mame*, add a dash of girlish femininity, and you pretty much have it. I'm five feet ***NINE*** and a half inches in my bare feet. **A few years** ago **I used to slouch along in flat shoes, trying to look shorter**. Then I read in one of my magazines that a girl who wants to get on in show business is very lucky if she is tall —especially in Italy. Miss Paul, Ilford-born daughter of a London printing-trade worker, who is **six foot one and a half in her best shoes**, exported herself to the Continent soon after she left school—to join the famous Bluebell Girls at the Paris Lido. PARIS isn't IN ITALY, I know, but still... That cured me of being embarrassed about my height. **Now I like** to think that by wearing high heels I may help to give other tall girls confidence. But being tall is not always a disadvantage. I can reach the tinned fruit on the top shelf of our pantry without having to fetch the steps and I'm tall enough to carry a big alligator bag without looking like **wee Jimmy Clitheroe** going on his holidays.

I held out my arms **like** an aeroplane. IT WAS THE FIRST TIME Mary HAD EVER measured me for anything, BUT SHE'D DONE IT MANY TIMES for Roy —getting his chest size for jumpers and whatnot— SO I knew the drill. She leaned in, and her arms reached around me as she passed the end of the tape measure from hand to hand behind my back.

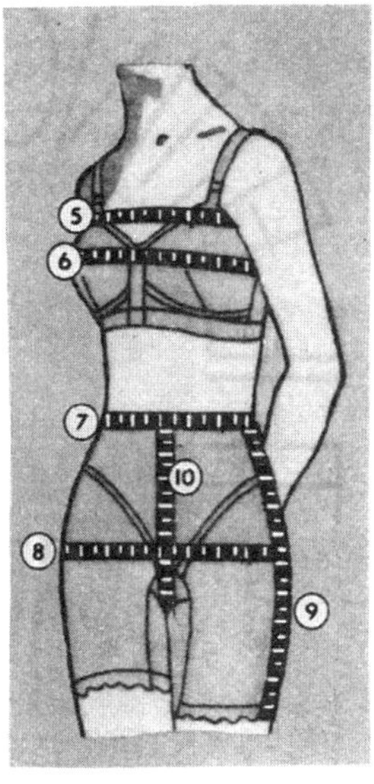

It was odd having her stand so near; **we're never normally that close. I half expected her** to give me a hug, to clutch me warmly to her breast in a loving *motherly* embrace, **but of course, she did not.** Mary never touches me, unless it's by accident. ***I don't know why;*** *Roy* **gets it all the time. EVEN when I'm suffering with**

a cold or flu, she'll **NEVER** soothe my fevered brow with a comforting hand like she does with ROY. With me, she prefers to keep her distance. Perhaps she's afraid of catching something.

UP until then, MY MEASUREMENTS had always been a matter of careless approximation— as remote as Dartmoor, as vague as CHEESE. Naturally I knew the basics, being pretty much the same as Roy, but there was nothing official in the record books. HAVING slipped the tape around my bust, then my waist and hips, MARY jotted the numbers down on the back of an old Christmas card, before she set about measuring my skirt length.

"Twenty-seven," she said. "We'll make it thirty. You don't want it as short as this one."

"I do. It's the fashion. Anyway, tall girls can wear their skirts shorter. It says so in all the magazines."

"Does it?" said MARY, unimpressed. "Surely you want to cover your knees?"

"No, why should I?"

Mary shrugged resignedly. She had decided not to fight me this time. "Oh, well. I suppose no one's going to see you," she said. "Right, so we need to add a bit extra in the back, and across the shoulders. I'll have to see if I've got a zip the right COLOUR."

In case you were wondering, I have a nice young figure, small-waisted and rather slim in the hip, with a full, strong bust and very square young shoulders. I could have wished my shoulders were a trifle more sloping, but a forthright, confident look sometimes comes at a price.

IT felt terrible to be deserting MARY and relinquishing the opportunity to forge the bond between us. For although of late we have been, I think, a pretty agreeable mother and daughter combo, we haven't always been a success in the woman-to- woman relationship. But what could I do? NIP out to the telephone box to try to arrange another evening with Mr. HANDS? Not without his phone number, I couldn't. My only option was to drive over there in the van to cancel in person and try to postpone my session until next FRIDAY evening when, assuming Betty had recovered from her cold, Mary would be out at the pictures. But if I was going all the way over to Egmont Street, it seemed silly not to stay long enough for Mr. Hands to take my picture. He'd probably have it done in an hour and I'd be back home again for my final fitting before MARY would have even noticed I'd gone. And to tell the truth, I didn't really want to cancel; I'd been looking forward to it all week. Yes, the mother — daughter connection is the most important thing *in the World*, but in spite of this my eye was on the MANTELPIECE CLOCK and I was already edging towards the door.

"I feel like I might be coming down with a cold." I said, slipping effortlessly into my ROYAL COMMAND PERFORMANCE.
"Really? You don't sound cold-y."
Sore throat, runny nose, aching all over. These are the first signs of a cold.
"Take a couple of Disprin," she said.
"No thanks. I might just go and lie down for an hour."
"Oh." She sounded a little disappointed. "I thought we were going to be doing this DRESS."
"We are. I'll be UP AGAIN later for TRYING ON and everything."
"Oh, go on, then. I'll make a start. I suppose you need to make sure you're fit for work on MONDAY. Why don't you lie on the settee? *Take Your Pick's* on later."
It was sweet of her because she's hardly ever seen it herself, with her usually being at the PICTURES, but she knows MICHAEL MILES is a favourite of mine. I do tend to TUNE IN, I must admit. I often tell her all

about it when she gets HOME. Last week a woman from Rhyll won the fifty pound treasure chest. Think of all the FROCKS she could buy with fifty pounds.

"No, I'll just go up to my room," I said. "Maybe you can wake me AT eight THIRTY for *Take Your Pick*." I looked at the clock. It gave me just under **TWO HOURS**. That should be plenty of time.

UPSTAIRS, I quickly applied fresh lipstick and titivated my hair, put on my red pixie jacket and grabbed my handbag. THERE'S LINO in the hallway at the bottom of the stairs so I had to make my way past MARY in the sitting room on kitten PRINCESS tippy-toes. Luckily, ROY had parked on the street instead of in our driveway so Mary wouldn't hear the VAN starting up. And, thanks to her twilight curtain ritual, she wouldn't be able to see out.

I tiptoed out on to the FRONT STEP, only to catch sight of Mrs. PRICE standing right next to the van, blocking my escape. Before She'd had time to see me, I jumped back into the HOUSE, closing the door quietly behind me. I felt very vulnerable there, facing the double-edged sword of being SPOTTED by Mrs. PRICE and having Mary open the living-room door and see me standing there with my coat on. Life is a bowl of pickles, and here I was, a butterfly trapped in the stuff.

I squatted down to peer through the LETTER BOX. I couldn't see too clearly through the front hedge, but Mrs. PRICE appeared to be locked in conversation with Dorothy Harvey and they showed no signs of budging. If Roy had parked on the drive, I might have been able to slip into the driver's seat unnoticed—but he hadn't, so there was no point in getting the best silverware out to entertain that IDEA. I couldn't just hang around in the hall. From behind the living-room door, I could hear the kronKING and chomping of the big, heavy scissors reverberating through the TABLE as they cut through the material, but I knew that MARY might at any moment decide to down DRESSMAKING tools and come out to put the kettle on or fetch her Liquorice Allsorts from the kitchen drawer. I had no choice: I had to make a dash for it—abandon THE VAN and go on foot.

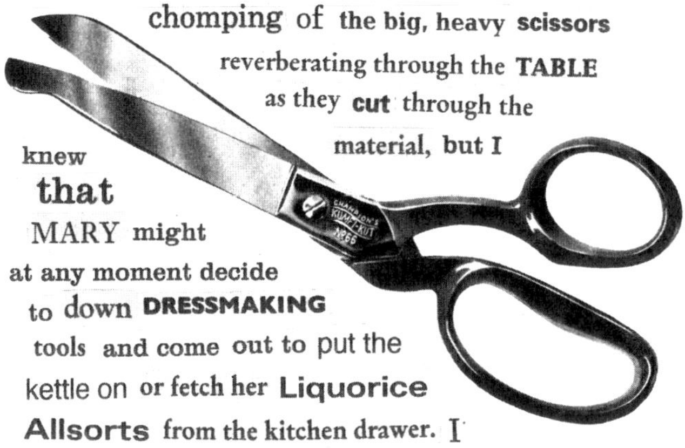

I gently closed the door behind me and there I was, out on the drive, exposed and vulnerable. Mrs. PRICE spun round instantly at the sound of the squeaky gate. She was barely twenty feet away. I kept my head down and marched briskly AWAY, feeling her eyes burning two perfect SAUCER- SIZED holes into the red fabric of my pixie jacket.

Egmont Street IS ABOUT A MILE AWAY. It's not on a bus route. Having to walk there put me at considerable risk of being spotted by other neighbours, but since Mrs. PRICE had no doubt already logged her sighting of me in her busybody book, the serious damage had already been done. Chances were, before I had been gone five minutes she would be making a follow-up visit to the HOUSE of LITTLE to quiz MARY further about 'that young woman in the red coat'. I certainly hoped I was wrong, because that really would blow my cover. My only chance was that perhaps she'd have the good grace to wait until MORNING when Roy might be able to head her off with a plausible explanation.

IT was a lovely evening, a night made for lovers of the PHOTOGRAPHIC image: the blue dusk and the drifting song of the nightingales. SEPTEMBER rain soon passes. It leaves nothing unlovely. In Bulsivar Street it left glistening jewels on every bush. The moist air was heady with perfume. I strode along the flagged pavement drinking it in. "Oh, I feel so happy!" It was as if tonight was going to mean something to me—something quite special. *My* heart rose so high in my chest that it was all I could do to stop it leaping clear over the wall into one of the gardens and picking a rosy red apple off the tree.

THE autumn leaves that had come too soon and the *Daily Mirror* that had come that morning had been slapped senseless by the recent downpour and were stuck fast to the pavement. High on a bough a bird was singing the theme tune to *Z Cars*. It was a glorious, luminous night of mystic beauty.

I turned into Magdelene Street, momentarily aware of no other sound but the cautious step of my fine, new red shoes upon the pavement. Walking in adverse weather conditions can be hazardous. MOST WOMEN step with sharp transfer from heel to ball of foot, letting mud fly. Not me. I like to walk the model way and overcome the fault. With knees flexed, I place my foot gently so that the weight falls evenly from the heel, along the foot and out at the toes. I practise the technique indoors—to achieve a graceful, gliding walk, come rain or shine.

The *trottoirs* of Paris astonish we British with the sophistication of the mesdemoiselles who promenade there, tight-skirted and tittuping in spike heels, and getting away triumphantly with outrageous accessories like cabbage-leaf *handbags* and miniature poodles ornamented with tiny choux pastry trousers. Nothing on the London pavements pulls you up short and staring, but there is much to delight the eye

in the lady with her

Can't hurry-Too Fat! legs

waddling along to the off-licence to fetch hubby's brown ale.

My confidence was growing with every step. I was out of the shopping zone, heading through drab streets far removed from the glamour of Paris or Rome, into a suburb of little houses with tiny front gardens and privet hedges. Most people weren't paying me much attention, but those that did eyed me up and down with quizzical curiosity, wondering if perhaps I was a popular recording star or someone they had seen advertising a new beauty product in a television commercial.

I'VE ALWAYS HAD a little private fantasy that it would be fun if there were some token—say a small silver thimble—that people could present unobtrusively without a lot of fulsome words to a woman whose appearance was superb—even if a perfect stranger. By the time I'd reached the corner, I would have had enough THIMBLES to play the washboard in a skiffle group.

TWO young, uncouth ruffian types (possibly skifflers themselves) were loitering with intent by the cigarette machine on Jessop Lane. Top Dog here was a thin, lanky boy with a TOMMY STEELE lick falling across his forehead, and knees and elbows so sharp that it seemed they might cut through the cloth of his cheap suit.

"Oi! Mae West. Give us a kiss, then," he shouted. They guffawed loudly. A young woman on her own is a sight that seems to amuse youngsters. I ignored them and carried on walking, but out of the corner of my eye I could see the other lad's arms were outstretched towards me in a mock embrace. He made a grotesque PANTOMIME kissing sound through his cartoon lips. Mae West indeed! Still, though not perhaps silver, it was a THIMBLE of sorts.

The rain had eased but there was a damp chill

in the air. I probably should have borrowed Mary's umbrella. English weather, as we all know, is typically unreliable, but tonight I felt invincible. In fact, I felt like 64,000 silver shillings, as the Hollywood types would say. Up until tonight, I had been recently feeling the pinch. Eve's a lovely girl, don't get me wrong, but the more time Roy spends with her, the less time he has for me. Take tomorrow, for example. I had been looking forward to spending time in my dressing room, experimenting with hair and make-up, lounging around the house in pretty nighties of nylon in pink and blue and lavender wearing perfumes from France and fluffy slippers. But with ROY getting up and going straight out to meet Eve, I will be left in limbo, waiting for him to come home again, just like on a WEEKDAY. Now, I certainly wouldn't want to squirt Weedol on Roy and EVE's blossoming romance, but I've been patient all week and think I deserve some time to myself. It was the same this afternoon with Roy sitting in the van with EVE instead of coming straight home, which meant less time for me to get ready for my PHOTO session. He knows how important this is to me. I suppose I just have to face it like a Woman. The only thing to do, I have decided, is to make my special times even more special. AND having my PHOTOGRAPH taken is the first step. A SET OF SUMPTUOUS GLOSSY prints of me in a variety of poses that I can pin to the wall of MY DRESSING ROOM, each one set at a jaunty angle like the ones of the

FILM STARS

outside the Odeon.

By the time I reached Beauchamp Avenue the streets had become less crowded and I was suddenly seized by the urge to skip. I hadn't skipped since I was young, but I remembered how good it felt. My favourite was sideways skipping. It is basically the same as forward skipping but you turn sideways to do it. The diagonal version of this was often adopted by the BOYS, imagining themselves on horseback, holding pretend reins in one hand and giving their bottoms an encouraging slap with the other. I was never much of a horsewoman; skipping sideways was more my thing. Feet together, feet apart, feet together—in great long

SCISSORING strides.

And the great thing is, you can get up quite a speed doing this.

THERE was no one about. I decided to give

it a go. It took me a second to get into the swing of it but then I was off, bounding along the pavement with the rhythm of a much-rehearsed dance—and the same rush of excitement I had experienced as a child. The locals, it seemed, were too busy watching CORONATION STREET or washing the dishes to notice me — a frisky young springbok in RED high heels, springing my way down their street. My ENTHUSIASM lifted me higher and higher, until I could see over their front hedges to the dull Television glow filtering through their front-room curtains.

IN THE end, it was *nature* itself that proved my downfall. The carpet of wet leaves was *Thicker! Slicker! Quicker!* here . Each one was a slippery customer to be avoided. But once I'd got up a good head of steam, I was blind to the dangers. More fool me.

My leading foot went skidding out from under me and I found myself with the WAYWARD leg stretched out behind me, my hands splaying the PAVEMENT as if I'd suddenly felt the need to adopt the starting position for the hundred yard dash. A little gentle stretching exercise can work wonders for the figure, but this was neither the time nor the place. I quickly recovered and got to my feet, more out of embarrassment than anything else. A GIRL across the road, who had been busy thrashing the GARDEN *wall* with a bamboo cane, paused to stare. I didn't want the little dear to have to witness my distress so I took a few courageous steps to hide myself from view behind a tree before checking for damage. I wiped my wet palms on my skirt and brushed the dirt from my sleeve. My RIGHT stocking was slurred with wet mud and had laddered at the knee. Blast! How was that going to look in a PHOTO? I took a KLEENEX from my coat pocket and pressed it to my leg through the hole. THE skin was grazed and stinging but I could see no blood. My WRISTS ached from jarring against the unforgiving pavement. Yet I did not whimper or wail. No, not I. Instead, I continued walking towards my destination with a nonchalant air AS IF NOTHING HAD HAPPENED, though

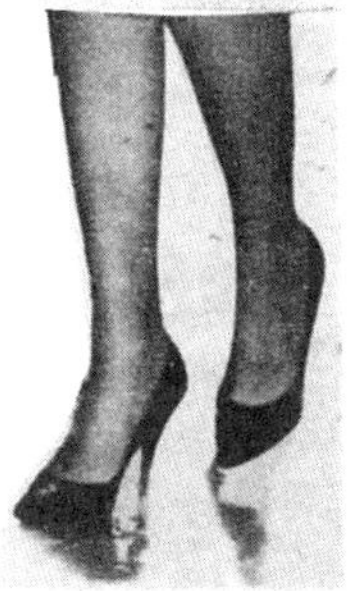

No. 204.

I could tell I'd done something to my ankle. The strange thing was that, despite this pitiful fall from grace, the warning system in my mind that alerts me to invasions of my privacy or threats to my sugar shell gave no signal as I drew near

13

THERE were a number of door-bells at number THIRTY-ONE. None bore the name of Mr. Hands. Had I remembered the number correctly? I opted for the one labelled Syms. I half wondered if I would be greeted by *SYLVIA SYMS*, star of stage and screen who keeps her skin so young-looking. There was a pane of frosted glass set into the front door but no light from inside the house, except a gleam here and there at the downstairs window where the curtains were not quite drawn. **After a moment,** there was movement from within and a light shone in the hallway. The door was opened by a **wheezy**, WIDE-HIPPED **WOMAN** whose resemblance to Miss Syms could be measured in nautical miles. She had thin, frizzy hair and cheeks that looked as if they had been slapped **FORTY** TIMES.

At her feet, a small, highly strung poodle WRIGGLED and worried itself into ***a rich, creamy lather.*** She hooked her index finger into its **COLLAR** to restrain it, though this did nothing to kerb its enthusiasm. It rasped and coughed, intent on choking itself to death.

"I was looking for Mr Hands. Have I got the right address?" I said.

The WOMAN strained to look up at me from her stooped position.

"First floor. Just go straight up."

She DRAGGED THE DOG aside and I stepped into the hallway, welcomed by the smell of old dinner and the sound of a television SET. Through the open door OF HER LIVING ROOM, I could see a young boy lying on the floor with his chin in his hands, watching what sounded like THE RUSS CONWAY SHOW.

There were BIKES in the hall and a thread-bare carpet running up the CENTRE OF the stairs. What you want from a carpet—apart from its looks—is long, long wear. And that is precisely what this carpet had not given. Believe me, that carpet was a disgrace—only 2 years old, and not fit to be seen, footmarks here, spill stains there, dirty and dingy all over. The house would have benefited from one of those heavenly carpets by Lees. A carpet ought to have a pretty face, not a tired old ONE covered in grime.

Mrs. Syms ushered the anxious PUP back inside the room and closed the door behind her. It was dark NOW and

I couldn't find the light switch. I felt my way up the narrow staircase, the banister was STICKY and there was *the smell of* IZAL and *Jeyes Fluid* coming from the lavatory on the half-landing.

TWO DOORS faced each other across the LANDING. From one, I could hear a saucepan being scraped and a woman's voice SHOUTING AT A CHILD. I'm sure this will be echoed by so many other parents with children growing up to the music of Rock 'n' Roll. On the whole, Mothers tend to expect their children to do as they are told promptly and without fuss, and often believe in a robust smack if the toddler will not conform. What housewife doesn't sometimes want to bang her child's head against the kitchen wall?

There was no sound from the other door so I knocked tentatively and put my ear to it. The door paint was chipped and old and the area around the handle was grubby with handprints. This was not quite the setting I had expected for a PHOTOGRAPHIC STUDIO. I was wondering whether perhaps I had made a mistake, WHEN the door swung open and Mr. HANDS stepped back to let me in. Like the lively little chap downstairs, he was boisterously glad to see me.

"I was beginning to think you weren't coming," he said. He brushed a length of hair over the bald patch on his head (NO HAT THIS TIME) and poked his shirt into his trousers with stubby fingers. Had he put on weight since I had seen him? In TEN days? Oh, I was being absurd! But **men will always** seek out the stodgy food their systems seem to crave. They simply must have steak and kidney pudding and hot jam roll on the menu. The foolish owners of these overworked stomachs are such slaves to habit that they think they will die of starvation if they lunch on chicken salad or an omelette. But there you are. Men are that way and I suppose we'll never change them.

"Don't you look a **Picture?"**

said Mr. **HANDS**, breathing heavily. "Get yourself sat down and we can get started. I've got ***EVERYTHING*** ready."

IT was hard to see exactly what he had got ready. The room was small and overcrowded with clutter. Seedy, down-at-heel, dilapidated — these were the only suitable adjectives that sprang to mind. The air was **choked** by the gas fire burning on the wall, and it felt AS THOUGH I was being forced to breathe through the ***FILTHY*** **rug** beneath my feet. A SCRATCHY-voiced **budgie was** SCRAPING **the metallic**

bars of its cage. In the corner there was a sink and a draining-board with a FISH TANK on it and, next to that, a STAINED Baby Belling Cooker. The wallpaper had faint roses, and a powdery look from damp. Two sets of curtains hung open at the dirty window, where grey light from the street-lamp outside drizzled in. The wardrobe door hung half open with clothes tumbling out. Perhaps I had overestimated Mr. HANDS as a connoisseur of quality.

Mr. **HANDS** went to switch on a Table Lamp, no doubt hoping that the frankly feminine pale pink shade and soft yellow glow would create a sophisticated and slightly exotic mood. If your shade is only slightly soiled, rub it over with cotton wool dipped in fine oatmeal, but if it is very dirty, clean it with a mixture of four ounces of methylated spirits to a quarter of an ounce soap flakes. He clicked the switch, but nothing happened, so he knelt to fiddle with the plug under the **bed**. Meanwhile, my eyeballs did

A ROUND-THE-WORLD TOUR.

There was much to take in. A DRESSING TABLE was littered with clothes and crockery, a row of empty milk bottles lined up against the wall NEXT TO a pile of worn-out SHOES, a dog's bone on the mat. Perhaps that's where the greasy lard smell was coming from. My nostrils prickled as Mr. HANDS (having given up on the lamp) leaned forward to take my COAT, adding his own special fragrance to the MIX. I stood tentatively on the threshold, reluctant to step inside for fear of soiling something dear to me. Mr. Hands was all a-fluster, tidying and straightening as he led me to a chair with BUDGIE SEED on it. I didn't sit.

"I'm not sure I can stay," I said. "I have a DRESSMAKING date with MOTHER *at home* as a matter of fact. And I've just remembered that I haven't had any supper."

"I'll get you something."

"No, it's all right. I'll have to run along."

"Don't be silly. "You've been here only a minute. Wait there."

While Mr. HANDS rummaged through the cupboard under the drain*ing-board*, I took the time to familiarise myself with my new surroundings. Perhaps I *was* being silly. As long as I got my PORTRAIT, what did it matter about the surroundings?

There was a small, low table at the foot of the bed with a stack of exercise books WITH home-made covers fashioned from a wide selection of wallpapers. There were also some magazines

—some of Mr. Hands's published work, possibly? On top of the pile was SOMETHING CALLED **MADAM**, a title I'd never seen before. I thought I was familiar with all the women's weeklies, but this was new to me. The cover showed a bride in her wedding dress demurely clutching a posy. I was both surprised and encouraged to see that she was quite heavily set with a FULLER FIGURE—not the normal cover-girl type. The dress was quite flattering, although I always feel that if you're broad on the shoulder like I am, a puff sleeve can be a mistake.

"***HERE*** you are," said Mr. Hands, proffering a TEATIME ASSORTMENT. ***ALL THE*** **CHOCOLATE** ones are gone but there are some **Cream** ones if you dig deep." I refused politely and he put the **TIN** down on the chair.

"Right, let's get started."

He took a packet of **cigarettes** and a lighter from his trouser pocket and lit one, holding a fat fist to his mouth as the ensuing COUGH raked his lungs. When he'd recovered, he offered me the pack. ***THE*** chivalrous charmer type. I'd have to be careful of him. I shook my head and he returned them to his trouser pocket.

"We'll have you on the **bed** to start, I think." He sat me down on the corner of it, and, indeed, for the first few moments I was conscious of nothing but a vast relief that I was no longer forced to stand on my own two painful **Boulevard Courts**. The SIDEWAYS **skipping** had taken its toll on my feet as well as my knee and ankle.

"Where's **YOUR CAMERA**? You do have one, I suppose." My nervous laugh was brittle as a bauble on a Christmas tree.

"No picture can hope to capture your true beauty." (At least that was the gist of what he said.)

"I wish the B.B.C. shared your enthusiasm," I replied. I wondered if, by chance, my remark made him think I was flirting with him. I was confused and thrilled by his outwardly colourless appearance and this inner, secret depth to his manhood.

"When I told you I was **APPLYING FOR A JOB** at **WHITE**'s **LAUNDRY**, the other day, I hope you didn't think it was as a delivery driver, or anything, **unsuitable** like that. The position was as private secretary to Mr. **WHITE**. It's a responsible position for the career-minded woman about town."

"Ah. So your application was a success?"

"Well, not exactly. But since then my brother, Roy, has found a job there."

"At **White's**?"

"Yes. We're very proud of him. He's an excellent **DRIVER**."

"Ah. So you have a brother.

That's interesting. Do you look alike?"
"Good heavens, no. Why would you think that?"

Once he had me sat down on the bed I could see my reflection in the dresser mirror. The face looking back at me was the face of innocence with a dash of Delilah, and a figure quite blatantly *Rubenesque*. Beautiful? Not strictly speaking. (Though that figure is perfect.) But the true secret of any woman's attraction is something much deeper—*vitality*. The incandescent vitality that captivates all eyes, all hearts. I'm not putting it half as well as Mr. Hands put it. He didn't generalise; he came right down to earth straight away. "Lovely *BOSOMS*. You could be on television with a figure like that."
Well, it's true I could. Like **Nurse Goodall** on *Emergency Ward 10*. 'The doctor will see you now. Don't try to talk; you've had a nasty accident. Yes, sister. Only for a minute, he's very weak. Would you mind sitting a little farther forward so that I can shake up your pillows ?'
I was fleetingly lost in the demanding role of being a woman, but I could hear Mr. Hands breathing now, slowly, as if each breath hurt. Closing my eyes, I surrendered myself to the rhythm of the waltz. To-night everything had a slightly unreal quality, like some exotic dream. To-morrow I would have to

revert to my ordinary bread-and-butter self, but now, for a few fleeting hours, I wanted to be someone gayer and more daring than the real me. I wanted to throw aside restraint and succumb to impulse.

"Let's see a bit more leg," said Mr. Hands, directing the proceedings from the foot of the bed. I complied, letting one slim hand rest lightly on my knee to hide my recent scrape with misfortune. My gaze ate itself in the mirror, fixated as I was by the image of my leg- flatter-ingly-lovely pose. Leaning, half-reclining with one slim hip flattened against the mattress, my eyes were hooded with a mock relish. I sensed Mr. Hands's approval, but I didn't turn to see if he had found his camera yet.

"YOU have no idea how romantic your profile looks from where I'm sitting." Except he didn't exactly use the word 'romantic' Or the word 'profile'. This was strictly serviceman's language —be warned! I threw back my head and laughed with the ease of two children. On his part, I raised a running, flashing flame in his blood because of my beauty and the sweetness which he knew lay at the core of my heart.

THE things he was saying may have lacked the poetry of Keats or Shelley, but it's only natural for artists such as Mr. HANDS to want to express themselves openly, to analyse the loveliness of women whom they consider near perfection.

PAINTERS have been trying to define beauty of face and form since the dawn of art,

Mr. HANDS showed a keen interest in my FOUNDATION GARMENTS and I bitterly regretted that I wasn't WEARing a PETTICOAT. The one I have at home shows the way to brighter underwear, in four-tiered taffeta edged with a feminine-look lace frill.

"You look just like RITA HAYWORTH," said Mr. Hands.

"I can imag-ine

you as a redhead with bright copper hair in two great long twists each side of your head, hanging down to your waist, and a loose peignoir thing on with a lot of lace about it, and I see myself just taking you into my arms and bearing you away."

"You'd soon put me down," I giggled, "I'm not a light weight. Besides, you're describing a scene from *The Scarlet Pimpernel.* That's all tosh and TABLE MARGARINE."

"You're lovely," he said, "do you know that?" There was a vibrant, primitive note in his voice. I threw my head back and with closed eyes let the words of admiration flood over me like a family-size can of Carnation evaporated milk. I imagined his eyes were resting appreciatively on my hair and lovely, expressive face. There was something about the urgency, the excitement in his voice. My emotions were all mixed up with wearing THE SKIRT and listening to the enthralling things he said about me. His words had flung open the french windows of my mind and forced me to step out on to the balcony of indiscretion.

MR. HANDS appeared to have mislaid his cigarettes. I could hear the coins in his trouser pocket jingle as he felt around for them. I wasn't sure how many PHOTOGRAPHS he'd taken. I hadn't heard the CAMERA click ONCE. It was glamorous and absorbing, but it was also an unrelenting whirl. At one point, I opened my eyes to find him fiddling with something at the foot of the bed. HE seemed in some distress and I wondered if perhaps he'd had a fall, so I started to get up to make sure he was all right.

"No, stay there. Don't move." He was trying to modulate his tone, but the irritation seeped through. I felt like a schoolgirl receiving a well-deserved reprimand. The next thing I knew he was standing over me, looking down at me with undisguised admiration.

"I hope you will pardon my boldness, but when I see something beautiful I am, how shall I say . . . without prudence."

I glanced at him drowsily through half-closed lashes and in one stark,

MOOD-CHANGING moMENT caught a horrifying glimpse of what he had been fiddling with ● MAN'S SAUSAGE MEAT — stiff with outrage and frustration. I scrambled quickly to my feet, but he caught at my hand.

"Barbie, Will you kiss it better?"

Speechless at such a request, I could only shake my head.

"I won't let you go until you do," he threatened quietly.

HIS HAND was wet and STICKY and I snatched mine away, instinctively wiping it on my Skirt. My mind fought to adjust to the situation. Who was Barbie? I was disoriented further then to see that Mr. Hands was no longer wearing Trousers, just his SOCKS, and realised too late that this was the wrong sort of man altogether, a libertine without consideration or even compassion.

"I . . . I must go home . . . at once!"

"Hush," he said, "stop that. Get hold of yourself. You've held me at arm's length all these weeks, and now you're acting like an outraged Victorian miss." His hungry eyes were devouring me, from my shining, disordered hair to my flushed cheeks, redder now than they would have been if they had not been stinging with effrontery. His gaze shifted to my slender throat and white neck, and came to rest on the delicately pretty white Bandeau bra which my opened blouse had partially revealed. My fingers flew to the loosened opening. But quick as I was, Mr. Hands was quicker. He caught my wrists and held them imprisoned in his ruthless grip. It was as if his cold, staring eyes could see beyond my clothes to my body.

"Don't," he said. "Everything about you is so lovely. You can't blame me for wanting to see all I can." His face was lobster pink. There are some men—just a few—

who are so scrupulous that they wouldn't even undo a parcel addressed to themselves ; but there are others, like my lobster-man, who wouldn't hesitate to shop-lift, if the goods on the counter happened to be women or girls. Mr. **HANDS** hasn't a conscience where 'affairs' are concerned.

Panic and fear flooded over me. I wanted to run but I couldn't find a clear path past the foot of the bed. The CANDLEWICK BEDSPREAD had become entangled round my feet.

"If you come near me I shall kill you," I said, staying him with my **POINTY** gaze. Searching for something to back up my threat, my hand groped in a curious blind fashion amongst objects on the bedside table and found an individual Bakewell tart in a foil tray with a bite taken out of it. With that instinctive sense of self-preservation which comes to us all in desperate moments, I picked it up and threw it at him. It struck him on the shoulder, showering **CAKE** crumbs everywhere.

I tried to find my footing but I'd lost a SHOE. My **tormentor** was coming towards me, his arms AIMING AT the parts of me he wanted to examine. When I rebuffed him, he lunged at me and began grabbing whatever he could get his hands on. I wanted him to **STOP**.

I wanted it all to **STOP**,

STOP,

but his hands were everywhere. He was tugging the hem of my skirt, trying to look up it, which is (or should be) strictly discouraged until after marriage. I was desperate to safeguard my modesty, but in the struggle the elasticated waistband was starting to slip. There was a scrabbling of hands and I didn't have enough OF THEM to fight him off and keep my skirt pulled up at the same time. In the end I simply let go and stepped out of it. He snatched it away then, AS IF he'd won it in a raffle. But THE SKIRT wasn't the prize he was after. He threw it behind him on to

THE BeD

and came for me again. He was staring at me down there, his eyes fixed and glowing like A PAIR OF MATCHING WALL LAMPS. The effect on him was physical. I quickly averted my eyes. "Let's have a look at you, then," he said, using the family's private word for the part of the body concerned. He began rummaging through the merchandise as if he was in a bargain basement and everything was on sale. I had not expected somebody quite so brusque, arrogant, and—not to put too fine a point on it—uncouth.

"Don't—don't be a fool!" I protested, struggling away from him. "You're being deliberately cruel to me, and I'll not have it."

He caught my wrists and pushed me against the wall.

"You'll not have it!" he repeated scornfully. "You'll have whatever I choose to give you."

I managed to free my trembling hands, and in desperation, I clawed at his face, ripping out his false teeth and kicking him with my feet. Had Mr. Hands (like so many men these days) underestimated the inner strength of the modern woman? Indeed he had, and vulnerable though I felt without it, having no skirt at least gave me greater freedom of movement. Seeing my Cinderella slipper caught among the folds of the bedspread, I stretched out my free hand and grabbed it by the toe. Fear and hate gave me strength as I brought the heel crashing down on his head. There was a HARD crack as the tip dug into his SCALP. He cried out in pain with the first blow, falling towards me, but before his cry had lasted any time, I struck him again and this time he only mumbled. His hands were on his head, protecting it as he began to TOPPLE. I shoved him hard towards the bed and he slid across it, taking the COVERS with him as he tumbled over the edge and crashed into the wardrobe on the other side. He came to rest in the the narrow gap between the bed and the wardrobe and lay there perfectly still. Perhaps he was subject to black-outs and would come out of this one presently.

He didn't.

I don't know how long I stood there. My **BRAIN** had dislodged itself and become a slice of peach slithering about on a spoon. I screwed up my eyes and tried to breathe steadily. A rushing sound in my ears swelled into a mighty roar, like all the winds of the world blowing through my head in one gigantic hurricane. THROUGH what aeons of time the hurricane blew, I never knew. When at last it quietened, the first thing I noticed was that I was sitting on the floor.

SLOWLY, I became aware of my surroundings again, as everything drifted back into focus: the budgie's THROATY cackle, a piece of BAKEWELL TART floating in the fish-tank, a leaky tap DRIZZLING into the washing-up bowl.

I leaned over the bed and looked down at Mr. HANDS. He was lying on his back with his eyes closed like someone in a coffin. His THIN bird legs stretched out before him. Thankfully, the front tails of his shirt covered his imprudence.

MY YELLOW SKIRT was trapped underneath him and I could see blood, **rich and thick,** seeping into it from behind his head, creating a

22'6

tough cleaning job for new Persil—though who would be tackling this particular job, I wasn't sure. Not me, because I knew I couldn't bring myself to TOUCH IT. Not Mr. Hands either. He wasn't going to be tackling anything; he wasn't MOVING at all. What's more, he didn't seem to be BREATHING. That's when I decided I should go back home to see how Mary was getting on.

Nurse Goodall would have checked his pulse, but for me there was no need. I could see he was DEAD.

I didn't think Hands had actually used the camera, but when I saw it on the DRESSer I opened up the back to check there was no film in it. There wasn't. This could have been a real concern. With my feminine loveliness captured on film, there would have been a DANGER that someone would FIND the film and produce a PICTURE of me as evidence. Luckily, Hands had been so caught up in the moment that he had not quite got round to that side of things.

He probably hadn't had film in the camera that day outside the PHOTO STUDIO either. It's an old trick. They do the same thing ON THE SEAFRONT IN WEYMOUTH. Roy and Mary got caught one year. Some young man with a Kodak Brownie. They take your money along with your name and address and promise to post the PHOTO to you. But there is no photo because there's no film in the camera, and all you're left with is a phoney receipt. At least I didn't give Hands any **money**.

STEPPING OVER Hands's DENTURES

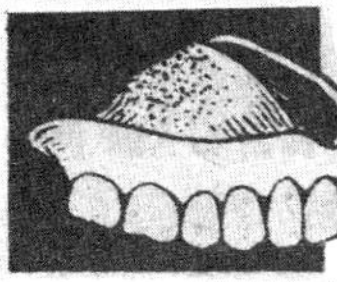

on the rug, I slipped my shoe on and gathered up my hand-bag. Then I drew the curtains, more for purposes of discretion than as a mark of respect. How could anyone respect a man like that?

Just then, I heard someone on the landing. There was a light knock on the door and a man's voice. "Are you all right in there, Mr. Hands?"

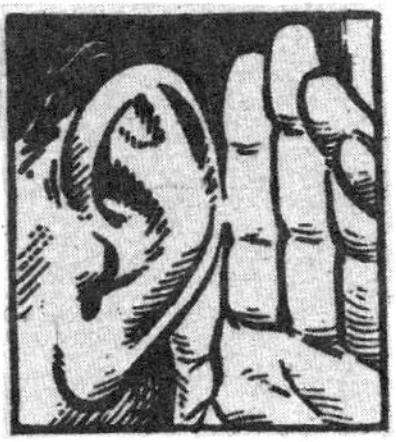

I froze for a moment, not knowing what to do. I could tell the man was listening on the other side of the door. We listened to each other LISTENING. Neither of us made a sound. He must have left his OWN door open because I could hear a television from across the landing. TAKE YOUR PICK was on. It was the yes–no game where contestants have to last sixty seconds without saying either of those two little words. Michael Miles (your quiz inquisitor) can always catch them out. "So you're from Nottingham?" "That's correct, Michael." 'You didn't say 'yes', then, did you?" "I did not, Michael." "You're quite sure?" "Yes, quite sure." Bong! The gong would go and that would be the end of that contestant.

A few moments of the game passed. Meanwhile THE MAN outside on the landing was still waiting for a reply. He knocked again but I knew better than to answer.

14

I hadn't wanted to

TOUCH

the *trousers*

at all—the situation was actually making me feel sick— but I couldn't have gone out into the street as I was: my coat was too short TO COVER THE NECESSITIES and, since I couldn't get to my **SKIRT**, the trousers had seemed the best option. They were much too big for me so I had to BUNCH the waistband **in my fist** to stop them from falling down. It only then occurred to me that they must have been the ones Mr. **HANDS** had taken off, because I had found them lying on top of my pixie jacket. **It must have been** an odd-looking outfit, but luckily the streets were relatively quiet and no one seemed to notice. Anyway, I wasn't thinking about that; I was thinking about

WHAT *I had* **DONE.**

In all the romantic stories I have ever read in my magazines, not one of the men, and certainly none of the women, has ever killed ANYONE. *Over the years, Evelyn Home* in **Woman** *has responded to hundreds of problems, dealing with matters ranging from* UNromantic HUSBANDS to *marital disharmony in general,* but not one single *letter* **has ever** asked advice on what do after having **beaten an** unwelcome suitor **TO DEATH** with the heel of **one's shoe.** If it had been something less serious — **MAKING CUSHION COVERS** perhaps, or dealing with a baby who suffers from a bloated tummy after feeding, **Evelyn** would have already pointed another reader in the right direction. As it was, the only solution I could see was to WRITE TO EVELYN DIRECTLY FOR ADVICE, and my fear was that that would only attract attention to the whole business.

I WANTED to get straight home but, as I neared Afferton Road, I realised I couldn't face Mary. Even if Mrs. PRICE hadn't spilled the *BAKED BEANS*, Mary would by now have discovered that I was not in my room. How could I explain to her what had happened? How could I describe the dirty, degrading scene? I was a murderer now. A proper murderer like you read about in the papers.

Someone was DEAD because of me.
Really, properly DEAD. And when they caught me — as they always did — I would be locked up in prison for the rest of my life. Or put in a home for the criminally insane. They might even hang me for it. Then I'd be really, properly **DEAD** too.

I took the long way round, past the railway arches, keeping to the shadows, fearful of running into A POLICEMAN. With each step, the coins in Mr. HANDS's TROUSERS chinked *against* my *thigh*, but I was reluctant to put my hand in the pocket to steady them. There were the shops in Great Colmore Street, shut now, of course. Some things in *Marcia Modes* I could have looked at, but I didn't want to linger and for once I'd lost my appetite for

window
SHOPPING.

In the chemist's,
a smiling Kodak CUT-OUT girl pressed her face to the inside of the glass. Some wag had stuck *CHEWING GUM* on her nose.

I didn't know what to do or where to go. I had never felt so alone in my life. As I passed THE CROWN, **beery** *smells* and jovial hubbub *wafted out on to the street.* I wanted to be one of the men inside, enjoying an average Friday night in the life of an average working man. If I hadn't been dressed like I was, **I might have gone in for a** *tonic wine to calm my nerves.* They do say you should never prescribe 'tonics' for yourself—

except, of course, those that do not come out of a bottle. A brief change of scenery, a visit to the cinema, or a new hat, any of these things may have the overall effect of a tonic. And so does a home given new colour. A coat of paint, some bright new cushions and a pot plant — a tonic for a room is a tonic for its occupants. But in my present state, I feared it would take all *FORTY-SIX SHADES IN THE DULUX MATT EMULSION RANGE* to bring the colour back to my cheeks.

There were more people on the street now, looking at me, or doing that thing where they try not to look. People on their own tend not to say anything but sooner or later I was sure to run into a group of know-nothing men, fired up by FRIDAY NIGHT ALE and ready for a little local sport. I turned off the main road and headed for HOME.

Luckily, I had the keys to the VAN in my bag. I just opened up the back and stepped straight in, shutting the door behind me, as naturally as if I'd been walking into my own house. I don't think anyone saw me. I had noticed that our downstairs light was on, which meant *Mary* was still up. It was only just gone ten, so she would be sitting down TO WATCH NO HIDING PLACE, having abandoned the DRESSMAKING as soon as she discovered that I was missing. I knew she'd still be furious, so I decided to wait in the van until she'd gone to bed.

I TOOK OFF Mr. HANDS's trousers and rolled them into a ball, setting them some distance away from me. My hands felt dirty and I was careful not to touch my face with them. Sometimes life is not at all like Hollywood would have us believe. Those who realise this truth will be the happier for the knowledge!

Even in the dark, I couldn't help noticing the dreadful state of my STOCKINGS. My RED Boulevard COURT shoes had ended up on a piece of waste ground near Egmont Street. AS *the murder weapon*, only the left shoe held the dark and terrible secret, but the right shoe was guilty by association so I had thrown them both over a fence, hoping that no one would see them among all the other rubbish that had been dumped there. HAVING walked home without them, the heels of my stockings had worn right through and there were big ladders up both legs, adding to the one originating at my knee. HAIRS poked out through the holes. I regret to say that mine, like the parsley in our garden, grows disgustingly vigorously. What remained of each STOCKING foot was caked in mud, which had seeped in and dried between *my prettily painted toes.* Hardly the perfect picture of leg beauty advocated in THE MAGAZINEs, but my concern for such things seemed to have waned.

IT had turned chilly and my feet were wet, but I was safe in the VAN. If I hadn't felt so uncomfortably dirty, I might have stayed there all night.

I SAT perfectly still, going over and over everything in my mind, thinking about what I should and shouldn't have done, and wondering what was going to happen to me.

"In your own words, will you describe to the court the events of the evening in question?"

"Well, Your Honour, I quickly became aware that I was in the presence of an unchivalrous rogue and was in two minds whether to pick up my skirts and run. 'Mayhap I have earned your displeasure but, surely, I've given you no cause for presumption,' I said."

"And what did he say?"

"His hand grasped my delicate and he turned me to to face him. 'Mistress, your protests are growing wearisome.'"

"Please continue, Miss LITTLE."

"When I raised my frightened maiden lashes, I saw naught but the cold narrowed look in his eyes. 'Pray loose my arm," I persisted. 'You are forcing me, sir,' I said, 'against my will.'"

"And what did you do then?"

"And then, Your Honour, I'd rather not say."

"And then, I put it to you, *in a frenzy of violence* you did *viciously* bludgeon *this man to death* with **the heel of your shoe.** Is that not so, MISS **LITTLE?**

"**O GOD,** help me. I don't want to spend the rest of my life **IN prison.**"

I wasn't sure if I'd said the **WORDS** out loud. I thought about running away. It didn't matter where — *A BEACH IN WALES*, under a tarpaulin on a building site. I could pretend to be one of the Black and White Minstrels or become an anonymous chorus girl and venture into that stickiest, trickiest branch of light entertainment, the musical. Maybe even just drive off in the van and never come back. But I knew I didn't have a dog's chance. **Murder,** in fact, can sometimes be a nightmare from which the murderer can't escape. "Run for it! Get out while the going is good!" is what the world so often advises, seeing, from the out side, a situation which looks intolerable. The sufferer knows that this is good advice and badly wants to flee, but can't budge a foot.

NOT killed Mr. **HANDS** —*that's what I should have done.* Not gone there in the first place. But instead of facing THE BIG PICTURE, my furtive BRAIN niggled at the details. What would happen to his **budgie** now? What was in those **wallpaper**-covered exer-cise books? Would someone feed the goldfish or would it be left to survive on *BAKEWELL TART* until it finally perished and floated, like the CAKE, to the surface? I stared blankly at the WALL of the van trying to make sense of it all. Then it seemED as though my spirit left me, wandered like a lost cloud among the unanswered questions. That wandering spirit went as far as Egmont Street, HOVERING at the upstairs window and peeking through a *GUILTY* chink in the curtain to glimpse the prostrate form of my tormentor, ***lashings of rich, dark cherry filling*** STILL ***oozing*** *from* his head. Presently the spirit would return again, dejected, battered and grieving, to re-enter my crouched form, holding the power to flay and torment me with its thorny stick.

So the party was over. There was no going back to the old peace and innocence now. No spinning sparkling, sugar-frosted, golden turreted castles in the air for me. I no longer deserved them.

The floor of the van was cold and I could feel my legs growing numb, but I made no attempt to ease my discomfort. The only time I moved during the whole HOUR was to open the back door and scoot the trousers into the gutter with my heel. I didn't want them in there with me. There was a chinking sound as the COINS in the pocket hit the TARMAC. EVIDENCE? I leaned out and hauled them back in again. My face soured like SPOILED MILK as I slipped my hand into the swaggering depths of the pocket, trying not to let the material touch my skin. At the bottom, I found a thick knot of personal effects, which I clawed to the surface.

There were two keys on a key ring, a handful of coins, and a ten-shilling note. There was also a DIRTY hanky and a tea card with a picture of a fish with its mouth wide open, looking surprised. In the other pocket was a little brown wage packet with his name on it. (HANDS's, not the FISH's.)

It had been opened and inside there was twelve pounds in crisp banknotes. ON the back of the envelope were various scribbled drawings in pencil. Whoever had done them — Hands one supposes — was no Michelangelo. One sketch seemed to be an attempt at a nightclub singer, brassy and heavily made-up; in another he had made a stab at a wide-eyed Betty Boop type who appeared to be smoking a CIGAR. Each one had been titled with a string of profanities that should never be used in polite company. The words were a testament to the MAN'S depravity. I stuffed the envelope, hanky, and TEA CARD back into the pocket before finally ejecting the whole repulsive bundle back on to the street. Only the keys could be traced to Hands, BUT I KEPT THE MONEY AS WELL. I WASN'T SURE YET IF I WANTED ANYTHING TO DO WITH IT, BUT THROWING IT AWAY WOULD BE SIMPLY *'throwing money away'*. **AND** ***not*** **throwing money away**

CAN SAVE YOU £££'s.

Shortly after eleven, our downstairs light went out. I waited for a further twenty minutes to make sure the coast was clear. As I stepped out on to the road, my LEGS jangled with **PINS and NEEDLES**.

I noticed that by chance the trousers had landed next to a storm drain so I paused briefly to poke the **OFFENDING** garment with my foot **T H R O U G H** the gap in the kerbstone.

Once inside THE HOUSE,

I looked into the front room. It was dark but STILL warm and cosy from the dying embers of the fire. Cocoa was asleep on the ARM of the SETTEE and I could see from the light in the hallway that Mary had eaten a TANGERINE and left the peel on a saucer. And there, hanging over the back of the chair, was the DRESS. I held it up to examine it as best I could in the poor light. There were a few LOOSE THREADS but otherwise it looked as though it was *pretty much* FINISHED. SINGER* machines really do make light work of *everything* you sew. It was then, more than ever, that I wanted the whole evening to have happened differently. I wanted to have stayed in with Mary, watching TAKE YOUR PICK and *Bootsie and Snudge*. I wanted us to have had our SUPPER SANDWICH and sipped *Ovaltine* together while I tried on the new home-made dress one more time before going off *to bed*. LOVELY CLEAN BED, where it's snug between sheets as white as your nightie. As shining white as all mother's white things.

I stood on the cold **linoleum floor** of the **bathroom** and peeled off the stockings before washing my mud-stained feet in the sink. I removed my wig and **slung** it on the linen basket. Normally, I'd be careful to ensure that it went straight back ON THE BLOCK, but tonight I didn't care. I couldn't imagine wanting to wear it again. It was rapture to toss off **sordidly** impregnated garments, underclothes that felt — although they could not be — dirty, and to abandon **the responsibility** of presenting myself as a charming and attractive **WOMAN** who is also a brilliant and experienced **flower arranger** and a pianist of more-than-average ability.

I WAS

hunched over the sink, washing the make-up from my face when a knock on the door startled me. **OUTSIDE, on the other side of the door,** Mary stood on the landing, her dressing gown pulled tight around her. She knocked again, and there was silence inside the room. She knocked once more, very loudly, and rattled the door-handle as if to disturb this silence. **After a moment,** the key turned in the lock, the door opened and there stood ROY

in his dressing gown. His face bore traces of make-up, which was streaked as if he had been crying. Why do men dislike make-up so much?

It isn't that men really dislike make-up; it's that they *think* they dislike it. It's the same sort of feeling that makes a man swear he can't bear to eat rabbit, but allows him to eat it quite greedily when it's on the menu as minced chicken.

"Where have you been?" Mary was seething.

"**Nowhere.**"

Her glance took in the **CLOTHES** scattered on the floor.

"I knew it. You went out **IN** *skirts*, didn't you?"

There was no need to answer.

"You promised." She was so angry, she could barely keep still. "Do you ever think of anyone but yourself? Does it ever occur to you to think how your actions might affect other people?"

Her voice was like an iron hammer knocking together the pieces of a strip-sprung bed. Each word screeched and vibrated like flayed steel.

Roy bowed his head. Through a mist of anger and misery and shame at her own betrayal, Mary could see that he was greatly distressed.

"Oh God, Mum," he said, putting his hands to his face. "Something **BAD** happened."

"What?"

"There was a man. He tried to take advantage."

"WELL, WHAT DO YOU EXPECT, looking like one of those golden girls with the come-and-get-me technique. Men don't look much further than a short skirt, you know. They're not bothered who's wearing it. They're animals, most of them, and their morals are disgusting. It's not even safe for decent girls to go out alone after dark, never mind you."

"It was awful."

"What did he *do?*"

"I can't say."

"Where was this, ON THE STREET?"

"No." Roy's hands were still covering his face, unable to bear the shame.

"Where then?" she demanded, impatiently.

Slowly, he answered. "At his flat."

Mary WAS INCENSED. "You went to a man's flat? Dressed as NORMA? ROY, what the devil were you thinking? That's just asking for trouble."

"I know."

"Did he think you were a WOMAN?"

ROY squirmed. "Yes . . . I think so . . . I don't know. He might have known."

THESE ARE THE DIFFICULT QUESTIONS, *delicate* as *daffodils in the snow.*

"And he soon found out for sure, I suppose."

Roy didn't want to think about what she might be imagining.

"THERE WAS A FIGHT," said ROY, unsteadily. "Then she hit him."

"Who did?"

"NORMA. She hit him really hard."

"Well, it's what he deserved, I expect, but it's your own stupid fault for going there in the first place."

"No, it's worse than that. He's **dead.**"

"What the devil are you on about?

TALK PROPERLY.

Dead?

He can't be." She stared at him, astonished and perturbed. *Roy* said nothing. There in the silence, Roy heard Mary's heart plummet to THE BATHROOM FLOOR like a weight on a cut rope.

Mary perched on the edge of the bath next to Roy. She was hunched over, resting her elbows on her knees with her palms pressed to her eyes as the terrible truth sank in.

" I knew something like this would happen. What have I done to make you do these terrible things? LOVED *you too much,* I expect. I should have been firmer with you when you were young."

There was nothing to say.

IT was a long time before she spoke again, but when she did she wanted to know all the ins and outs. After the obvious WHO WAS HE? HOW DID IT HAPPEN? her questions became more practical. Who had seen me? Who knew I was there? Was any evidence left at the scene of the crime? Fingerprints?

Had anyone seen us together?

Roy tried to speak objectively and give it all as it had happened, though he didn't mention the SKIRT; he didn't want to have to describe the events that led to its REMOVAL. HE didn't mention the shoes, or the

TROUSERS

either, which he knew he probably should have done. He was embarrassed at having handled the whole affair so badly and knew his foolishness would only have irritated her.

WITH all the relevant information to hand, or so she thought, Mary became more decisive. "Right. This is what we do. We put all Norma's

CLOTHES in a suitcase and you take them down to the *Salvation Army* like you were supposed to do TWENTY YEARS AGO. Get rid of everything — clothes, wig, make-up, jewellery. Then that'll be the end of it. For good, this time. There'll be no more DRESSING up from now on."

"Should I go to THE POLICE?"

"Don't be stupid. They'd have you for MURDER."

"I could tell them it was self-defence."

"Why don't you tell them about WEARing women's clothes while you're at it? Then the other prisoners can give you a good kicking before they HANG you."

The familiar harsh tone told *Roy* he had better back down and let her take charge.

"And what's more," she went on, "it would be all over the papers."

IT SEEMed ODD THAT she was as concerned about the '*family secret*' getting out as she was about Roy's imminent execution.

Nevertheless, a **MOTHER** who stands by you in a crisis is worth a thousand rubies.

"No, my lad," she went on, "your best bet is to GET SHOT OF all Norma's clothes and hope no one spots the connection. THE police will be on the lookout for a

WOMAN,

won't they? In a **RED** coat. Well, they're not going to find her, are they? Because there'll be no **WOMAN** and there'll be no COAT. They won't be looking for A NICE YOUNG MAN WHO WORKS AT a laundry."

It was too much for *Roy* to take in but he supposed she was right. Following her instructions, he had the BIG BLUE suitcase down off the WARDROBE and was mechanically packing my clothes into it WHEN MARY returned with the DRESS from downstairs and the underthings that had been drying by the fire. She threw them on the bed next to the case.

"On second thoughts, don't take it to the Salvation Army," she said briskly. The police might find the clothes and trace them back here. We'll have a bonfire in the garden tomorrow and set fire to THE LOT."

Mary had turned into a character from a cops and robbers programme. I wondered if she'd picked up any of this from INTERPOL CALLING.

"Thanks for making the dress," said Roy. "It's lovely."

"Sling it with the rest. It's no USE now," she said dismissively.

"But you've only just finished it. All that effort."

"Just get rid of it."

Roy sensed she was fighting to control her temper.

He searched his mother's face for signs of weakness or tearfulness, but saw only *her dogged resolution. She was determined not to* let them take him away. He had a mental image of a woman bracing herself against the pull of a roped bullock, and those *squat* heels churning up the red earth like a miniature pair of bulldozers.

ROY'S briefly considered BRILLIANT IDEA had been to acquire all new clothes and buy a long, RED *Rita Hayworth* wig to make me look DIFFERENT — to create a new me, a new NORMA, but he knew it wouldn't work. And the truth was, he didn't want to do it any more. If this was the way women were treated, it was better to make sure I didn't go OUT at all. It seemed clear now that whenever I got dressed up and made myself beautiful, I would inevitably attract the attentions of men like Mr. HANDS. Mary was *right.* NORMA had to GO.

GETTING RID OF the clothes in the suitcase wasn't going to be enough. I knew that. There were too many other things stacked against me — the CANARY YELLOW skirt, for example, which I had been seen wearing by Mrs. Price, not to mention Sylvia Syms and a full cast of supporting players. I couldn't have chosen a more vividly memorable colour if I'd tried. With my RED pixie-hood COAT adding its own contrasting hue, I might as well have tied a bunch of balloons round my neck and played 'My Old Man's a Dustman' on the trumpet. Nevertheless, with MARY taking control of the situation, a part of Roy believed—or wanted to believe—that everything would be all right, that somehow MARY would sort things out. Her brisk, matter-of-fact approach gave him confidence, and he had an odd sense of excitement about this bold new adventure. For once, it felt like the right thing to do.

HAVING the big blue suitcase out on the bed REMINDED HIM OF THE last-minute packing he and Mary would do the night before going on their annual summer holiday. They'd visited many popular seaside resorts together, but I was never allowed to go. (Mary had strict rules about '**DRESSING**' on holiday.) The difference was, now it was me who was GOING; ROY and Mary WOULD BE STAYING BEHIND. And unlike Roy and Mary who, at the end of their holiday, would return home to Afferton Road, tanned, rested and invigorated by the sea air, mine was going to have to be A ONE-WAY TICKET. This was a permanent HOLIDAY, one from which I could never RETURN.

15

Roy held the wheel at ten to two, though it was actually twenty past. He drove through dark, unfamiliar streets, urged by the looming presence of the suitcase behind him in the back of the VAN. His eyes danced from side to side looking for a suitable place to rid himself of his guilty burden. Mary had told him to wait until morning, but Roy was unable to sleep, and his escalating panic about getting caught by the police had spurred him to action.

IT scared him to think how easily they might pick up the trail. The neighbour from the flat across the landing would have found HANDS dead and alerted the police. After questioning Sylvia Syms, officers would have a full and accurate description of a striking-looking woman in a red pixie jacket seen arriving at (and later departing hurriedly from) the Egmont Road bedsit. Roadside witnesses would furnish them with descriptions of the before and after versions, which together with the canary yellow skirt found at the scene of the crime, would paint a complete picture in oils or watercolour.

Mrs. **PRICE** would have somehow elbowed her way to the front of the queue to help the police with their enquiries and told them of the woman fitting the description who was staying with us. Even without a degree in **mathematics,** it wouldn't take the boys in blue **L – O – N – G** to **tot up the score,** and then it would be **rat-a-tat-tat** or ***'Ding-dong; Avon calling'*** at

48

Afferton Road.

BUT NOW,

thanks to **ROY'S** evasive action, **there would be no point in them setting out the board to play that little game** because, as Mary said, there'd be no woman and there'd be no red coat. Mary had it *vice-versa,* but it came to the same thing.

There were few other motorists on the road but at a set of traffic lights, a ***Ford Anglia***, the same colour and model as Mr White's, pulled up alongside him. Roy dared not turn his head to look at the driver, fearing that it might be HIM. He tried to concentrate on the road ahead, and told himself that it was just a case of nerves.

Imagination could play strange tricks on people. He had read a story once about three men alone in a lifeboat who all swore that they had seen and heard a fourth, eating crisps.

THE new Ford Anglia is a popular car, he reasoned, enjoyed by many families across the land. There must be thousands of cars like it on the road.

One thing was certain: his only chance of safety lay in getting rid of the suitcase without any delay. The slightest mishap and he was done for.

Once a suitable 'dropping off' spot had been found, there would be a number of options. HIS FIRST CHOICE would have been to set fire to the clothes in some desolate area, but at night, he feared the flames might draw unwanted attention. Burying them might have been a better idea, but he had FAILED to take the spade from the garden shed before he set off, and without the appropriate tool for the job, the would-be handyman is likely to make a bodge of the whole thing. Several large stones added to the contents of any SUITCASE should ensure that, once tossed into the river, it will not resurface to incriminate the suspect. But *Roy* couldn't think of a river nearby and the Blue Danube seemed a very long way away.

It was getting later and later and he was tired. He was right on the other side of town **now**, completely lost, and miles from home. Surely, he could just dump the case somewhere? Was anyone really **EVER** going to trace it back to Afferton Road now? The most important thing was to get rid of the evidence quickly. The longer he drove round with it in the back, the greater his chances of being caught, bowled or run out.

THE

first possibility, a building site, looked promising until he noticed that it was overlooked by a warehouse **where** one or two windows were still lit. A **MILE** or two later, he spotted a high chain-link fence with what looked like waste ground on the other side. He drove up close and changed down into second gear, looking for a suitable **point of access.** His headlights picked out the shape of an iron footbridge about a hundred yards ahead.

HE drew up to the

kerb and turned off the engine. It was dark and quiet and there was no one about. The houses on the other side of the road had obviously been condemned and were sealed shut with corrugated iron. It was the perfect spot.

Nipping out to take a closer look, he saw that beyond the fence, the ground fell away sharply, sloping steeply down towards some railway TRACKS below. Shrubs and bushes grew capricious and wanton on its slippery slopes, and amongst them, all manner of rubbish had been thrown. It was obviously used as a local dumping site and neither British Railways nor the local council seemed willing to take responsibility for clearing it up.

ROY took the suitcase *from* the back of the VAN and made his way on to the BRIDGE. The whole structure reverberated with a dull metallic boom in response to his footsteps. Through the criss-crossed pattern of the IRONWORK, he could see the HOUSEHOLD detritus below. There were clothes there already, strewn and dirty, like a risqué story told by a *farm worker*. A broken *RADIO*, newspapers, and moth-eaten carpets, along with the usual BEER BOTTLES, CIGARETTE *packets, and sweet wrappers* contributed to the sordid tale. Most of the stuff looked like it had been there for years. The difference, as ROY saw it, was that unlike the contents of the suitcase, the CLOTHING here had been weathered through time into muddy, sodden rags which would not interest even the most poverty-stricken scavenger — whereas the sight of my sparklingly fresh, resplendent wardrobe, *displayed in some informal arrangement* along the railway embankment, would be sure to catch the eye of every remotely fashion-conscious passer-by. *A* WOMAN like **myself**, with an eager sense of style, would be unable to resist an attempt to retrieve them from the mire. **ROY**'s main aim was to make sure the **CLOTHES blended in.** And lead us not into temptation, but deliver us from evil.

HE was just wondering if it would be better to **throw the whole** SUITCASE overboard, or to scatter the **CLOTHES AS** separates, when the nearby railway signal suddenly dropped and made him jump. A train was coming. He decided to wait until it had **PASSED** before making his move, in case anyone saw what he was doing, but as it approached, he realised it was a goods train. **OF** course, passenger trains would have stopped RUNNING hours ago

●

Then he had an idea. What would happen if he dropped the suitcase off the footbridge into one of the open wagons as it passed underneath? *Was* that a sensible solution? Where would the train be going? To another town hundreds of miles away. It could easily end up in Kilmarnock or Dundee. Wasn't sending the suitcase to Dundee as good as burying it? No one would be interested in its up there, surely? They had better things to do: listening to Moira Anderson records and *tossing the caber.*

CONTENTS

HE had an uneasy feeling that there had been something like this in a film — where something gets dropped off a bridge into a goods wagon. Alec Guinness was in it. The Ladykillers? He couldn't remember the details but he sensed that in the film things had not turned out well.

He had to think quickly. It was now or never. The train would soon be underneath him. He moved further along the bridge, positioning himself over the tracks, and swung the suitcase over the side, letting it dangle from his fingertips. All he had to do was to LET go at the right moment, and all his troubles would be over.

Thick chuffing clouds of smoke and steam choked the bridge as the noisy BLACK DRAGON passed underneath. Roy INSTINCTIVELY turned his head against the ferocity of the

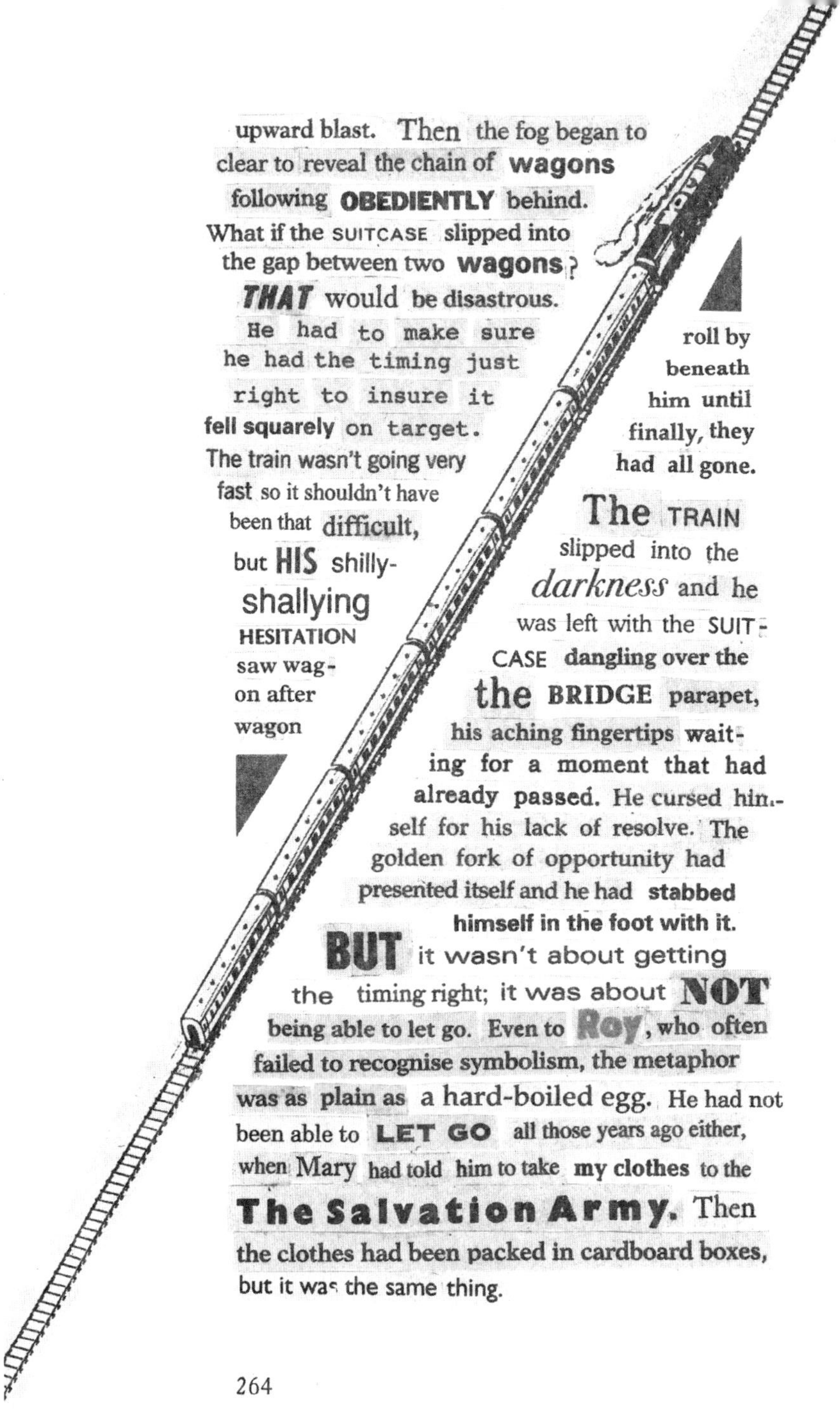

upward blast. Then the fog began to clear to reveal the chain of **wagons** following **OBEDIENTLY** behind. What if the SUITCASE slipped into the gap between two **wagons**? ***THAT*** would be disastrous. He had to make sure he had the timing just right to insure it **fell squarely** on target. The train wasn't going very fast so it shouldn't have been that difficult, but **HIS** shilly-shallying **HESITATION** saw wag-on after wagon roll by beneath him until finally, they had all gone.

The TRAIN slipped into the *darkness* and he was left with the SUIT-CASE **dangling over the** the **BRIDGE** parapet, **his aching fingertips** wait-ing for a moment that had already passed. He cursed him-self for his lack of resolve. The golden fork of opportunity had presented itself and he had **stabbed himself in the foot with it.**

BUT it wasn't about getting the timing right; it was about **NOT** being able to let go. Even to **Roy**, who often failed to recognise symbolism, the metaphor was as plain as a hard-boiled egg. He had not been able to **LET GO** all those years ago either, when Mary had told him to take **my clothes** to the **The Salvation Army.** Then the clothes had been packed in cardboard boxes, but it was the same thing.

Mary went a bit strange after my accident.

Part of her seemed to disappear without trace, while the other part remained resolutely detached and uncommunicative. Roy was left very much in the dark. I spent four days in hospital, but that's as much as Roy was told and even that came from Mrs. PRICE. He wasn't allowed to visit. Mary went up there on her own while he stayed with the PRICES, pretending nothing had happened. Endless meals of **beans on toast** and stale JAM TARTS. On the fourth day, MARY came home and drew the curtains. *It was the middle of the afternoon* so he knew what that meant. He stood on the pavement outside, not knowing what to do. There was no KEY UNDER THE MAT and he was too afraid to KNOCK.

She never actually said it was his fault but he knew that was what she was thinking. And after that, there was nothing. It was as if Mary had shut up shop and moved out, leaving her cold, empty carcass behind to cook the meals and vacuum the rugs.

Even as an eight-year-old, Roy knew it was somehow wrong to get rid of everything, to remove all trace of someone's *existence.* Still, he did as he was told, loading the boxes on to his little cart and taking them along for redistribution to the commonwealth.

NoBODY at THE SALVATION ARMY BUILDING paid him much attention. They didn't seem particularly GRATEFUL FOR THE DONATION or to appreciate its sentimental value, so he kept ONE BOX back and took it home again, stowing it away in the bottom of his wardrobe.

FROM TIME TO TIME, when Mary was out of the house, he would take the clothes out and look at them. They had a familiar smell, something he'd never really noticed before, a 'little sister' smell. He would hold THEM to his face and breathe it in. Then he'd lay them out on the bed, creating outfits I might have worn. They were like those paper dress-up doll outfits that had the FOLD-OVER TABS — flat and lifeless because there was no DOLL to put them on.

Mary must have been aware of the

clothes box, known what was inside it, but she never mentioned it. Nothing about the whole matter was ever properly discussed. MARY's unwillingness to come to terms with what had happened was really no different from Roy's, except that Mary's STRATEGY was one of excommunication — rejecting and ejecting in one big spring cleaning operation, to ensure that there was nothing of mine left in the HOUSE to remind her — whereas Roy's was the opposite. IT IS HARD FOR ANY boy TO shut the wardrobe door on his little sister.

So, ONE DAY he put the clothes on. Glancing at himself in the mirror, he could imagine it was ME standing there. And that's how it all started.

"What are you doing with that suitcase, sir?" Roy turned to see two policemen standing behind him. Thickset broad-in-the-beam plodders with *bruise* blue uniforms with bulging pockets. He had been so lost in the past that he had not heard their flat-footed approach. The policeman was waiting for an answer to his question, but Roy could not think of one. What *was* he doing with the suitcase?

"Nothing," said ROY, *wearing the face of innocence* like an ill-fitting toy mask. He swung THE CASE BACK over the parapet and set it down.

One of THE POLICE men

bore a striking resemblance to PC 'Fancy' Smith off *Z Cars*. The older one— the one who had spoken— was cast more in the seen-it-all-before Dixon of Dock Green mould. It was reassuring to see that he had finally **been promoted to the rank of sergeant.** At the same time, they looked like the TWO who had turned up at the house to talk to Mary about my accident. Yet they couldn't have been the same ones: that was twenty years ago. ***We all get telltale signs of ageing around the eyes, even*** police*men.* Besides, nobody had a television back in those days.

"Nothing?" said Dixon of Dock Green. "It doesn't look like nothing to me. What have you got in there?"

"Just some clothes."

"Your clothes, are they, sir?"

Roy hesitated.

"You don't have to say anything unless you wish to," he told him. "Whatever you do say will be taken down in writing and may be given in evidence."

"Yes, they're mine," he said.

"And where are you going, this time of night?" asked P.C. Smith. You could tell he was from ***Z Cars*** because he knew all the right things to say.

"Nowhere. HOME."

"And where have you been?"

"Nowhere, as far as I know." It wasn't a very clever response.

The two policemen exchanged glances.

"Key," said the sergeant, holding out his hand like a ham.

"It isn't locked," said Roy, wishing now that it was, and that the key was at the very bottom of

A COAL MINE IN WALES.

Dixon of Dock Green unsnapped the catches and examined the contents of the case. He took out, one after another, gossamer garments and shook them out and held them up in the moonlight. A nightdress befrilled and delicate as the wisp of the white mists that were forming now on some romantic Scottish moor. A petticoat, a brief pair of panties.

"Yours, did you say?" sniggered Sergeant DIXON.

It was seeing the nightdress like that, desecrated in the moonlight by their great hands and puffing breath, that made Roy mad. It was more than he could take and caution flew. "Put them down," he said, furious, "you've no right . . ."

THEY paid no attention. Constable Smith measured a filmy petticoat against his vast thighs. Dixon of Dock Green had slipped his arms through the straps of my Contesa 'LITTLE EXTRA' EMBROIDERED BRA which, without being fastened at the back, sat limply across his TUNIC while he rummaged through the suitcase for more things. Humiliation bubbled in the pan as the heat was turned up to gas mark six. Roy could scarcely believe what was happening, that officers of HER MAJESTY'S CONSTABULARY would be so brutish in their teasing.

"Here you are, Sarge," said Z Cars, finger-ing the dangly earrings he had clipped to his ears. "What do you think? Wrong colour?"
"No, they're lovely. They go with your eyes." He himself was stepping into the petticoat and HIKING it up round his thick middle.

ROY stood and watched. All this had a tinge of unreality. He was not sure whether he was dreaming or awake. P.C. Z Cars had forced his arms through the sleeves of my PETER PAN collar blouse. It was much too small to go over his TUNIC, besides which HE HAD IT ON back-to-front. His shoulders were pinned back by the restraining fabric until he jerked them forward, causing the fabric to tear. Oooh! His mouth made a LITTLE O *Perfect* as he turned to ROY, WIDE-EYED *with* PANTOMIME surprise.
"Are you sure these are your clothes, sir?" said Dixon. "They seem a bit on the skimpy side to me."
It was not a moment for broken Spanish, so in the plainest English he protested furiously.
"I told you. They're my sister's and you've no right to touch them."
"No, sir. That's not what you said. I distinctly remember you saying they were yours," said the sergeant.
The pearl earrings trembled a little as the PC turned his head. "Yes, that's right, Sarge, I've got it written down here.
He said *'they're mine!'* "

Sergeant Dixon held out a pair of lace-look pantie briefs. "Let's see you in these, just to make sure."
"Please. Put them back. All I want is a chance to explain."
"NO NEED TO EXPLAIN. Come on. We want to see you in them."
The SERGEANT knelt at Roy's feet, stretching the waistband of the PANTIES between his PORK SAUSAGE fingers, ready for him to step into them. When Roy hesitated, the policeman prompted him condescendingly, as if he were helping a small child to dress. "STEP," he said brightly.
Reluctantly, Roy did as he was bid, wincing as the heel of his muddy brogues caught in the delicate fabric. The policeman

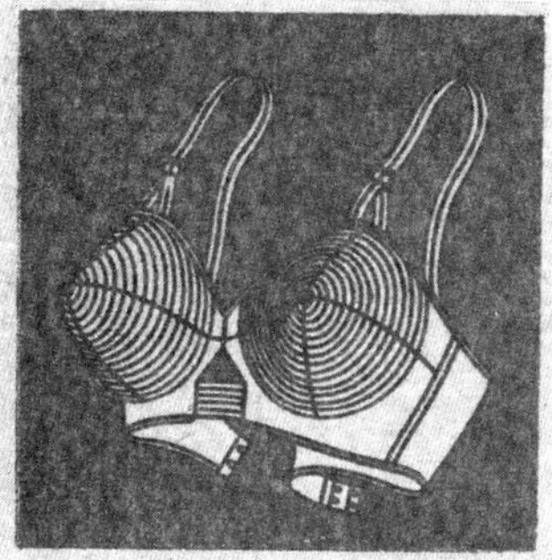

hoisted the pants up over *Roy's* TROUSERS.
"There now. They're a perfect fit. Don't they look lovely?"
"Oh, wait, SARGE. Let's see them with the bra," said P.C. Smith excitedly.
"Oh, yes. Of course. I was forgetting THE BRA." He shrugged it off his own shoulders and held it out by the straps.
"Arms," he said.
Roy reluctantly raised his arms and Dixon slipped it on him.
"Oh, yes, that's much better," said Fancy Smith.
"Wait, though, I think he needs A BIT OF LIPSTICK."
OLD Dixon agreed and the enthusiastic young

P.C. quickly found one in THE CASE.

Dusky Rose for a Lovelier Mouth.

He handed it to Sergeant Dixon, who undid the cap and propelled THE BASE to expose its entire pink length, rude and moist like **a dog's thing.** Stepping forward, he studied Roy's mouth with marked concentration before pressing the lipstick to his lips. **Roy** could feel a big ***Cupid's Bow*** being drawn on his upper lip, and underneath it a full lower lip pout.

The sergeant stood back to admire his handiwork. "What do you think? Too much?"

"No, SARGE, not enough. Here, let me have a go."

The younger constable's lack of experience *with* **COSMETICS** was more than compensated for by his enthusiasm. He circled Roy's MOUTH several times, LIKE something in the classified section OF THE ***Police Gazette*** that had caught his attention. Roy could feel the thick greasy **cosmetic** sprawled up to his nose and down to his chin. **WHY DO MEN FIND LOVELY LIPS SO ALLURING?**

"Oh, yes, that's much better," he said, tossing the still-open

LIPSTICK

into the **suitcase.**

Roy's eyes were closed now and he could not open them. The humiliation had forever stripped him of all dignity. **HE** felt the tears form under his eyelids and fought to staunch the flow. According to the code by which men are brought up and made manly, there's something shameful about blubbering. This schoolboy embarrassment at tears lingers on. There was a time, two or three hundred years ago, when it was considered by no means unusual or shameful for a man to weep. Not in the twentieth century, though, and certainly not in front of a policeman. He realised that he would have to pull himself together somehow.

ROY heard the **suitcase** being SNAPPED shut. He opened his eyes to see Sergeant Dixon handing it to him.

"Well, thank you for your cooperation, sir. Just routine. We'll be on our way."

DIXON was no longer wearing the *underskirt*.

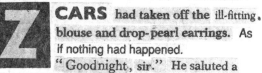

Z CARS had taken off the ill-fitting, blouse and drop-pearl earrings. As if nothing had happened.

"Goodnight, sir." He saluted a little salute, just like he does AT THE END OF THE PROGRAMME, and wandered with his Z Cars colleague back towards the road.

Roy was trembling. He was seriously starting to doubt his sanity. This could not have really happened, surely? And yet there he was, in the middle of the night, standing on a railway bridge in BRA and pants, *with lips so full and luscious they would put* CARMEN MIRANDA *to shame.*

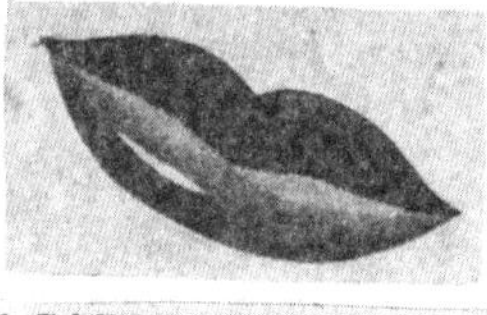

HE crossed to the other side of the bridge, crouching in some bushes to quickly remove the UNDER-

GARMENTS. He spat on to the panties and wiped the daubed LIPSTICK from his mouth, before stashing them along with the brassiere in the suitcase.

THERE was NOTHING TO DO NOW BUT TO GO home.

●

6TEEN

dodged round him in circles. **It had been a long night, crammed into a few short twilight hours of worry and speculation.** What made Roy so sure **HANDS** was **really dead?** The wound had seemed severe **at the time** but Roy is no more a doctor than I am

Nurse Thompson

Perhaps he had only been unconscious; the human body is a very resilient muscle **man**. Then again, Hands may have been **ALIVE** when I left the bed-sit **but, for want of appropriate medical attention, had bled to death** on the floor. **Should I have called an ambulance?**

The combined effects of worry, guilt and lack of sleep made him queasy. He had no appetite for breakfast. It was just as well it was Saturday. He couldn't have faced going in to work. A glass of Lucozade might have helped. Lucozade is a very delightful way of giving Glucose, a rapid source of energy. It does not upset the most delicate stomach. Invalids take Lucozade willingly because it is so delicious and refreshing.

But there wasn't any.

Renie PRICE had already been over, blabbing about seeing the tall girl in the red coat again, but by then, her gossipy tell-tales were old news to Mary. Luckily, Mrs. P had only seen me going out, not coming back.

Roy stepped up with an explanation, telling her that his 'cousin' had gone to live in Dundee. Permanently. "She's going to join a convent, as a matter of fact," he said. It was all he could think of on the spur of the moment.

Mary shot him a glance to let him know he had gone too far. "Yes," she said, with a light dusting of icing sugar, "so we won't be seeing her again."

" A convent?" said Renie. "Fancy that. She didn't look the convent type."

Mary smiled awkwardly: Roy looked at the wall.

"She's a big girl, isn't she, Mary?" said Renie, seeking confirmation.

Roy stepped in. "She's not that big."

Renie wasn't having it. "Ooh, she is. She's taller than you, Roy."

"That's just high heels," he said.

"And she likes her bright colours, doesn't she?" The tone was mocking.

Mrs. PRICE was beginning to get on Roy's nerves. He said: "Not always. She wears subtler hues as well. Anyway, there's no law against bright colours, is there?"

This was not strictly true.

IN 1960, AMENDMENTS TO THE 1938 FOOD, DRUG AND COSMETIC ACT **outlawed** THE USE OF THE STRAWBERRY-TONED RED NO.3A COLOUR ADDITIVE USED IN MARASCHINO CHERRIES, BUBBLE GUM AND CERTAIN LIPSTICKS BECAUSE TESTS SHOWED THAT LARGE AMOUNTS CAUSED THYROID TUMOURS IN MALE RATS.

They finally got rid of her, and *Mary* went out to the garden. When she came back in, *Roy* **was adjusting his tie in the hall mirror.**

"Where do you think you're going?" she demanded.

"Out. I've arranged to meet EVE."

"You can't. We've got to get a bonfire going and get rid of all those **clothes**. Or have you forgotten?"

"No need. I went out last night."

"Last night?"

"Yes, I couldn't sleep for worrying, so I DROVE OUT TO THE COUNTRY **and buried them in a field**."

"I didn't hear you get up. What time was that?"

"AROUND TWO."

Mary shook her head. "You should have told me what you were doing. I thought we were going to **BURN** them down the garden."

She sounded almost disappointed, as if she'd been looking forward to it.

"I know, but it's done now."

"Did anybody see you?"

"No. There was no one around for miles. So they're six feet under now and no one will ever find them."

"Did you bring the suitcase back?"

"Yes."

"Where is it?"

Roy thought for a moment. "Oh, no I buried it. THE WHOLE THING," he said with a vague air.

"Well that was daft. Why didn't you just empty the clothes out?"

"I thought it would be less suspicious, in case someone saw me coming home with it. Anyway, it's all done and dusted now. There's nothing to worry about"

"Well, let's hope so."

Mary remained dubious but Roy had slipped comfortably into his story as if it were an Armstrong reclining chair. He was actually quite convinced by it himself. It sounded much more plausible than his true recollection of the previous night's events. Perhaps he really had BURIED the case, and the whole Gilbert and Sullivan rigmarole on the BRIDGE had merely been a piece of fanciful invention for theatre-going audiences everywhere.

"And if the police turn up asking questions, you were here with me last night. Got it?" Mary sounded like a seasoned criminal, used to frequent brushes with the law. "We watched TAKE YOUR PICK and Bootsie and Snudge, then we turned over for the news. After that we watched No Hiding Place." Of course, THE POLICE knew very well that he hadn't been at home watching television, since they had questioned him themselves on the RAILWAY BRIDGE, but he couldn't tell Mary that.

"What happened in No Hiding Place? —In case they ask," he said.

"Well I wasn't really watching because I was making that BLOOMING FROCK but Chief-Superintendent Lockhart was tracking down an elusive safe-blower who was using a new and dangerous type of explosive."

"Did he catch him?" asked Roy, though the programme's TITLE had already suggested the answer to his question.

"Oh, yes. The Police always get their man," she said. "On telly, anyway," she added with a note of uncertainty.

Before setting off, Roy checked in the back of the VAN to make sure the suitcase was where he had left it when he got home. There was no reason it shouldn't be, but something about the peculiar shenanigans on the FOOTBRIDGE had made him mistrust his own memory of the incident. He hadn't BURIED it, of course. Nor had he thrown it over the bridge. It was still there, as plain as sunlight on a garden wall.

DURING the night, between bouts of fitful sleep, *Roy* had formulated a plan. He would take the suitcase to the left-luggage department at the railway station.

IF *Hands* had merely been UNCONSCIOUS, as now seemed possible, there was less urgency to deal with the matter, and this way, he could dispose of the **clothes**, prudently, in his own time, without having to rush into any hasty decision-making that might put him at risk.

Nothing had really changed. It was a practical solution that HE FELT SURE had nothing to do with any reluctance to relinquish the clothes, and at least they would be out of harm's way, which was necessary to safeguard his relationship with **Eve**. It wasn't that they were ever going to be worn again. He was adamant about that. Mentally, he had already purchased a one-way ticket to Dundee; it was simply that he had not yet specified the date of departure.

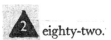

HE had planned to drive over to the STATION before meeting EVE, but now there wasn't time because he was supposed to be

there

at 8.30 and, like

any young man

bringing

his vegetables

in to market, he

didn't want

to be

late setting out his stall.

Part of him was desperately keen to see Eve, but another part of him dreaded it. He wasn't sure if he was quite up to pretending everything was all right. Besides, he knew that as soon as he looked into her eyes, those three 'i's'—instinct, intuition, inspiration would see through any bluff he put up, and he did not want his wretched mood exposed. He had to act naturally, but his performance would require all the acting skills of a LAWRENCE OLIVIER or a Richard Chamberlain. He'd tell EVE he had to run an errand first. Nothing suspicious about that. Surely storing a suitcase at the left luggage office was the most natural thing in the world, as natural as a squirrel storing nuts for the winter?

"HELLO", he began brightly.

She had been waiting at the shop door, and came running out with a picnic basket on her arm LIKE A character from a fairy tale. Yesterday's BRA seemed to have been swept under the CARPET, and she greeted him with a smile that washed over him like KIA-ORA.

THERE was a fly-away character to her dress, and it was as pretty as a dancing summer cloud. **B**anded at neck and front. Smoothly cut in EMERALD rayon givrine, scoop-necked and sleeveless, with a deep inverted front pleat.

She wore just enough make-up to ensure that on a clear crisp day, in brightest sunlight, or in the soft glow of a candle, she **would look** radiant, wonderfully natural.

ROY **was so pleased to see her that,** in spite of an inner sense of foreboding, his heart sang a song from the hit parade. **He hoped that her feminine intuitiveness would** not **tune into its** faltering **melody.**

"Do you like crab paste?" she said, getting down to business.

"Yes."

"Tomatoes?"

"Yes."

"Pork pie?"

"***Yes!***"

"How about Robinson's lemon barley water?"

"Yes."

These easy first round questions are just to get the contestant started.

"I've made a flask of tea as well," she said. "Have you decided where we're going?"

"EVE, before we set off, I have an errand to run. I can be back in half an hour."

"Where are you going?"

"I've just got to take A SUITCASE to the left-luggage office at the station."

"What's in it?"

"Just some old clothes."

"Whose clothes, yours?"

Roy wasn't going to get caught with that one again.

"They're my sister's." HONESTY IS ALWAYS THE BEST POLICY. (Well, not complete honesty, obviously.) "I'm putting them in storage for her," he added. "She's going away for a while."

"Where to?"

"DUNDEE."

"How long will she be away?"

"I don't know. Perhaps indefinitely. She's thinking about becoming a NUN."

"A nun?"

"Well, not a nun exactly, it's more like

The Salvation Army.

Well, it is The Salvation Army, as a matter of fact."

"Is she religious then?"

"Religious? No. Well, yes I suppose she is. It's just something she's decided to do."

He put his hands in his pockets. It pained him to think that he should have stooped to such wilful deceit, but what else could he tell her? That his sister had committed murder — or at the very least — assault with a deadly SHOE, and was on the run from the police? That, of course, would never do. Nevertheless, he wished he'd polished his story a bit more vigorously.

"Won't she need her clothes?" enquired Eve.

"No, they have a

UNIFORM

and she gets that free."

Roy was on creaky floorboards. His

His understanding of The Salvation Army and its activities lay somewhere between rudimentary and non-existent. People in funny outfits with trumpets and tambourines standing outside Woolworth's singing, "Will you come to the mission, will you come, come, come? With a free cup of tea and a bun, bun, BUN."

A young MOTHER with a dog and a little 'Good as gold' girl of about ten approached, providing a welcome interruption. The girl shouted Eve's name and the dog barked.

"You're O F F today, aren't you, EVE?"

said the woman. She had an attraction of sorts, but was not in Eve's league.

THE WOMAN'S eyes shifted briefly as she gave Roy the once-over.

"Yes. We're going on a picnic," said EVE, with girlish excitement bubbling up to the boil beneath the calm, assured smile of the

"Well I hope it brightens up for you," said the woman, looking up. There were indeed few breaks in the cloud. The **She** handed the dog's lead to the little girl. "You wait here with **Bruno**," she said. "I won't be a minute." **ROY** wasn't sure if **Bruno** was a

Lovely Laddie

—the kind of dog that was pleased to see everybody, **but** he certainly seemed pleased to see **Eve.** The **WOMAN** turned to speak as she entered the POST OFFICE. "Don't let that big ugly brute jump up on your dress, ***EVE*** ; his feet are dirty."

EVE gave Roy a quizzical look as she ruffled the dog's ears. "*Are* your FEET dirty?" she said.

"No, I washed them last night," he said innocently.

"It's OK," she reassured the little girl. "He

washed them last night." She delivered the line with theatrical sotto voce.

The little girl giggled. "Not him. BRUNO."

"Oh! I see." Eve pretended she'd just understood.

"Is he your new boyfriend?" said the little girl.

"He might be. What do you think? Is he handsome enough for me?"

She looked at him with the warmth of a spring day. Roy smiled, trying not to think about his dirty feet.

The little girl went all shy. "I don't know. His eyebrows are a bit funny."

"Are they? Why?"

"They're too little."

"Too little? No, I think he's got nice eyebrows." Eve lightly touched the side of Roy's face and smoothed his eyebrow with her thumb.

The MOTHER came out of the shop, closing her purse.

"You off somewhere nice?" she said.

"We haven't decided yet," said Eve.

"Well. I'll have to get going," said the WOMAN. "I've got my mother coming. Come on, sweetheart."

She took the little girl's hand and they set off with BRUNO in tow. Eve waved to the little girl as they turned the corner.

It was time to deal with the matter at hand.

Eve peered in through the little window in the back of the van. "Can't you keep it at home?" she said, referring to the big blue SUITCASE.

"My mum doesn't want it in the house," said Roy.

"She says there isn't room."
"There must be room."
"No, there isn't," he said. "She was quite firm about it."
"Oh dear," said Eve, pulling a bit of a face. "It sounds like they've had a fall out."
"Hmm. Sort of. Mum's rather over-protective."
"Is your sister older or younger?"
"Than my mother? Younger."
"No. Than you, silly."
"Oh. Younger. Just a year."
"Doesn't your mum want her living at home?"
It was a hard thing to admit.
"Not really." ROY was trying to keep a lid on the beans in case they spilled.
"I'd be livid if someone threw all my clothes away. Even if I was joining the Salvation Army. Does your sister know?"
"Oh, yes. NORMA's in full agreement. The clothes are part of her old life and she doesn't want to go back to it. She can't be that person any more. I'm supposed to get rid of them for good! Everything must go!"
Roy was right, of course. It was the only way.
"And you can't help thinking that your SISTER might one day have a change of heart and want her old life back?" Eve suggested.
There was a quarter of a teaspoon of something in what she said but he denied it. "She can't come back. I know that."
"But you're keeping them for her just in case," said Eve. She had him properly pegged.
Roy shrugged. He wasn't sure what he was doing.

"You can't leave her SUITCASE indefinitely at left-luggage; it'll be expensive. Why don't you store it at my place?" she said.

"No. It's very nice of you, Eve, but . . ."

"Honestly, it's no trouble," she said. "There's plenty of room in my wardrobe. And it would save you all that money. . . which you can spend on me," she added teasingly.

He couldn't think why he was even considering it, but now that she knew about the Case and what was in it, what was the difference where it was stored?

"Well, perhaps just for a week or two, until I sort something out."

"It can stay here for as long as she likes," she said with a smile.

Roy agreed, though as he followed her SHAPELY LEGS up the stairs to her flat, he couldn't help thinking he was probably doing the wrong thing. What was it about EVE that made him think everything she suggested was a good idea?

EVE'S room was at the top of the house in the attic. It was a cosy all-in-one bed-sit *affair* with a sloping ceiling. There were pictures and books and everything had been made nice as a new pin. The bed was a double with a pretty, hand-made bedcover. In the far corner was a gate-legged table, already laid for dinner *à deux*, and under the skylight, a little two-seater settee.

Its appeal to the man of the house is its classic simplicity and reasonable price. Its appeal to you, madam, is its colourful contemporary spirit. **P**atterns that vary from the crisply modern to the richly traditional.

Other furniture items were— a narrow sideboard of Utility pedigree and a small bookcase In the corner near Roy's elbow, there was a tiny kitchenette with a stove and a larder.

If you live in a bed-sitting-room or have to cook in a very small kitchen-ette a pressure pan can be a special pleasure.

And what woman does not want to possess one ?

EVE opened a little door and showed Roy where to put the **Case**. **It** was a closet space built into the eaves. As *Roy* slid the suitcase inside, he could see dresses and blouses hanging up on a rail.

There were shoes too, STANDING TO ATTENTION IN A NEAT ROW. The Twinco shoe tidy, made of high-impact polystyrene, is sold in kit form and can be placed in the bottom of the wardrobe or in any convenient corner of the room. It is available in lemon, blue and tan, holds six pairs of shoes and costs 10s. 6d.

THERE wasn't time to look at everything properly, but the set-up suggested a girl ***who*** took ***pride in her wardrobe.***

"We'll sort out a proper place for it later, " she said, shutting the door.

"I feel as if I'm moving in," said Roy. "I wish I really were. It's cosy."

It was inappropriate to suggest such a thing, but Eve was too refined to take his remark the wrong way.

HE wanted to apologise about the bra incident, offer some sort of explanation, but decided it might be BETTER to let the whole matter lie.

"I love it here," she said, *revelling in the luxury* of her own good fortune. "I've got everything I need. I can cook my own meals, read or listen to the radio, and there's a bathroom just on the next floor."

"Have you got a television?"

"No, have you?"

"Yes, AT HOME. But I wouldn't need one here."

Roy longed to connect himself with her goodness, her very perfect loveliness. He wanted to be quarantined there with her always, reading and cooking meals and sitting next to her on the settee listening to the radio. He yearned for the *snow-perfect* peace and security it offered and the chance to disengage himself from that other world where sordid beastliness rules the roost, and where perverted policemen and skirt-lifting hands-on types ply their ugly trade.

Kissing her then might have helped to reserve a seat on that settee but he was all too aware that even the tenderest and most feeling man can offend his sweetheart by a hasty or clumsy movement in the intimacies. Consequently, he failed to seize the moment, and before he knew it, they were back out on the street.

They were just putting the picnic things in the back of the VAN when Eve touched his arm.

"Sorry about yesterday," she said suddenly.

"Good heavens, no. You shouldn't be sorry. It was my fault. I just didn't know what to say when you found. . . that thing in the GLOVE compartment."

"*Ladies' unmentionables*," said *Eve*, with a shy laugh. "It was my sister's actually. She took it off one day when she was HOT in the van. I didn't want to embarrass her."

"I didn't know what to think. You were in such a state. I felt sure you were hiding a wife or girlfriend. If you hadn't been so lovely, I might have kept away, but I simply couldn't."

Roy closed his eyes for a brief moment, letting her warm words wash over him. When he opened them, he saw Mr. WHITE crossing the road towards them. He quickly closed the VAN door.

"Ah, hello, EVE." Mr. WHITE straightened his tie as if he were there on official business.

"Morning, Mr. WHITE," she said.

Roy lost his footing and stepped backwards off the kerb, involuntarily bending one knee. It looked like a curtsy.

"So you two know each other, do you?"

"We met, er.. yes, sort of," said EVE, going the long way round and not quite getting there.

"What are you doing here, Roy? You're not working today."

Roy knew he wasn't supposed to be using the van for recreational use.

"No, I was just . . ."

"He came to pay something in . . . into his POST OFFICE book," said Eve, quick as a ballerina.

"Yes, well, you shouldn't really be using the van for that, Roy. It's only for COMPANY BUSINESS, and for travelling to and from work," said Mr White.

Yes Sir! "So you really shouldn't be using it at all at weekends. You know, it's the cost of petrol, oil, general wear and tear, etcetera."

"Yes, sorry Mr White. I'll take it straight home."

"Mmm," said Mr White. He clasped his hands behind his back and sauntered over to the VAN, peering in through the back WINDOW.

If he saw the PICNIC BASKET, he chose not to say anything.

He turned to Roy and looked at him without speaking.

"RIGHT. I'll be going," said Roy, taking this as his cue to depart. He glanced at EVE and there was a tiny flash of panic in her eyes. He was going to have to drive OFF without her. "I'll see you later, EVE," he said, feigning nonchalance. He slid behind the wheel and started the engine. As he pulled away from the kerb, he was hoping Eve would give some kind of secret signal that would tell him what to do, but instead she gave him a 'yikes!' CARTOON FACE, widening her eyes and turning her mouth down at the corners.

The van moved slowly as if being pushed by two teenage boys from Dagenham. It was a runaway vehicle, gently rolling by, with nobody at the wheel. In his rear-view mirror, Roy saw that Mr WHITE was still there on the pavement, talking to Eve. What was he supposed to do? Drive back and pick her up later when Mr White had gone? What if he was watching from the outer office, and saw the van again?

He turned into the first side road and waited by the kerb with the engine running. After a few minutes he got out and went to the corner to look up the road. *Nobody there.*

HOW WOULD

EVE know where he was? She wouldn't. She'd be waiting for him at the SHOP, expecting him to double back. He set off again, driving round the block. He sailed past—The Post Office on one side, the laundry on the other. The ideal vehicle here would be one that was INVISIBLE when

2⁹⁵

viewed from one side, yet completely normal from the other – though this, of course, would prove impractical in virtually all other areas of motoring. Even in this situation, it would be more than useless if one were travelling in the opposite direction.

NO sign of Eve, but glancing to his RIGHT, he saw Mr. White in the yard, who looked up as Roy went by. *Darn those socks!* He'd been spotted. Now he couldn't stop at THE POST OFFICE. He had planned to slow and pip his horn but that would have been too obvious so he carried on. Then he saw *E V E* at the corner, standing on tiptoe, looking along the side street. He pulled up ahead of her and shot open the door. ***She* ran** towards him, and threw herself into the seat. She was a bank robber and he was the getaway driver. She was bubbling over with excitement. "Quick. Let's go." She laughed nervously. "Oh my lord. I thought you weren't coming back."

"He saw me," said Roy, clutching her hand. He was excited too. "Mr. White was in the YARD and he saw me go past."

The giggling released a little of their nervous tension. **It was fun!** And as **Roy** looked across at her, he doubted if there was anyone more wonderful. Sylvia Peters ON HER

BEST DAY, in a sequined, off-the-shoulder gown with ten tiers of frilly white lace, could not have held a birthday cake candle to EVE's loveliness.

HANDS couldn't possibly be DEAD, could he? Surely he had merely fainted OR SOMETHING and was now up and about attending to his head injury with Elastoplast and a c'est la vie attitude to the whole affair. ROY felt sure of it. How else could he be experiencing this BUOYANT sense of well-being?

"Oh dear," said Eve, with a laugh. "Do you think he figured out what we were doing?"

"He must have seen the PICNIC BASKET," said ROY. "Good job he didn't see the SUITCASE. He'd have probably thought we were running away together."

"Oh, Heavens. *You're right!*," said ROY, flustered by the very notion of it. It was exactly what he wanted to be doing.

"Nevertheless, I'm still going to get the sack," he said.

"No . . . you're not," she said, with calm confidence, urging him to dispel the idea from his mind.

"Aren't I?" he said. Eve seemed to be 'in the know'.

"Well, maybe," she said. And she laughed again.

17

THEY parked at the edge of a field.

POETS have always sung of the witchery of spring. When the cuckoos **spit,** when the air is rich with the scent of living clods and the uprising sap, and the earth glows green and gold. There is music in the countryside— the golden chain of lark-song, the whispers of the squirrels in the larches, blackbirds and **BLACK-CURRANTS** in lovely rivalry. And the world walks by two by two in the loveliness of a newly-wakening earth. Spring-time is love-time.

THE charm of Autumn was **just as lovely, and EVE** stood on the **brow of a hill,** drinking it **all** in **with a big spoon.** She **could feel feel the warm** wind **tugging** at **her skirt.**

The morning sun danced on the

soft, warm brown hair that she wore almost unwaved and falling to the base of her neck. Her wonderful white skin was underlaid with rose—the sort of skin that looked like a translucent enamel. Against dark, dull blue, and painted with a very low- keyed palette, that skin would glow as if it were lit from within by all the suns of spring.

ROY came up behind her and slipped his arms round her slender waist. It was easier to MAKE a move like this when she wasn't looking at him. As if sensing this, she held her position but crossed her arms over his, urging him to hold her tighter. This he did. The soft skin of her shoulder beckoned and he kissed it lightly. He nuzzled into her, smelling the sweet fragrance of her HAIR — HAIR without a trace of dulling scum—scum that takes the edge off real cleanness — and feeling *the round pertness of her fine young figure* against him **through the thin dress**. Her body relaxed, yielding to his firm embrace. "Mmm..." she murmured contentedly. "It's lovely here."

"You're lovely," he said.

Out of the corner of his eye, he was surprised and somewhat alarmed to see a rosy red mark on the skin of her shoulder where he had kissed her. At first, he thought it might have been a rash or one of those STRAWBERRY FLAVOURED birthmarks, but he felt sure he would have noticed something like that. How could it have appeared so suddenly? An insect bite or a sting, perhaps? Then it came to

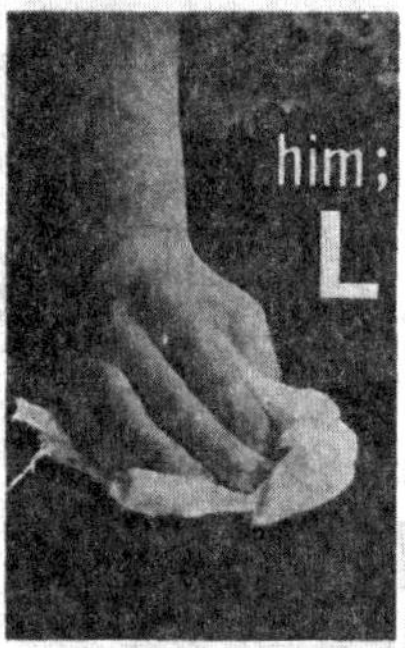

him; he knew exactly what it was. **LIPSTICK.** It was the very same SHADE he had been forced to wear during his police interview. So it was he who must have put it there, transferring it from his own lips to her shoulder. But he couldn't have, could he? His mind wrestled itself to the ground in search of an explanation. When he had arrived home in the early hours he had scrubbed his mouth thoroughly clean with a soapy flannel until there wasn't even the faintest trace of the policemen's handiwork. **THE** redness he had seen around his mouth afterwards in the bathroom mirror had surely been a touch of soreness from rubbing, not from any remaining cosmetic residue? Was there really a mark on her shoulder or was he imagining it? Still contained within the circle of his arms, she turned to face him, and he could no longer study THE SHOULDER discreetly. She lifted her head and looked him straight in the eyes. Even a rose, a red rose, could not have expressed itself more plainly. When she raised herself up on tiptoe, the kiss was inevitable. She pressed her lips lightly to his and the feel of her in his arms made him yearn for the inner peace that would enable him to take this up as a full-time hobby.

She rested her head on his shoulder and he took a moment to recover from the dizzying sensation of her nearness. THE DELICIOUSLY metallic TASTE OF her lipstick WAS ON HIS LIPS, but little by little he began to taunt himself with doubt. Perhaps it wasn't *her* lipstick he could taste; perhaps it was *his*. EVE wanted to be kissed again but Roy was seized by panic. He gazed at her beautiful, inviting lips but now the colour seemed stronger—stronger than it had been two minutes ago. It must have been his imagination—he knew that. Unless she had applied fresh lipstick while she was in his arms—which she could not have done—it could only have come from his own mouth. She leaned towards him, but all he could see were those full red painted

lips—lips that were now besmirched and sullied by their contact with his own.

Confusion and uncertainty played across her *lovely* face. She must have noticed his hesitancy and the way he was looking at her ***mouth***. What on earth must she be thinking now? I know what I would have been thinking.

"my LIPS look COMMON!"

IMAGINE! And yet 'common' is just the word any man would use for that painted look. And her lips *did* look painted! Poor Eve. She should have listened to the women's magazines. Look critically at your own lips... have they that obvious look that men detest so? Do they look actually coated with paint? **In Hollywood (where a girl's face is her fortune)** Fire-in-the-basement Red, Yardley's sensational new "Petal-Finish" Lipstick is being acclaimed by the loveliest ladies, and will make your lips young, gay and appealing. *And that's why* Yardley's sensational new Lip Lovely range *is starring on Hollywood's smartest lips.*

She pulled away. "What's wrong?" she said. "Nothing." How could he tell her that he was temporarily deranged?" Suddenly, like a hawk dropping, a sense of futility fell on him. It seemed an eternity before she spoke again. "Sit down for a moment. I want to talk to you." Roy sat down beside her on the little blanket she had laid on the grass. He felt apprehensive, but there was no way to avoid her questions. Something in the way she sat, her bearing, the motionless way she looked at her hands told him that round two was going to be trickier.

"I feel so many things in the air," she said, "so many things I don't understand, and I can't put my finger on any of them."

She watched him draw a shape on his trousers with his fingernail. He was so quiet, intent on what he was doing.

"You can tell me," she said tenderly.

Roy didn't look up. "It's just that there's a bit of trouble I have to sort out," he said.

"What sort of trouble?"

"Oh it's just family business. I can't go into it."

"Is it about your sister going away?"

"Well yes, in a way I suppose it is," he answered guardedly. He carefully negotiated a precarious path through the truth. "She's got herself into a bit of a fix and I'm rather worried about her."

HE looked at her and just then found a curious sympathy in her expression.

"Is there anything I can do to help?" she asked.

"No, it's something I have to sort out."

Eve saw the sadness in his eyes and her heart went out to him. She wanted to give him comfort. Scarcely realiSing what she was doing, she began a delicate, light action with her fingers on the back of his neck. He was afraid to move, wondering what to say next.

What struck him most about Eve was her kindness. She was staring up at him and he thought she looked like the loveliest thing he had ever seen —a face you're glad to have in your home because she's sweet and pretty and nice, A FACE you'd hang over the fireplace or embroider on a cushion.

"I don't want anything to come between us, Eve."

"You sound as though you think something might."

"I don't know. I'll have to see if I can get things cleared up."

"What are you going to do? PERSUADE YOUR SISTER to come home?"

"No, she can't come home. She has to stay where she is."

There was nothing whatever wrong with Eve's *lips*; he could see that now. His mind had been performing conjuring tricks. But, no doubt unsettled by the way he had looked at her before, Eve seemed reluctant now to kiss him for fear that she was doing something to offend him. She turned and lay on her front, supporting herself on her elbows as she plucked some blades of grass at the edge of the BLANKET.

He could tell she was preparing the questions for the final round.

"Roy? Is your sister . . . Is she . . .?" Eve hesitated.

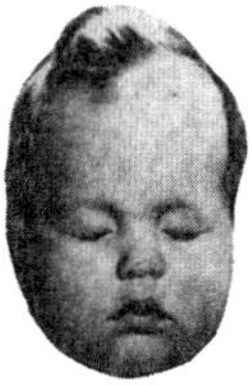

"What?"

"Is she expecting a BABY?"

"Good God, no. Nothing like that." He was appalled that the very idea had crossed her mind. "She's not that . . . Well, she just isn't."

"I'm sorry, I didn't mean to suggest . . ."

"No, it's all right. I'm sorry."

"It's just that when you said she was in trouble and was going away . . . There was a girl at school who got herself into trouble and had to go away."

"Trouble?"

"In the FAMILY way."

EVE was a clever customer. Given the story Roy had told her, it was a shrewd conclusion to draw. These unfortunate situations can occur when a young courting couple have not learned to master the temptation of the " one flesh " union. If they can happily occupy themselves in other ways than by love-making,—marquetry, needlework, flower arranging, for example—they can overcome this difficult time and come through to the quieter days of companionship and more peaceful love. Then, when marriage is possible, both young people can approach their wedding day with clear consciences and no tainted memories to mar the **nuptials.**

Eve's **second guess would have been that** 'little sister' had to go to prison for some misdemeanour—which, in a funny way, was not too far from the truth. Neither **scenario** held me in very high esteem, but I supposed it's what I deserved.

Eve **told** Roy **she'd do anything she could to help. She even offered to put me up in her flat. All very confusing for** Roy, **of course, for where would that leave him? The last thing on earth he needed was** me showing my face **at the post office.** He was emphatic that it should never happen, and told her so.

"I'm emphatic that it should never happen," he said.

Eve **assured him that everything would be all right. Of course, she didn't know the full story, so it was pretty easy for her to see things** IN THE ROSY GLOW FROM A BEDSIDE LIGHT. Nevertheless, **the infectious warmth of its gentle radiance spread over him and hope stole into him.** All that he wanted seemed tantalisingly within his reach.

They ate the delicious lunch she had prepared, at the end of which, as a treat, she produced **a paper bag of Everton mints.** "I know you like them," she said. **It occurred to** Roy **that it is most extraordinary how a day can be grey and rather dreary one minute and then bright and shining as a new pin the next.**

It was warm and pleasant, a good day for a

picnic. Roy lay back luxuriously in the sunshine with Eve beside him. It seemed wrong that he should be enjoying these normal, pleasurable things after the previous night's TERRIBLE incident, but he couldn't help himself.

Even if HANDS were dead and I confessed—told them what I had done—would they really blame me? I could imagine old Dixon adopting a sympathetic approach.

"Take it easy, old girl, you've been through a lot. I wouldn't worry too much if I were you."

"It's true, I tell you! I killed him!".

The policeman would pat my arm reassuringly.

"Steady on, madam, nobody is blaming you. It's pretty clear what happened. We know all about this Mr. HANDS and his wrongdoings. You can't *make* yourself responsible, you know. It wasn't your fault."

Roy felt a curious lightness inside him—a feeling of freedom.

"That's right," he mumbled thickly. "Not my fault. . . . didn't think anybody would believe me."

"Are you talking in your sleep?" asked Eve.

"Hmm?" said Roy. He must have drifted off.

The hours rolled gently on and ROY put the nasty bits to the back of his mind, bringing the nicer items up from the basement and putting them on display in the window.

With the nightingales overhead crossing out the date in the calendar, Roy and Eve chatted as they lay side by side in the lazy SEPTEMBER sun. She told him about herself – how her parents had been killed in the war and how she had been brought up by her auntie. The more she talked, the more he adored her. She was natural and warm and caring. *Roy* opened up a little too, talking about **Dad** dying and how Mary —'please call me Mother'— had been left to bring us both up.

It was good to be able to tell her things – though the enormity of all that he *wasn't* telling her, all his dark secrets, hovered over them like the Hindenburg. The sun was momentarily lost behind its dark form, and in the chill of its shadow Roy looked up to see the ominous shape looming overhead — and he knew that it was only a matter of time before the whole thing came crashing down AROUND THEM. "Oh, the humanity!"

A
18
K
L

What is it that defines a typical suburban Sunday morning? THE HOUSEWIFE in her pinny, peeling potatoes and getting the joint in, ready for lunch? Spindly-kneed paperboys buckling under weighty issues in the news. Dad in the garden pulling up a few radishes, while MOTHER washes up the breakfast things, with WILFRED PICKLES 'having a go' on the wireless with Mabel at 'the table'.

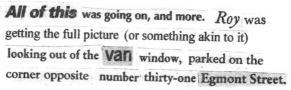

All of this was going on, and more. *Roy* was getting the full picture (or something akin to it) looking out of the van window, parked on the corner opposite number thirty-one Egmont Street.

IN his mind, he had envisaged an entirely different scene. A police car, the area cordoned off, with a line of BOBBIES on their hands and knees combing the street for clues; a hearse parked outside, waiting for the coffin to be brought out. But EITHER all of this was yet to happen, OR it had all happened already.

AT least he had come to his senses and was facing the facts. After all, ROY was surely not the first young man to have kidded himself into believing that someone was alive when really they were dead, in order to give himself sufficient respite from the guilt and worry to enjoy pork pie and lemon barley water in the company of a loved one. But seeing the curtains drawn shut at Mrs. Syms's downstairs window confirmed what, in his heart of hearts, he knew to be the truth. And with that in mind, it was now imperative that he somehow find a way to retrieve the skirt and dispose of it. It was the only piece of physical evidence that could possibly be traced back to THE LITTLE HOUSEHOLD, and therefore the one contestant that had to be eliminated from the game to give him a real chance at the star prize.

EVERYTHING was quietly normal. A typical suburban SUNDAY morning. Roy watched unnoticed from the van as the WEEKLY ritual of events played out before him.

Spinster ladies on their way to church, all pressed, ironed, folded, and starched. SOMEONE taking the dog for a walk. A man at the kerbside with a bucket of water and a fat, soapy sponge, slavering his car with suds. A teenage boy on the front lawn, mending a puncture on his bicycle. ALL perfectly typical, and typically

PERFECTLY **NORMAL.** Yet the more ROY WATCHED, the less convincing it all seemed. The activities looked STAGE-DIRECTED AND OBVIOUS. This is what people do when they're told to 'act natural'. No one was paying Roy any attention, but he imagined they would have been instructed not to, LIKE film actors avoiding eye contact with the camera. But who would have set up this elaborate charade, and for what reason? The police? Trying to make things look natural so that they could NAB the suspect when he or she might unsuspectingly return to the scene of the crime, as criminals are wont to do?

ROY had to **CHECK** himself. His mind was running away with itself, and was halfway down the street before he could bring it under control. Of course it wasn't a police trap. **RELAX.** This was simply what people really did on a Sunday. Just to be on the safe side, ROY decided to continue his surveillance for a while longer before making his move.

A handsome CLIFF RICHARD type stood on the corner, combing his hair into a *FONDANT SWIRL.*

Are good looks in a man an asset or a liability ? And in order to avoid an effeminate appearance, should such men grow a moustache or a beard ? Cliff's verdict? An emphatic "No."

A man strolled by, counting out the change in his pocket, **probably off to** spend some of his hard- earned wages on a news- paper, some BLUE BIRD Toffees, and a football coupon. ***MEN!*** **They'll never change.** We must take them as they come.

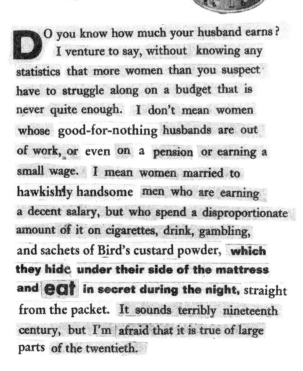

DO you know how much your husband earns? I venture to say, without knowing any statistics that more women than you suspect have to struggle along on a budget that is never quite enough. I don't mean women whose good-for-nothing husbands are out of work, or even on a pension or earning a small wage. I mean women married to hawkishly handsome men who are earning a decent salary, but who spend a disproportionate amount of it on cigarettes, drink, gambling, and sachets of Bird's custard powder, **which they hide under their side of the mattress and eat in secret during the night,** straight from the packet. It sounds terribly nineteenth century, but I'm afraid that it is true of large parts of the twentieth.

At NINE forty a big, lumbering boy with a head the size of A TELEVISION SET turned into the driveway of number thirty-one. He was wearing a badly knitted jumper and had a family-size packet of Sugar Puffs under his arm. Sugar Puffs are the tasty breakfast treat made from crisp wheat puffs glistening with sugar *and golden honey!* Energizing honey — to give kids extra "go"! (No need to add sugar.) This 'Gormless Gregory' however, had dispensed with the usual cool, fresh, creamy milk accompaniment, along with the bowl-and-spoon METHOD of eating them, in favour of burying his arm elbow-deep in the BOX and pawing sticky handfuls of the cereal directly into his mouth. Breakfast on the go! Golden puffs of wheat clung to his knuckles, SLEEVE, and CHIN as he chomped them DOWN. Those that failed to stick left a telltale trail of breakfast enjoyment behind him on the pavement.

Having rung one of the bells, the boy stepped into the front GARDEN, cupping his sticky hand to his *HEAD* as he peered through a gap in the curtain at the front window. The average number of children per family today is 1.75, but the average child is handicapped by having no complete brother or sister—it usually has to make do with about three-quarters of a companion, unless it can find a friend who lives nearby.

THE door opened behind him and the BOY I had seen watching television in the SYMS flat on the night of the murder emerged. Without speaking, the two BOYS walked off together and crossed the road, heading towards the van. Roy's worry was that the BOY might recognise the family resemblance, even though he knew that this was unlikely. On the night of the PHOTO SESSION, the youngster had hardly glanced up from the television, and anyway it was probably an unnecessary concern. In truth, neither of the boys looked intelligent enough to recognise their own reflection. As if to demonstrate this shortage in the brain department, when offered the Sugar Puffs packet, the SYMS boy stuck a piece of cereal up each nostril and proudly snorted them out on to the pavement.

So had THE POLICE been and gone? Perhaps at that very moment they were inside Hands's flat, conducting their investigation, picking things up with pencils and wrapping them in their hankies.

Today's modern policeman thinks on his feet and has no trouble at all putting two and two together and coming up with the correct answer. Maybe they'd already found the SKIRT. EXHIBIT A. They'd probably take it along with them as they carried out door-to-door interviews. Or put a picture of it in the newspaper. Even in BLACK-AND-WHITE, Renie **Price** would be sure to recognise it because the **PRICES** watch a lot of television and never use COLOUR FILM in their CAMERA.

THE only way to find out was to ***SEE FOR HIMSELF***, though the idea of a return visit to ***HAND***S's flat held little appeal. **HE** thought about the squalid little room and how starkly it contrasted with *EVE*'s **PERFECTION OF COMFORT.** Where Hands's bed was an untidy jumble of **grimy** bedclothes, hers was fresh and pretty with crisp, clean white sheets.

ROY's thoughts slipped out of gear for a moment as he imagined Eve getting into her bed at night. She discards a frilly negligee, discloses a flimsy nightie and sinks into an

Englander mattress (with appropriate intermission for Commercial). She makes big eyes, pantomimes a little over an imaginary hairdo, and puts out the light as a procession of doubly exposed sheep leap over her bed.

A tap on the window jerked him awake. It was the WOMAN who had opened the door to me the other night, the WOman I had thought might have been SYLVIA SYMS. She was standing on the kerb, peering at him through the GLASS. A feeling of dread SEEPED into his stomach. Had she found him out? It was too late to come up with a short story or a novel; he had to confront her. As she bent to speak to him a fluff of white HAIR appeared momentarily at the base of the window: the scratching on the door told him it was her little poodle pup TRYING TO GET HIMSELF NOTICED. *Roy* wound down the window a little so Mrs. SYMS could speak.

"Your coat's in the door," she said.

The words meant nothing to Roy; he felt groggy and disoriented. Your coat's in the DOOR? How can a COAT be in a DOOR? He stared back at her blankly, his face a tablecloth of plain and simple design.

"You've got your COAT in the DOOR," she said again. She pointed to something on the kerb.

Slowly he realised. He must have trapped his raincoat in the door when getting into the van. He gave it a tug; it was indeed stuck. Without thinking, he jerked his DOOR open to FREE it, not realising quite how close Mrs. Syms was standing. The sharp top edge of the door must have caught her just above the lip. It was only a little bump but she reeled back holding her hand to her mouth. Realising what he had done, Roy apologised through the gap in the window. Mrs. SYMS pulled a face and felt around with her TONGUE before pressing her fingertip to her gums to check for blood.

"Sorry," said Roy.

Looking a bit disgruntled, she wandered to the corner and headed along Egmont, away from NUMBER THIRTY-ONE. No serious damage done, and certainly no need to call Nurse Babcock or the handsome young Dr. Hastings. The good thing was, Mrs. SYMS had not noticed any family resemblance either. The key witnesses had been tested. The only person who might have made the connection was HANDS, and he was dead.

With Sylvia Syms out of the way, Roy decided this would be the best time to make his move. It was impossible to say who else might be at home, but because he had Hands's keys, he was hoping he could slip in and out without anybody GETTING INTO A FROTH OR A FIZZ about him being there. THE Police, he imagined, would have done their sleuthing on Friday night, or at the latest, Saturday. They'd be long gone by now.

He was on the step, working out which key was which, when he saw someone's blurry approach through the frosted window of the front door. Roy stepped back into the FRONT GARDEN as the DOOR opened and a man came out. He had some letters in his hand and was opening one of them, using his index finger as a letter-opener. Yesterday's

POST,

Roy assumed. No delivery on Sunday. The man lingered on the front step, reading the envelope's contents. He hadn't noticed Roy, who stood on the front lawn with his arms by his side trying to look natural. Roy wondered if this was the man who lived in the flat opposite HANDS and who had called through the door on the night of the accident.

Suddenly the man looked up. He had a STINGING red face with a forbiddingly masculine atmosphere.

"What are you doing?" he demanded, his accusatory tone instantly stabbing at the COCKTAIL SAUSAGE of Roy's guilty demeanour.

"I er . . ."

"Eh? What are you doing? Is it you who's been taking our milk?"

"Milk?"

"Off the step. Is it you?"

"No, it's not me. I don't drink milk. Except on cereal."

"Well, what are you doing in our garden?"

"I was just looking."

"Looking? Looking at what? Looking to see if anyone was at home? I know. Well, you can clear off before I call the police. Go on."

ROY did as he was bid. Forced into a humiliating retreat, he headed back towards the van from whence he had come. He was fishing around for the key when he glanced back and saw that the man was still watching him from the gate, so he carried on walking instead.

A group of *shops* had gathered at the top of the hill, and Roy decided to hang around until the coast *was crystal clear and there was no static or interference* back at number thirty-one.

In the newsagent's—the only shop that was open—he bought a quarter of Murray Mints, the

'too-good-to-hurry' mints. The characteristic **SHOP** smells reminded him of ***EVE*** and her enticing post office goodies. He wanted so much to be back there, with all the ***HANDS*** business cleaned up and neatly tidied away.

While he was waiting for the shopkeeper to weigh out the sweets, Roy scanned the national newspapers to see if the **Murder** had been reported, but found nothing. The local paper didn't come out until **WEDNESDAY** so there was nothing to check there, but what he did notice was that this week, a most exciting week, there was a fine, brand new **WOMEN'S** magazine with the most practical approach to home-making yet.

The temptation was great, especially as the woman on the cover was sporting a modish BLOUSE in an unusual double-breasted style with threequarter-length sleeves – for which there

32/6

was a pattern inside – BUT Roy KNEW THAT HE MUST RESIST. It would do no good at this stage in the game to put ideas into my head about the latest fashions, beauty tips, and handy hints for the home. Young Salvation Army officers do not need to know about such things.

Roy made his way back down the hill. As he did, he unwrapped a MURRAYMINT and popped it in his mouth. MURRAYMINTS last a wonderfully long time and they cost only 10d. a quarter.

As he approached the

CORNER

the street seemed to go suddenly quiet as if **all the locals had stepped indoors and were waiting quietly** for *Roy* to make his move. The **red-faced** man had gone. This was his chance. The time was nigh.

NOW. DO-IT-

Just go straight in, he told himself, straight up **into** Hands's **flat.** Each second he hesitated meant the opportunity, which hung in the **AIR** like a balloon with a '***MY BIG CHANCE***' label

No.327

on it, threatened to drift over the rooftops and out of sight. In two shakes, he was heading resolutely towards number thirty-ONE. Keep going, keep going. Don't look round.

There was hardly a change in his determined pace as he bounded up the steps, and let himself in through the front door. It was as if he were a robot programmed by a talented young hypnotist at the London Palladium.

THE hall and STAIRway looked even more depressing in daylight. And though he tried to focus on the job in hand, he noticed that on the third step a Royal Scot biscuit LAY trodden into the CARPET.

ROY HOVERED quietly OUTSIDE Hands's door, listening for policemen's voices. When he heard no sounds from within, he knocked very lightly on the door, and then a few seconds later tried the same knock again, slightly louder. Satisfied there was no one inside, he turned the key in the lock. As he nudged the DOOR open with the knuckle of his forefinger, chez Hands's special fragrance greeted his nostrils like an old familiar refrain.

The body was gone; a quick glance behind the bed confirmed it. So the police had been.

Other things in the room had been moved in their search to find clues that would lead them to the killer, though it took a few minutes for Roy to put his finger on exactly what was different.

There were little things. The PIECE OF BAKEWELL TART was no longer floating in the fish tank. The curtains had been opened. On the bedside table were a bottle of Lucozade and a packet of 'ASPRO'.

The most noticeable difference was that the BEDCLOTHES were back in place, albeit in a slapdash fashion, and that Hands's shabby brown suit had been carefully laid out length-ways on top of them. The buttons were done up, and the trousers had been tucked neatly under the hem of the JACKET. But for a cravat at the neck and a handkerchief in the breast pocket, the ensemble might have been on display in the window of a gentlemen's outfitters. *Roy* assumed this to be the work of Mrs. SYMS rather than the police. AS his landlady, it would probably have been left to her to lay out Hands's SUIT ready for the undertaker. It was the SUIT in which he would be buried.

Roy scanned the tableau of tat with

a mental picture of the skirt's fabric —for that was his main objective— hoping its

COLOUR

and PATTERN might register a connection and render it visible amid the tawdry squalor of the room. But there was nothing in Hands's world so lovely in hue and spirit, and a match was not immediately made. Roy bent to look under the bed, just in case the SKIRT had somehow found its way under there. As he knelt, something from THE RUG soaked into the knee of his trousers. Not blood. Cold tea, possibly. Lifting the CANDLEWICK BEDSPREAD he uncovered more of HANDS's personal effects —— an abandoned SOCK and, next to it, a small plate with what he took to be egg smeared on it. The plate had clearly been there for days, if not weeks. A short soak in Fairy Liquid would soon shift that. There were some more SHOES, dusty and worn out, and another pile of school exercise books, but no *skirt.*

Though it might have seemed an obvious spot to look, the WARDROBE was the last place he had expected to find it. Unlike EVE or myself, Hands had not seemed the house-proud type, given to meticulous WARDROBE orderliness. Most of the clothes in his collection were DRAPED across the furniture or lay in SMELLY bundles on the floor. But there was the skirt, hanging neatly on a hanger, its shining YELLOWness given pride of place in the wardrobe. The other CLOTHES had been scooted to either end of the rail so that nothing came near it; nothing touched it. It was the coveted prize in someone's trophy collection, displayed like an exhibit in a museum. But it was no longer the pretty sight it had once been. In the right setting, the splash of russet brown adorning the front of the skirt might have been something daubed on to canvas by some spirited young artist from the 'modern' school but now, having dried creased and crusty, it looked more like a rag that had been used to mop up spilled paint.

ROY was surprised that the police hadn't taken it away with them to examine it for forensic evidence in their laboratory, as he had seen them do on *Interpol Calling*. It wasn't as though they could have missed it, but perhaps without any witness descriptions they had not yet recognised its significance.

The sudden sound of the front door shutting down-stairs had Roy **scrambling eggs.** With his heart racing like **A WHIPPET** on a motorbike, he **snatched** the skirt from its hanger and sprang across the room. Within the blink of an eye, he was out on the landing pulling the door closed behind him. He had expected to hear **approaching footsteps on the stairs, but there were none. Instead,** there was a woman's voice in the hallway downstairs. "Come on, Mick. Get in." **DOGGY** toenails on the lino and then the inner door shutting, followed by quiet. The Syms woman must have returned from taking the dog out.

TIME TO GO.

With the skirt under his coat, Roy slipped quickly down the stairs and out

ON TO THE STREET.

Even though **he was anxious to make his getaway,** he **STILL** stopped at the kerb to observe the rules of road safety. ***Sensible chap.*** As he stood waiting for a car to pass, he noticed that **a little** of the YELLOW skirt showed beneath the hem of his raincoat, but not enough to be noticed.

Once inside the VAN, he bundled the skirt under his seat. It felt grubby and it had also retained some of the lingering odour of Hands's bed-sit. Suffused with shame, it was no longer the same lovely garment I had worn on the night of my ADVENTURE. Roy knew that even if I had still been DRESSING, no washing powder could ever make it clean and bright enough to wear again. It was irretrievably impregnated with HANDS's UGLINESS.

Shifting uneasily in his seat, ROY wound down the window and SPAT his Murraymint on to the road.

●

19

The film was a comedy. Roy had managed to talk EVE out of *Victim*, saying he didn't like Dirk Bogarde's hairstyle. It was a lame excuse but she seemed to accept it. The real reason was not so much that Sylvia Syms was one of the stars, but more that the show-card pictures outside the Odeon suggested a serious theme and he was WORRIED there might be something about a dead body in it. So they'd gone to the Regal instead.

THE CINEMA felt safe and secure. They slid down in the prickly plush velvet and BLEW Smoke into the dark space above them, watching as it spiralled up into the projector's beam. The filter tip is the extra refinement that adds to the enjoyment of smoking.

MARY used to have a friend, Mrs. Chambers, whose husband was a Rotarian and who fancied herself as a bit of a socialite. She smokeD De Reszke Minors. Red Tips for Red Lips! Minors Red Tips boasted the inclusion of a red tip to ensure that no telltale traces of lipstick showed on the cigarette. After she had gone, Roy would inspect the ASHTRAY and count what looked to him like discarded fingernails.

DE RESZKE RED TIPS were clearly a ladies' cigarette, but after the Lipstick business on his picnic date with Eve, Roy had considered buying some for himself. As it turned out, they didn't MAKE THEM any more so he bought KENSITAS instead —which was probably just as well.

The supporting film was a travelogue thing about timber in Canada.

"Are you interested in natural history?" ROY whispered recklessly.

"I've never had it," Eve replied enigmatically. Her skin was soft and delicately pink and white and her light brown eyes looked wonderingly at the screen.

HE thought perhaps they had sat too far forward. Most of the COURTING CAPERS seemed to be going on in the rows behind them, and tonight Eve looked bewitching! The confection she was wearing had real style and she had the figure to set it off – the figure and the skin. It was all to the good that, having draped her cardigan over the seat in front, she was now showing rather more of the latter than BEFORE.

FASHION writers sometimes mock at our love of 'little cotton dresses'—but who in the world wears a cotton dress so well as a young British girl with clean hair, not too much make-up and the long, easy-walking legs that are the secret envy of the more dumpy Frenchwoman ?

Inspired by other COUPLES nearby, Roy slipped his arm around EVE and she snuggled comfortably into his shoulder. A WOMAN sitting behind them tut-tutted and shifted in her seat. Roy and EVE *exchanged knowing glances; they could just imagine* NEXT WEEK's LETTER to

Mary Grant's

PROBLEM PAGE:

In my courting days couples always sat in the back row of the cinema. Not so today—they sit anywhere and have no consideration for other cinemagoers who have to keep moving their heads to see the screen and are often obliged to witness "goings-on" that on the screen would merit an "X" certificate. There ought to be a law against it!

They heard the WOMAN get up and move to another seat.

When EVE looked back at Roy, her gaze settled on his upper lip.

"You haven't shaved today," she whispered.

"I'm growing a moustache," he replied. "Like DAVID NIVEN."

"Are you now? I'm not sure about that."

"Don't you like it?"

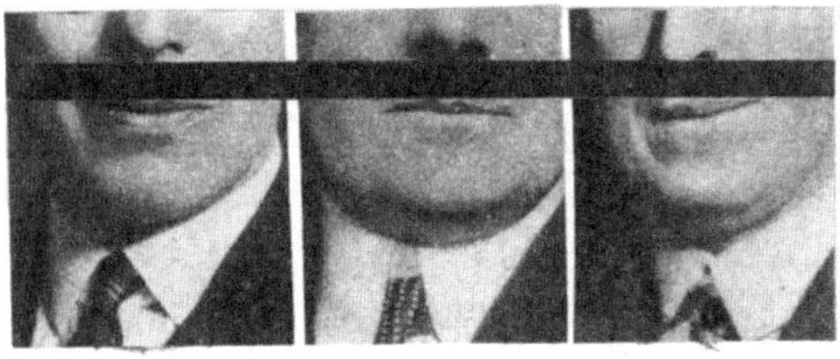

IT was a fair question. MOUSTACHES can be a rather ticklish subject. Many ladies simply loathe the things and cannot understand any reasonable woman liking them. But then they may be biased by the fact that when one of their favourite men grew a moustache, he turned out to be Jimmy Edwards or Adolf Hitler, and they have never quite recovered from the shock.

"I think it might suit you," whispered wise old EVE, having weighed up the pros and cons on a pair of modern-looking kitchen scales. "I'll let you know when you've kissed me goodnight," she added, with a tantalising flick of her eyebrows.

THE scent of her *SOFT SHAMPOO* filled his head. He kissed her lightly on the temple and this time there was no LIPSTICK aberration. Immediately yielding to this tiny tender advance, she looked up at him, her eyes sending out an invitation, to which *Roy* could not help but RSVP. Their lips melted together like CANDLES on a hot day, yet there was NO confusion about whose *lips* were whose. HIS lips were his, and hers, sweet and tender as BATCHELORS PEAS, were her own.

As the lights went up for the intermission, Roy turned to EVE.

"Do you want a *choc ice* or anything?"

"No, I'm **ALL RIGHT.** Are you having one?"

"No. Unless you're having one."

" They're expensive here. They're only threepence in **OUR** **shop.** "

"It doesn't matter. I've got enough."

It was actually thanks to the money from **HANDS**'s trouser pocket. He somehow knew it was wrong to spend it, but until he got paid, he had no other MEANS.

While they were dithering, a long queue had formed in front of ***THE ICE CREAM*** salesgirl. ***That's the trouble.*** You have to be **QUICK OFF THE MARK** or you find yourself still up the front, blocking everyone's view, when the film starts up, and then you discover that whatever the girl has left on her tray has melted. Usually **JUST** the Neapolitan tub, which is **the most** expensive member of the Ice Cream family.

EVE had her purse out and was sorting through it for change. "Are you going, then?" she said. "I'll pay." He stood up. "Yes, I'll go and see." Ever the gentleman, he waved her money away. He'd paid for her ticket too. She'd insisted on 'going Dutch', but he thought it wasn't quite human to make her pay for

herself. It was Hands's treat, anyway.
"Choc ice, then, is it? You can have a tub if you like."
"No, I prefer a choc ice."

AS He stood at the end of the queue, the spotlight shining on THE ice cream girl caught him on the back of the head. He turned round and, bathed in its glow, with the audience all facing him, he felt as if he were on stage. This must be what it's like for Adam Faith or Matt Monro, he thought. He had never considered himself suited to a life in the entertainment industry, but rather than experiencing the stage fright that many seasoned performers complain of, he found he felt quite comfortable in the spotlight, and wondered if show business was a career path he might, under other circumstances, have chosen. It was hard to see through the light's glare, but he gave a special little showbiz wave in EVE's direction, hoping she would be watching him.

When he finally reached the front of the queue, all THE GIRL had left were ice-lollies. So Lollies it was. ROY and Eve enjoyed their cool, refreshing sunshine taste and settled down again as the curtains slid back in readiness for the next SLICE of CINEMATIC ENJOYMENT.

A few late arrivers drifted in to catch the end of the forthcoming attractions prior to the commencement of the main feature. Roy watched one *chunky chap* grope his way along the row in the dark until he settled in a seat a few rows in front of them. He noticed that the man did not remove his hat. At the theatre or cinema, failing to remove one's hat (along with rattling sweet wrappers and SPITTING BUTTERKIST POPCORN from the balcony) is considered the height of bad manners.

Carry on Constable had some funny moments. Three raw police recruits getting into all kinds of hot water while being bobbies on the beat. The LITTLE one with curly hair was pathologically superstitious and refused to make a move without consulting his horoscope chart. "That's just like my **aunt**ie," said Eve, breathing the words close into Roy's ear.

HE watched her laughing at something on the screen and realised that he hadn't been paying attention. Try as he might, ROY could not take his eyes off her. It was as if they were attached to her very being by two lengths of strong garden twine. A lesser girl might have found this adoration overwhelming, but when **E V E** caught him doting on her loveliness, she merely smiled and squeezed his hand.

O **N THE SCREEN** a young policeman and a young woman *in a negligee* were contemplating having that privilege that is reserved for the married. They should ask themselves: is it worth it? Would it not be better to wait one, two, three years, until they can afford to marry, rather than run the risk of bringing so much misery upon themselves ? Even in marriage, the full joy of consummated love may not be known for many months. **So** how is it likely to be achieved in the furtive and uncertain atmosphere that must surround intimacy that is not accompanied by the vows of the marriage ceremony ?

THE difficulties of the unmarried remain an ever-present problem. ROY had to be strong. It would do him no good to have thoughts about EVE wearing the latest boudoir styles. The adjustments of courtship are troublesome enough without making them any more so by these kind of prenuptial imaginings.

WITH her eyes still **fixed on the screen,** and **with the minimum of paper-rustling fuss,** **EVE** produced a quarter of chocolate limes from her handbag. She had *the canny knack of choosing* **THE PERFECT CONFECTION FOR EVERY OCCASION.**

Later on in the film, there was a scene in which **two of** **the police**men **disguised themselves as women in an attempt to foil a gang of shoplifters, but who ended up getting nabbed themselves instead.** And it served them right because **they were thoroughly unconvincing.** **IT'S ALWAYS THE SAME** in comedies. Whenever they have someone impersonating a female, the interpretation is invariably a grotesque caricature of WOMANLINESS. *Roy* and I have never enjoyed this aspect of comedic horseplay. It makes a mockery of *femininity and the female role.* THICKSET Theodores tottering BANDY-LEGGED in HIGH *HEELS*, with BIG RED LIPS AND *flowery* HATS asking, 'Are my seams straight?' Not one of them would pass AS A WOMAN in real life.

ROY remembered once seeing Cary Grant in some film or other successfully passing himself off as a female American army officer by SIMPLY donning a skirt and wearing a makeshift wig fashioned from a horse's tail. Well, I'm sorry, *CARY*, but that just won't do. *Any women's magazine would concur.* It takes much more than an A-line skirt and a ponytail hairdo to become the woman of today.

But how many others share this view?

Eve, like the rest of the audience, seemed to find the whole thing *HILARIOUS*, so ROY resisted the urge to leap to his feet, throw his hands on his hips, and shout "I object!"

THE man in the hat sitting in front of them was laughing too. The laugh was distinctive —thick as custard with a rasping cough at the end of it. ROY recognised it at once; it sounded exactly like **HANDS.** Then he noticed the little RED FEATHER in the **man's HAT.** *Oh, Lord Lucifer.*

SO, *HANDS* *WAS ALIVE!*

IF it really was him, it changed everything. *Roy* was unsure how he was expected to feel about it. A pair of conflicting emotions leapt into the ring to fight it out. In the blue corner, there was a giddy sense of relief, because this meant there had been no murder, and therefore there was no **murderer.** (All Hands had got was a bash on the head, which he clearly deserved.) In the red corner was the cuticle-biting concern that his adversary might now choose to reap some kind of revenge.

Of course, 'not being a *MURDERER*' won the bout, far outweighing his other concerns, but he was nevertheless anxious that they should leave the cinema before HANDS saw him. Although he had failed to recognise ROY that day outside the Post Office, perhaps after the familiarity of THE PHOTO SESSION, he would be more likely to spot a likeness.

Roy couldn't concentrate on the rest

of the film ; he kept staring at the man,
a dozen Questions trotting in
an endless circle round his head LIKE ponies
in the circus. He was desperate to know for
certain if it was HANDS, but realised that
his safest bet was to steer well clear of him.
"Shall we

GO?..."

he whispered.
EVE looked puzzled. "Now?"
He nodded.
"Aren't we going to watch THE END?"
"Yes, OK. If you want," said Roy quickly switch-
ing direction with a three-point turn.

"Don't you like the FILM?"
"Yes, it's good."
"Why do you want to go?"
"I don't. I'm fine."
The audience guffawed. They'd missed a a funny bit. Eve turned back to THE SCREEN, looking a bit perplexed. Roy strained to make out HANDS's LAUGH amongst the crowd.

After 'GOD SAVE THE QUEEN', they shuffled along their row to the aisle, where they waited to file out with the rest of the audience. EVE had her compact out and was deftly applying fresh lipstick before they hit the night air. In his bid to appear unruffled, Roy had lost sight of his target.

He sent his EYES on a rec-onnaissance mission around THE CINEMA, but neither Mr. Hands nor his TYROLEAN TITFER, were anywhere to be seen.

HE finally caught sight of the hat over on the other side of the CINEMA, exiting by another door. But the man WEARING IT was younger, slimmer, with glasses—nothing like HANDS at all. Clearly, CONTINENTAL-STYLE headgear was not as unusual as ROY had imagined. They probably sold these hats in the market for seven and sixpence. After all, what was it really? A cheap piece of moulded felt with a dyed CHICKEN feather in it. That day in the Excella café THE FEATHER had seemed to symbolise individuality and a spirit of artistic flair, but now it was nothing more than the shaming emblem of perversion.

SO, we were back to square one. But, when they came out into the LOBBY, Roy saw the man again, standing a few yards ahead of them, facing out towards the Street. NOW he looked fatter, his coat was different, and Roy quickly realised that though it may have been the same HAT, it was not the same man.

Suddenly he swung round to face them. It was HANDS. NO QUESTION. He even had a bit of WHITE *bandage* showing under his hat. He stared blankly into the middle distance, and then, as if he had left something behind in the cinema, he began to push his way BACK through the oncoming traffic of the emerging audience. Eve was *oblivious to the* THREAT.

Roy took her hand and tried to sidestep him, but, caught up in the flow of the crowd, they were being jostled *nearer and nearer to the foe.*

Hands wriggled his way between them and Roy and Eve were forced to break apart their clasped hands to let him by.

"Sorry," he said. "Excuse me."
He looked Roy straight in the eye as he said it, and though his gaze appeared to bore right through **HIS HEAD** to the back of the foyer, *Roy* felt sure that, on some unconscious level, this time **the FAMILY** resemblance had been positively identified.

N°350

20

"I LIKED the bit where those policemen dressed up as women, didn't you?" she said, shuffling forward. They were in the queue at the chip shop, where Eve had been telling Roy all the bits in the FILM she'd found amusing.

"Sort of," said Roy. "They didn't look much like women. They weren't even wearing WIGS."

"I know. That's what was funny. I like that one with the glasses. What's his name?"

"I don't know," said Roy, a little dismissively. "Men are never any good at it. You can always tell."

"Always tell what?"

"If it's a MAN DRESSED UP as a WOMAN."

ROY found himself heading towards dangerous white-water rapids, unable to steer his way clear. He struggled to come up with a fresh topic of conversation, but Eve beat him to it.

"Hey. Guess what?"

He did not want to guess. HE had an uneasy feeling about what might be coming next.

"You know that SCARF," she said, "the one you found in the waiting room at WHITE's? Well, Miss Harrow said that the woman who left it was rather peculiar-looking. And do you know what she thinks? She thinks she was really a man."

"A *man*?"

"Disguised as a woman."

Within the briefest of moments, Roy was suffering from one of those stomach upsets that can quickly spoil one's leisure enjoyment.

"Why would she think something like that?" he said, his voice shaking a little.

"Well, apparently she had a deep voice and her make-up was really thick."

"That doesn't make her a man. Look at **Rosalind Russell**."

"I know, but . . . "

"Isn't it ridiculous, how gossips always seem to get hold of the wrong end of the stick?" he said. "Before you know where you are, they've started a scandal that hasn't an atom of truth in it.

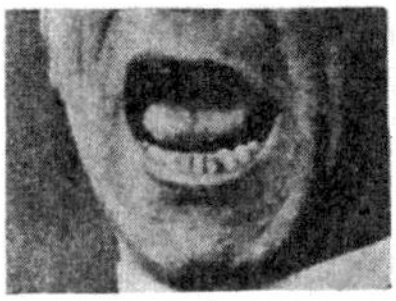

I think Miss Harrow should stop spreading vicious rumours about people."

EVE was a little taken aback by his confrontational stance. It was a side of him she'd never seen before.

"It isn't vicious, *Roy*." There was tenderness in her voice. "It's simply what she thought. There are those kind of men about, you know."

"Are there really?" he sneered cynically. "What would Miss Harrow know about it? What would either of you know about it?"

"It's true, **ROY**. *You must* have seen them. **Men** who put on Women's **dresses** and go walking down the street. **There was one who lived near us who** used to go to the park pushing a pram."

THE ***woman*** in front of them in the queue

turned to look over her shoulder. She had obviously been eavesdropping and now felt sufficiently involved to offer her opinion on the matter. There were no **WORDS**, just a little TUTTING noise, with a slight wobble of the **HEAD** to convey her disapproval. Roy wondered if she might have been the TUTTING woman who had sat behind them in the cinema. Fortunately for *Roy*, the interruption was enough to halt the flow of their discussion, so that by the time they'd been served and were heading into Great Colmore Street, the subject had been dropped. Anyway, it didn't matter what Eve's views were on the subject. Not any more. The important thing now was that **HANDS** was alive and (reasonably) well; there was no murder inquiry to answer to, so Roy could get on with the serious business of COURTSHIP. He wasn't even convinced any longer that HANDS had recognised him. Besides, even if he had, they were just two floating balloon **HEADS** in the crowd and the chances of them ever bumping into each other again were pencil slim. Roy hardly ever saw anyone he knew. Michael **PRICE**, Roy's childhood CHUM from across the road, lived over **BY** Egmont *Street*. They walked the same streets, shopped in the same shops, travelled on the same buses, but in more than TEN years they had not run into one another once.

EVE and Roy were standing in the doorway of the CHEMISTS, sharing six pennyworth of chips before catching their bus. HE HAD thought it best not to take THE VAN after what Mr. WHITE had said the other day.

Anyway, the 76 dropped them right outside the POST OFFICE, and from there Roy could easily walk home.

THE only other shop in the block that still had its light on was Marcia Modes. A beacon to welcome true lovers of stylish apparel. Roy noticed that the window display had been changed since THE NIGHT OF the PHOTO SESSION. He had promised to himself—really, truly promised this time—that he would steer clear of the shop, BUT something in the window had caught EVE's eye and she stopped to look at it.

THERE were a number of new dresses that Roy had not seen before. EVE's eyes were fixed on a romantic blue creation with flattery in every seam. The yoke, softly gathered each side of the V neckline, the fitted, darted bodice and three-quarter set-in sleeves gave a trim but essentially feminine outline.
"Oh I like that," she said, pointing.

HE agreed. "Yes, it's femininity all the way in the new styles. A dress to delight every woman's heart. And every man's too! So very becoming, it would show off every figure to best advantage. Smart and up to date, it has a timeless elegance that will be fashionable for years. You could wear it proudly all day long. Perfect wear for the **post office** during the morning and afternoon, it's ideal for social evenings too, dressed up with the prettiest beads."

"It *is* nice," she admitted. "I wonder how much it is. It looks expensive."

"It's probably LESS THAN YOU THINK. Marcia's is very reasonable."

"More than I can afford, anyway."

SHE had started to walk away, but ROY had not finished his appraisal of the dress. "The fabric is wonderful woven rayon with a raised finish. Substantial yet soft, it has marvellous wearing qualities."

"When did you become such an expert in WOMEN'S FASHION?"

"I've always been an expert in WOMEN'S FASHION," he said playfully. It was true, of course—he had. But he realised his reply may have sounded strange and needed further explanation. "Over the years, I've done a lot of clothes shopping for my sister. You know, when she was unable to go out. YOU LEARN THINGS, looking in shops and in

Magazines.

I like Women's **FASHION** anyway. It interests me."

It was a bold admission for a man to make, but Eve didn't seem the least bit fazed by it. "Well, I think it's wonderful," she said. "It's nice to have a boyfriend who takes an interest in a **WOMAN'S** clothes. It's normally so unlike a man to know about such things."

•

21

It was funny. All that time HANDS had been ALIVE, SO there had never been any murder investigation, and Roy had never been a fugitive from justice. HANDS had not recognised *Roy* —or at least had failed to 'Name that Tune' —so there was no threat there either. As long as he kept out of Hands's way, and I stuck to my end of the bargain and remained in Dundee (... yes, mother, I promise ... and no dipping in to the SUITCASE again ...), there was nothing whatever to worry about. But before Roy had chance to settle into an easy chair with the GOOD NEWS, there was another family-sized portion of TROUBLE ready to be served up.

"What's this?" said Mary, shaking a canary yellow fist in his face. He was barely in the door. Oh, Lord —she'd found the skirt. And now he'd have to go through the entire routine. Roy steered past her into the front room, hanging his jacket on the back of the chair.

ON the way home from Egmont Street that

SUNDAY, THE SKIRT

had been singing out to him from under the SEAT. He had planned to keep it in the VAN until MARY was out and he had a chance to burn it on the fire, but its incriminating yellowness pecked away at his conscience, and with Mr. WHITE's suspicions already aroused, and the POLICE sniffing around, he felt it was not safe to leave it there. So, while *Mary* was PREPARING SUNDAY LUNCH, he had sneaked it upstairs and stashed it rolled up behind the WARDROBE where he hoped it would remain undiscovered.

"I don't know what's the matter with you," she said, throwing the skirt down by the hearth. "Why can't you just stop?"

"I have stopped."

"Well what's this then? Scotch mist? And what's all that?"

She was pointing to the **stain.**

Roy tried to explain how in the struggle that fateful night the SKIRT had slipped its mooring and become trapped under HANDS's seeping head. He told her about the embarrassment of having to walk home without it, and how he had gone back to get it a couple of days later, in case anyone traced it back to THE HOUSE.

HE was hoping Mary might applaud this bit of fancy footwork, but she didn't. "I was going to get rid of it," he assured her.

"When? Next week? Next year? And what exactly are you planning to do with it until then? Hang it in a frame over the fireplace, perhaps? Or stick it on a flagpole in the front garden? You do realise that if the police find this, you'll be had up for murder and carted straight off to prison?"

"Well, actually, it turns out there wasn't any murder. THE man isn't DEAD."

"Not DEAD? You told me he was."

"I thought he was, but I've just seen him at the PICTURES. He must have woken up."

"Woken up?"

"Yes."

"He's alive, then?"

"Yes."

"So you're not a murderer?" She sounded almost disappointed. She thought for a moment. "But you still hit him. They'll have you for that. Grievous bodily harm." It was another term she'd learned off the *Television*.

"I don't think so. I can't imagine this man reporting the incident to the police. He wouldn't want them to know what he had been up to. He's got just as much to lose."

"You think so?"

" Yes."

"So you think you've got off scot free?"

"Well, hardly. It was a most unpleasant experience for NORMA."

"But you thought you'd keep the SKIRT as a souvenir anyway?"

"That wasn't THE PLAN at all."

THOUGH the skirt was no longer the incriminating evidence he had previously thought, and in spite of the fact that it had always been a favourite, it was forever tainted by its association with that dreadful evening and he longed to be free from its cursed memory. Roy knew that **the most stubborn (and for any young woman, the most shaming) stain of all can only be banished by one foolproof method:** purification by fire. **—With its three in one action, it effectively** cleanses the mind, body, and soul — **all in one go!** — **thus preserving the spotless** innocence of youth **in its eternal flame.**

Yet even in its CONTAMINATED STATE, it was hard to think of the skirt going up in smoke like **an ounce of Golden Virginia**.

It seemed so final. And though he was determined that the SUITCASE CLOTHES should never again see the light of day, so long as they were STORED at Eve's, they were, at least, suspended in a kind of limbo until he disposed of them properly.

OTHER things went on the fire after my accident: Photographs mostly, but also stories and drawings I'd done at school. It was as if Roy were looking down a tunnel twenty years long, and there was Mary, a distant figure at the other end of it, wearing the exact same expression.

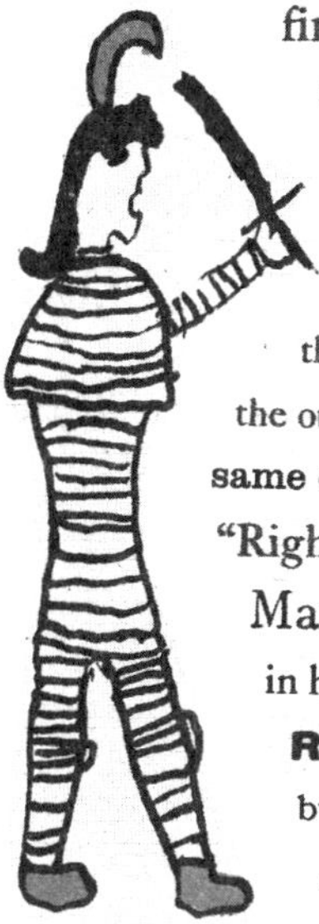

"Right, let's get shot of it," said Mary, anxious to deal with the job in hand.

ROY put himself in charge. He bundled the SKIRT into a ball and rammed it firmly into the back of the grate. Mary stood with her arms folded, looking on. He searched in the KITCHEN drawer for the can of lighter fluid, but it was empty. He didn't need it. Being made of a thirty per cent rayon tricel, the skirt went up surprisingly quickly, blazing intensely out of control for a moment like a holiday romance with a girl from Hartlepool, before dying away to nothing in the grate. He stirred the flimsy ashes with the poker before emptying dank coal from the scuttle on top of them. **Buried and cremated** all in one go. Ashes to ashes, dust to dust.

When it was all done, **MARY** went out into the garden to hang some duster s on the line. *Roy* washed his hands in the kitchen sink , turning the soap over and over in his hands until the water ran cold.

TWENTY 2

Although the merchandise is reasonably priced, **Marcia Modes** is not for the everyday purchase — unless you have a healthy clothing allowance *OR* **£2,050** CASH

All over the country, for just a few minutes of their spare time, over 100,000 ordinary men and women are making **EXTRA** pounds regularly —but unfortunately Roy is not one of them. My red pixie jacket was a **Marcia Modes** purchase, but that was with his Christmas bonus from **Mackintosh's**. **It's nearly a year ago now,** but I STILL wear it all the time (or did until recently). More often than not, especially during his periods of unemployment, *Roy* has TENDED to rely on the rag market, charity shops, and jumble sales.

LUXURY styles at a budget price . . . that's what we're all looking for in clothes these days. You can find some marvellous bargains: my navy **scribble print skirt** was from our local jumble. It was practically brand new and cost only sixpence.

"I nearly didn't recognise you with the *moustache*," said Mrs. **Marcia**.

"Well, it's still growing," said Roy, fingering his upper lip.

"What brought that on? Fertiliser?"

Roy's laugh was not as hearty as her own.

"Well, what can I show you today, Mr. LITTLE?" she asked, slipping back into her professional routine.

"Well, I was interested in the beautiful powder blue V-neck in the Window."

"Oh, it's gorgeous isn't it? It's a MILADY. They do some lovely things."

Roy could see that the waistline was defined by its own stiffened belt, and the smart straight skirt had a flat pleat at the centre back, making walking easy. It was one of the autumn's prettiest silhouettes, specially designed with an eye to every occasion.

"It only came in last week," she said. "The prettily shaped cuffs on full three-quarter sleeves, are an attention-winning feature of this young, demure, easy-to-wear style. It's the very latest thing. There's something very like it in one of the magazines this week. *WOMAN'S OWN*, I think."

"Really? I haven't seen it RECENTLY."

She told him the price. It would take care of nearly half of *Hand*s's money, but it was worth it. "It comes in romantic blue, **fashionable tan, soft grey** and **glowing red,** all with a black speck weave that gives a fascinating tweed effect. I think the blue's the nicest, though. It is sure to suit your SISTER perfectly. I'll just make sure I've got it in an EIGHTEEN," she said, flicking along the rail.

"No, that's too big. I need a size ten."

"TEN?"

"YES. This isn't for my SISTER; it's for someone else. My fiancée, actually."

Mrs. Marcia raised her eyebrows. "Fiancée?"

"Well, I haven't actually popped the question yet, but I'm hoping she'll say yes."

"Good heavens, I had no idea. Well, whoever she is, I'm sure she won't turn you down when she sees this DRESS. It's lovely. I hope your SISTER isn't going to be jealous."

"Jealous? No, I don't think so. EVE—that' s my girlfriend — is a wonderful girl."

"I'm sure she is. And she's a very lucky girl, too. So, you don't want anything in a SIZE EIGHTEEN then?"

"Good heavens, no. EVE's much smaller than my sister. She has a petite, doll-like figure with Brigitte Bardot proportions.

She's quite perfect.

In fact, I won't be buying clothes for my SISTER any more. She's gone away."

"'Gone away?'" said Mrs. Marcia, adding her own quotation marks.

"Yes. She's gone to live in Scotland for GOOD."

"I see. Well, that's a shame, but they do say three's a crowd, don't they?" She was carefully folding the dress in tissue paper. "Ah," she said, "now I understand about the moustache. RONALD COLEMAN, is it?" Roy looked away, feeling a little self-conscious. "David Niven, actually," he said.

● ● ● ● ● ● ● ●

"For me?" EVE slipped the dress out of the carrier bag. "Oh, Roy. You thoughtful darling! You bought it. You shouldn't have. REALLY. You can't afford to buy me things."

"I got a size TEN, but if it doesn't fit, I can take it back," he said excitedly.

"No, TEN is perfect. How did you know?"

"I'm an EXPERT, remember?"

"Well, I'm impressed."

"I can't wait to see you in it," he said. "Try it on."

"Now?"

"Yes, why not? I'll turn my BACK."

"No, you wont," she said, firm, yet playful. "You'll wait outside."

HE readily agreed. He stood on the LANDING with his hands in his pockets. The decor was cheerful and bright, with prettily framed pictures on the wall. EVE WAS TAKING HER TIME. When he put his ear to

the door, he could hear the rustle and swish of soft fabric. *Almost immediately,* he deviated from the path of rectitude, IMAGINING her in mid-change of toilette. He forced his mind back on track *by* studying an embroidered picture of some goblins fishing in a pool.

"All right, you can come in," sang *Eve*.

The dress was **a sensation and** she **looked sensational in it.** He could see it was destined to play an important rôle in her wardrobe this autumn and winter. She stood in front of the wardrobe-door mirror, turning slowly, in order to see her reflection from all angles, then she backed away for a full figure view. "How do I look?" Her eyes shone with the glamour of sparkling diamonds, her face youthful, clear, and flawless. She was a vision of loveliness. Even with her hair in rollers, which it wasn't, she would have given the appearance of being '*somebody*'.

"You look gorgeous," he said.

She transferred her gaze back to the mirror, and smoothed down the dress. "Roy, it's much too extravagant. How can you afford it?"

"I can't, normally. I just happened to have some cash

burning a hole in my pocket. Don't expect me to BUY YOU CLOTHES every week."

"Every fortnight?" She laughed and slipped her arms round his neck. "Oh, ROY, I don't expect anything from you. You're all I need."

"Really?"

"Yes, really."

She looked at him with such sincerity that he felt slightly embarrassed.

"So it fits?" he said, touching her SLENDER WAIST.

"It's perfect. I love it."

She lifted her face. He would have kissed her forehead, but she gave him her young and fragrant lips instead. He was merely making advances of friendship, because that's all it is to a decent young man.

" I don't know why you're so good to me."

"It's an old German custom," he said.

It wasn't, of course.

He sat down on the edge of the bed and pulled her down on to his knee. She offered no resistance, draping one arm across his broad shoulders and flexing her knees like A CHORUS GIRL. The dress was crisp as the morning, sparkling as springtime, irresistibly, enticingly, lastingly fresh. He was admiring the elegant, embroidered motif at the hemline when his eyes drifted to the SHAPELY LEGS and the 15-denier sheer stretch stockings that fit like your 'next of skin'.

N° 374

Flattering as a cosmetic, provocative as a stolen kiss, and infinitely more delightful than any stockings you've ever worn. He drew her closer to him and it was clear that the curves of EVE's body had the power of calling out the strongest feelings in him. His mind started wandering down forbidden avenues.

This is the constant danger. A young man and young woman who are frequently going about with one another quite naturally embrace each other in a manner they would not do with other, more casual friends. As month succeeds month and their affection develops, they find themselves almost perpetually under a strong temptation to allow all kinds of intimate caresses and embraces to take place. And, of course, human nature being what it is, 'one thing leads to another' and often enough, although this may not have been their intention at the outset, the couple find themselves staying on the bus and going all the way to the Cannock Hill roundabout, and we are only too well acquainted with the unfortunate consequences that follow that kind of pre-*nuptial* journey.

"Is it all right my being here? Will your auntie mind?" asked ROY, concerned that his intentions should be deemed honourable.
"No. Why should she?"

"Well, you know. Entertaining a gentleman after dark." He'd somehow made it sound sordid and untoward.
"I'm over twenty-one," she said, "and it *is* my flat." She sounded both GROWN-UP and a little childish at the same time. "Anyway," she went on, "it's all perfectly respectable.

We're just having a DINNER

date. AUNTIE trusts us. She knows this isn't just some casual affair."
Eve raised her head to look at him, her eyes questioning. "It isn't, is it?"
He shook his head.
"Oh, Roy, " she said, putting her hand on his arm.
It was then, when she smiled her enchanting smile, that he knew that neither Hands nor anybody, nor anything could ever reach them so long as they were together.

How much happier he felt about everything now, with the burden of guilt and the fear of retribution released from his shoulders. Only a few days ago the hangman's noose had been a very real threat, but now it was merely the name of a pub on Jessop Lane.

HE toyed with the idea of telling EVE about

HANDS,

or at least that the thing that had been worrying him (and his sister) was no longer worrying him (or his sister). **But how could** he **explain any of this to** her **without telling** her **more than** she **should know?** It is impossible to say definitely that a courting couple should have no secrets from each other—in fact, to my mind, in most cases it is better to avoid revelations about the past. Some secrets should be shared, while those that may be harmful to a loved one are best kept wrapped in airtight parcels, using either plastic bags or thick brown paper sealed with plastic tape, with a handful of mothballs sprinkled between the layers of deceit. They can then be placed on a high shelf out of reach.

"Did you manage THE ZIP?" he asked, spinning her round.

"Yes, thank you."

"You missed the little catch at the top."

She lifted her

HAIR

while his deft fingers set to work on it. He could detect the sweet perfume of a dewy rosebud, or a freshly plucked violet, or something.

"Nice smell," he commented.

"Roast lamb," she said.

He was still fiddling.

"Don't bother, Roy, I'll have to change in a minute."

"Why?"

"I've got food to serve up."

"That's OK, you can wear an apron. You do have an APRON, don't you, or is that something else I've got to buy for you?" He liked the idea of being her CLOTHING benefactor.

"No, I've got an apron thank you. I just don't want to ruin my DRESS."

"Don't change," he pleaded. "I want to see you in it."

SHE relented, making him sit at the little table by the window while she donned a CHARMING DUTCH APRON (prettily gathered with contrasting bound edges and large, floral-printed cotton patch pockets) before preparing the dinner in her happy, unflustered way. She had set the table with two place settings. There were TABLE MATS with castanet-clacking flamenco dancers, and fancily folded paper napkins that looked like PARTY HATS.

A recipe book might suggest that a casserole is really nothing more than stew, but to Roy it was a **symphony conducted by Mantovani.** He thought he had never tasted such a delicious meal, though poached eggs on toast would have tasted like Ambrosia Creamed Rice to him that evening. Throughout the meal, **EVE** and ROY were in a fog that was one part low-flying cloud and ninety-nine parts shimmering excitement. They couldn't stop looking at each other.

Eve cleared away the things, with the rest of the **TREACLE PUDDING** he couldn't manage, insisting he relax while she set about making coffee. ***Made in an instant-right in the cup!*** The best drink in the world for your complexion as well as your thirst.

THERE were no curtains at the little window. They sat on the sofa together, looking up at the night sky.

"That's URSA MAJOR," said Roy, pointing to a cluster of stars.

"Is it?" said **EVE**.

"And that's the plough. And over there is Ganymede." He was making it all up; he didn't know anything about THE STARS.

WHEN he had finished explaining about the Milky Way and the universe, ROY suggested she might TRY her NEW DRESS WITH DIFFERENT SHOES AND EXPERIMENT WITH OTHER BAGS AND ACCESSORIES. EVE was happy to do so, demonstrating an innate sense of style, with the confidence and the know-how to make even the most simple outfit look elegant. It was wonderful to see her choosing just the right gloves, or a piece of jewellery that complemented *the* DRESS so perfectly. FOR *Roy* it was like coming **home**.

The coffee she had drunk made her cheeks glow, her eyes more lustrous. She had never looked happier, more alive. *Roy*'s eyes were alight with the fire which is only lit by one torch in the world.

He even got to see some of her other CLOTHeS.

SHE had left him alone in the room while she popped downstairs to show the DRESS to her Auntie, promising she'd only be gone a couple of minutes. The door to the built-in wardrobe had been left open and the light from inside beckoned. He stepped inside for a searching inspection of the things he had merely glanced at before.

EVERYTHING was so drastically, delightfully tidy. He looked along the rail and he saw her dresses hanging there, all neatly fitting in, with the little coverings over their shoulders. So many mouth-watering styles that were a perfect delight. Everything you'd want, from a saucy wear-it-four-ways beret, to a suit designed by Michael (late of Lachasse).

He touched the dresses one by one, his hands shaking a little in their clumsiness. It was all too much to take in.

HE spotted a Gay Gordon made-to-measure tartan skirt. Spirited, gay, and oh! so young-looking, deeply flounced for saucy swing at the hemline, in the softest taffeta plaid. There was that 'lighter than air' all-day dress in delphinium blue gossamer linen that she had been wearing on the day of his interview. He wished now that he had told her she looked beautiful in it, worrying that she might never wear it again. But she must—she must. The blue suitcase, he noticed, was now stored neatly at the back of the wardrobe. There was a Renaissance-inspired gown in luminous stained-glass red and green. He also found a little white linen skirt and a daringly up-to-date Russian-looking sort of blouse with long, full sleeves, quite tight at the wrists, a dream of a blouse for off-duty hours. And next to that, a dark dress that was the colour of a thousand acres of evergreen forest, with a panel of brilliant red poppies down the front which Dreft had restored to their original colour. Faultlessly tailored in pure wool Harris tweed, it was threequarter lined with rayon taffeta and a side zip fastening.

HE didn't hear EVE come BACK into the room. She found him holding one of her dresses up to the mirror.

"Sorry," he said. "I was just sneaking a peek in your wardrobe. I hope you don't mind. It's so wonderful to see all your *lovely* CLOTHES. You have some **delightful** things. Perhaps we could spend an evening sometime with you showing me all the different outfits you have. Some of them I've seen *YOU* in already, of course, but I'd love it if you could show me everything you've got. We'll have some grand times."

Enthusiasm warmed his voice and he failed to notice the reserve in hers. "Are you sure you wouldn't be bored? There's nothing very special. Except this, of course." She was referring to the NEW dress. "I don't have much, really. It's mostly MAKE DO AND MEND. I shall never be able to afford the model gowns and coats in the MAGAZINE

FEATURES on the London and Paris shows, **but I read every word about these fabulous clothes and study the photographs for hours.**
The words were balm to his soul. **"Do you really?" he said. "So do I."**

He took her hands, hesitated, then, losing his head because she was so very beautiful, he took her into his arms and kissed her again and again. " You lovely thing ! " he said .

She heard the words, she saw the **MAGICOAL** fire burning in his strong cheekbones, she felt his arms—the hunger of them. Under his kiss her blood grew warmer, and her **fainting** heart regained its **galloping** momentum with a glowing, lovely seeping strength. It was as though he had poured into her veins his own vitality. Yet he was all tenderness, for all the fire and passion. She felt steeped in great amazement, yet strangely content. In some **age**, somewhere, she had dreamed a dream. Now the dream had come true.
"Oh, **EVE**," he said.
"Oh, yes," she said with a fervour that surged from her deepest being.
She felt giddy with desire. This was something that had never happened before. There were too many things happening for the first time.
Afraid that her worship might be too noticeable, she **turned away to the window, breathing in the clean night air and trying to steady herself.**
"Does anybody want some more coffee? " **she trilled.** "I believe your cup's empty. Oh dear,

am I a very bad hostess?"

ROY didn't answer. He was already thinking of ways to RAISE EXTRA CASH so that he could buy her the clothes for which her heart and her wardrobe yearned. Perhaps he could become one of those 100,000 men and women who, for just a few minutes of their spare time, are making extra pounds regularly.

She heard him say quietly behind her: "It's an awful nerve, I know. I don't have much to offer. I suppose I shouldn't have started with you, but I couldn't help it. I liked everything about you, and next thing I knew, there I was in love with you."

"You're in love with me," she repeated slowly, and he nodded. And for a moment they stood toe to toe, breathing deeply at each other, and she felt warm and good inside ——

like

A FRESHLY BAKED PIE.

"I still have a little money left," he said. "Do you think there might be enough to put down a deposit on a RING?"

"A ring?"

"Yes, an ENGAGEMENT RING. Would you like that?"

She said very softly, "Do you mean what I think

you do?"
"I do," he said.

Her voice was low and shaken when she spoke, but there was a little song in her heart. "Well," she said " it's not as though I have one already, and I suppose **an engagement ring** would go nicely with my new dress. Don't you think? **I mean,** *YOU'RE THE EXPERT* ."
"I think it would look perfect."
"OK, then," she said. "But you really must let me pay for something soon."

Their eyes locked, and she was shaken from that composure to which she had been clinging so bravely. She hardly seemed to be breathing. **He took her in his arms and the time for talk was over.** Words, however eloquent, cannot convince a man that his wife-to-be belongs to him in body and spirit unless he knows that in the supreme moments of their loving, she is completely and utterly his, that she willingly and joyfully gives herself to him in the fullest sense of the word.

She stirred against him, no longer afraid, no longer holding back any part of herself, longing only to give as he wanted her to give. She could not fight, had no will left for refusal. As though her limbs were liquid, she melted into his waiting arms and they were as one. That extra kiss swept aside defences, seeming endless and sublime. She had a strange sensation as though her body had released a **record, which went straight to number one in the charts.** It happened then, with the old, rich surge of a rebellious sea. The material side fell away, disregarded, unworthy. That lovely glowing thing which had escaped met and united with another, soared and in unity found ecstasy. "My beloved is mine and I am his!" sang her heart, and **EVE** entered the heaven for which she had waited.

They lay with hands and shoulders touching and talked, and the talk had the quality of dreams. They talked of the thousands of years that lay ahead of them, and all they would do. According to the MAGAZINES, this was the way you talked when you'd been married almost nine days. They'd only just got engaged, **but it** was **good to get a bit of practice in.**

ROY lay quite still, listening to the quiet ticking of the little TRAVEL ALARM CLOCK by the bed and the muted sounds of traffic from the front of the building. He turned to Eve, watching the lovely face, peaceful now in repose with the eyes closed and the lashes very dark against her cheek. The recent display of emotion had given an apricot flush to her smooth cheeks and her welcoming mouth was as red and as perfect as a carpet rolled out for a royal visit.

Neither **of them had** any regrets. There were no feelings of guilty remorse normally associated with such an exchange because what they felt for each other was pure and real.

A car backfired out on the street. It may have been that, or the very intensity of his gaze on her, but in a little while her lashes fluttered open and he was looking down into her lustrous eyes, the colour of wet wood violets. Transfixed, they stared at one another, Roy spellbound in wonder; EVE bemused by sleeping sheep in the meadow of her mind.

She said softly: "Weren't you ever in love before?" "I guess not. Anyway, not like this. I had one or two affairs which petered out eventually because there was no reality behind them. There was something wrong with each one of them, at least by my standards. Love had begun to seem to me simply a nice-looking emotion writers wrote about in the weekly magazines." He propped himself on one elbow. "What about you?" "No-one serious. When I had only been working in the shop a short time, I had a — call it an adventure —similar to yours. I wasn't in love with this man but he was attractive and he turned my silly head. But it wasn't any thing. Even at first."

So, that was all right, then.

They talked of practical things. They even discussed where they would live. These days the housing shortage is a popular topic of conversation, and a very real problem for the newly-married. Every couple trying to build a happy House of Marriage will obviously stand a better chance of doing so if they can start their new life together in a home of their own than if they have to share with in-laws or friends.

"We can live here," said **Eve**. "It's big enough for two. Auntie only charges a nominal rent and it would be handy for the LAUNDRY. You'd only **have to nip across the road.**"

"Yes, that's true."

"And I could go on working until we get a bit put by," said Eve.

"What about your auntie? What's she going to say?"

"She'll be thrilled. She won't get in our way. It will be our home. Just us here together."

ROY could not believe his luck. He had met the most wonderful girl in the world and she had agreed to marry him. He imagined himself coming home to the little flat above the shop to find her waiting for him, with the sun in her hair, a song in her heart, *a kiss on her lips*, and something tasty in the **CHOCOLATE** drawer.

And in the wardrobe the prettiest flowered dresses, **and his lovely young bride** looking absolutely darling in each and every one of them. The ideal of free marriage is the coming together of two persons, emotionally mature, to share their lives and to unite for mutual enrichment in the closest possible manner open to human beings. And if a husband can support his wife in all matters relating to her **WARDROBE**, true happiness will never be far away.

But was he in a position, financially, to ask for her hand? Would he be forcing her to remain a 'MAKE-DO-AND-MEND' girl?

"I've got no money," he said, " except my wages." "Money!" she cried. "Who cares about money?" And she really meant it.

She put a finger on his upper lip and gently stroked the bristles. "Will your SISTER come to the wedding?" she said.
It was sweet of her to ask. In all the passion and excitement, 'LITTLE SISTER' had been left somewhat on the shelf. On occasions such as these, of course, one is prepared to step gracefully into the background, but it was clear now, more than ever, that this was going to have to be a permanent arrangement.
"No, I think not. I believe it would be a very bad thing if she turned up now. She's got to stay PUT," he said, squaring his determined jaw and doubling his resolve. "In any case, she wouldn't be able to stand the strain of a wedding just now. I can write and tell her, and ask for her blessing—I think that she'll give it to us and that she'll be pleased. That is— if you're sure you'll marry me."
"Of course I'm sure. For goodness' sake, I've thought about little else since I first saw you." She touched his hair. "What will your MUM do? She'll be all on her own now that your sister has gone."
"She'll be fine," said Roy. TELEVISION is an excellent medium of entertainment, and in the long winter

months, helps to while away the time most pleasurably."

"But she can't watch television *all* the time," said Eve. "She'll hardly notice I've gone."

"But will she approve of our getting married? She hasn't even met me yet. Won't she think it's too soon?"

"**MOTHER?** Good gracious, no. She'll be thoroughly delighted."

She would too. He was certain of it.

●

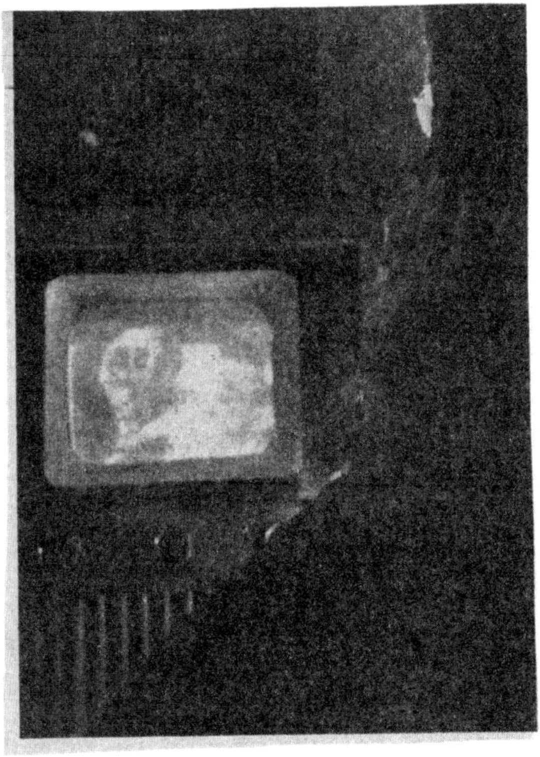

THE TWENTY THIRD

MARY took the news surprisingly well, even the bit about moving in with EVE after they were married. Worried less, it seemed, about being left on her own in Afferton Road than she was about having me HANGING AROUND THE HOUSE dressed to the nines, looking for all the world like some glamorous Hollywood star. NO MORE fretting about what the neighbours might see through a chink in the curtain. Besides, she'd always been keen to see Roy settle down with a nice girl, and there was no nicer girl than EVE. He'd arranged to take her for tea on Sunday 'TO MEET MOTHER'. It was all very decorous. Though as always, there was the usual *song and country dance* to go through first.

"How can you get married? You haven't got a penny to your name. Where are you going to live?"

"**Eve's** got a little flat above the shop. We're going to live there," said Roy.

"What about all the other expenses? Have you any idea how much a wedding costs?"

He had, of course, because WOMAN AND HOME had recently run a feature entitled

HOLY MATRI-MONEY

THE HIDDEN COST OF MARRIAGE

which answered exactly thEse sorts of questions.
"We're going to do it in a registry office," he said.
"Eve's not bothered about a big wedding."
" DON'T BE DAFT. Of course she is. It's every girl's dream to get married in a church. REGISTRY OFFICE ? EVERYBODY will think you've got TO GET married." Then the thought occurred to her. "You haven't . . . have you ?
"No, of course not." Roy looked at the CARPET.
Mary had an embarrassing habit of rolling up her sleeves to deal with those delicate subjects others took such pains to avoid.
"Well, you wouldn't be the first. What do her parents say about all this?"
"They don't say anything. THEY'RE DEAD."
"So she's got no family? Who's going to pay for the WEDDING, then? Because it's no use coming to me. I've only got my money from the school and your Dad's PENSION. How am I expected to save anything on that?"
"Eve has an auntie."
"And is she paying for it ?"
"I don't expect so. Anyway, none of this is important. What's important is that we'll be TOGETHER."
"You only met her two weeks ago. You can't possibly know her."
"TWO WEEKS is long enough, if you're certain about someone.

THIS IS *the real thing,* **Mum.**
Guaranteed 100% genuine!"

Mary softened a little. "All I'm saying is, why do you have to rush into things? I haven't even set eyes on the **GIRL** yet. Why not wait a year or two until you get settled in your job. GET a bit put by." Mary clearly felt, as many of **THE women's magazines** do, that marriage should not be a risky adventure based on the idea that romance will compensate for every lack of comfort and for years of hard struggle against adversity.

"We don't care if we're broke. We just want to be joined together to share the joys of wedded bliss. The *raison d'être* of marriage is to be found in the very nature of mankind itself. It is a great and glorious relationship—and I believe we should *APPLY NOW WHILE STOCKS LAST.* True Love Conquers All."

"You've been reading too many romance stories," she said. "It isn't like that in real life. **It takes money to set up home,** you know."

"**EVE**'s already **set up home** in her flat. ***It's charmingly cosy.*** *She's got* gay teatowels and a settee and **PRESSURE COOKER**, plus there are table mats with Spanish dancers on them."

The look was scornful. Mary shook her head. "**SPANISH DANCERS**"... But a tiny crack had appeared in the plasterwork, and **ROY**, knowing her like he knew his own WRISTWATCH, had spotted it. Beneath the staunchly defended façade, he could see that she

was really quite delighted by the idea.
"Well, I'll have to give my *APPROVAL* first," she said, determined not to appear too RELENTING.
This was a FREQUENTLY ADOPTED STANCE and *Roy* had been familiar with it since he was a boy. He would say, "Mum, can I get the HOSEPIPE out?" or *"Can* MICHAEL *stay over at our house?"* or "Can I have some E-L-A-S-T-I-C to make a HEADband?"— and even when she had no objections whatsoever, permission was always granted grudgingly. It was never: "Of course you may, darling." IT WAS ALWAYS: "Oh, go on then." As if she'd been cajoled into it. AND the agreement was never unconditional; some proviso, some extra clause would be added. LIKE: "—but make sure you put it back where you found it" or "— but mind my flower bed," or "— so long as you put newspaper down first."

"She's the most wonderful girl in the world, *MUM*," said Roy, excitedly. "You'd be proud to have her as a daughter-in-law."
"WOULD I?" Her arms were still folded BUT *Roy* COULD DETECT a core thread of tenderness.
Crunchy nut coating on the outside; soft, creamy filling on the inside.
"I could bring her round for tea on Sunday."
MARY tutted and rolled her eyes.
"Oh, go on then," she said. "But make sure she wipes her feet."

FRIDAY was a COLLECTION DAY, so when he'd unloaded the van Roy went into the front office to drop off his COLLECTION sheet and takings. He'd skipped lunch so that he could finish early, so eager was he to see Eve again. He wondered if, like himself, she had floated through the day on a candyfloss cloud.

This was a whirlwind courtship and it would be a whirlwind marriage. And when it was all over he would congratulate himself on his good fortune, looking forward to all the years that he would have Eve completely to himself. Roll on the day when there would be no more partings at her door, no more meetings to arrange, because they'd be married and together for always . . . wonderful words to a man in love.

"I hear congratulations are in order. EVE told me." It was Miss Harrow. She was looking rather pleased with herself. She sprang up from her desk *like* a dog after a biscuit, and before he knew it she had taken him by the shoulders and *planted a sloppy kiss on his cheek,* exaggerating THE SOUND lest he should mistake it for something else. It took him by surprise and he was unsure how to react. **He'd had little to do with** Miss HARROW **since he began working there, but this** little NEWS soufflé seemed, in her mind, to have set their relationship on a new footing.

"Yes, YES, THANK YOU. Thank you." He tried to respond graciously.

"You're getting a lovely girl there," said Miss HARROW, who CLEARLY ONLY SPOKE in clichés. She was wiping Lipstick off his cheek with her thumb.

"I know. I know." He couldn't concentrate because of the lipstick SMUDGE, and the confusion was making him SAY EVERY-THING TWICE.

"Did your friend find you?"

"What friend?"

"A chap came in looking for you earlier. Ooh, I don't know, about twenty minutes ago? I told him you'd be out on your ROUND, or else over at The Post Office canoodling with your new fiancée. He was back two minutes later so I guessed he hadn't found you."

"Who was he? Didn't he leave a name?"

"No. He said he'd catch up with you at HOME, so I gave him your address."

"What did he want?"

"Dunno. He didn't say."

"What did he look like?"

"Sort of fat. Round face. He had a funny accent. WELSH, I think."

"My home address? You gave him my home address?"

"Yes. Is that a problem?"
"No, that's fine," he said, feigning calm. "About twenty minutes ago, you say?"
She nodded.

How had HANDS known where to find him? He must have remembered ROY's name that day at the bed-sit when I told him about Roy getting the DRIVING job at WHITE'S. Find the BROTHER and you find the GIRL: that would have been his thinking. **And vice-versa.** To him, it was *a piece of cake with Bird's Dream Topping.*

The whole thing was like an ugly wave suddenly lurching up out of nothingness, rejecting everything gentle and kind and pitying, making chaos and nonsense of the carefully woven loves of the characters in our romantic drama. HANDS was on to him and he was playing games. But these games were NOT **'FUN FOR ALL THE FAMILY'** *as advertised on* **TELEVISION.** What did he want? Revenge? Was he the kind of man who might retaliate in a **VIOLENT** way? MARY would be at ***HOME*** and Roy was concerned that *all the cosy castles he had been building were about to come crashing down,* and that she might get HIT BY FALLING MASONRY.

"SO when are you going to name the day?" asked Miss HARROW

"Later," said Roy distractedly. "I've got to sort something out first."

AS he pulled up outside, Roy could see Hands standing on the DOORSTEP talking to Mary.

"What do you want?" Roy called, as he made his way up the garden path.

"What's it to you?" sneered HANDS over his shoulder. "Who the dickens are you anyway?" A light went on in the upstairs bedroom under his hat. "Oh, wait, I know you, don't I? Yes, yes. Now I see it." His eyes did a tour of inspection *as if he were* looking over a second-hand car. "You looked a little different last time I saw you. Your hair was longer. I think I prefer it long."

ROY joined ranks with Mary. United in defence of THE FAMILY HONOUR.

"Look," said *Roy*. "If your object is to punish me for the other day I can only say that I consider it in extremely poor taste."

"DOES that mean you're going to HIT me again?"

Then Mary piped up. "We never resort to violence to resolve any of our problems."

It was not her best choice of argument and HANDS was quick to pick up on it.

"I suppose he did this with a FEATHER DUSTER, then?" He lifted his hat to reveal the bandage on his head.

"YOU were in the wrong," said ROY. You quite definitely were the aggressor."

"You don't agree, perhaps, that aggression might be a matter of opinion, subject to evidence, factual evidence?"

HANDS pointed at Roy's BRYLCREEM bonnet. "I don't see any STITCHES in your head."

It was a waste of time trying to reason with a man like HANDS. Somebody tries to do it every so often and for all the good it does, one might as well recite the two-times table.

"Look, *HANDS*. What do you want?"

"What do I want? Eleven stitches, I had. And you never even sent me a GET WELL CARD. I thought you'd get a discount with your girlfriend working at THE Post Office."

Hands had strayed into unprotected territory.

"I'll deal with this, Mum," said Roy.

MARY folded her arms and widened her stance.

"No, I want to hear what Mr. *Hand*s has to say."

*Hand*s stepped up to state his claim. "What do I want? I'll tell you what I want. For a start, there's the small matter of my twelve quid you stole."

We all know that some people put pounds before persons and shillings before sentiment — and of course, HANDS was one of them.

"I didn't steal anything," said *Roy*.

"Well, where is it, then?"

"It's gone. I've spent IT."
" Roy, did you take his MONEY? " MARY wanted to know the facts and she was not prepared to ALLOW TWENTY-EIGHT DAYS FOR DELIVERY.
"No," said Roy. " THE MONEY was in his trouser pocket. I wore the TROUSERS HOME because of THE SKIRT. I didn't know IT was there until I got home."
"But you still kept it, didn't you?" sneered HANDS. "And that's stealing."
He sounded like A child.
"Is that true, Roy?" demanded Mary. "Why didn't you give it BACK? You shouldn't be SPENDING MONEY that doesn't belong to you."
Suddenly she was wearing Hands's HAT and standing on the other side of the fence.
"WHOSE SIDE ARE YOU ON?" he wanted to say, but he was reluctant to show DISSENT IN THE RANKS.
"I thought he was dead!" explained ROY.
"I very nearly was, thanks to you!" said Hands.
"That doesn't make it right, Roy," said Mary. "It's still stealing. How much was it? Twelve pounds?" Mary went to the HALL TABLE to fetch her purse.
She looked at Roy. "Have you any of it left?" she demanded, her palm thrust out. He had. Five pounds, and ten shillings in change. It was the money he was going to use for EVE's ENGAGEMENT

RING. He handed it over to MARY. Mary ADDED ANOTHER POUND from her purse. "There's SIX pounds ten. You'll get the rest next week," she said stiffly.

Hands took the money, counting the notes again. "SIX pounds? That's not enough."

"It's all you're going to get," said Roy. He was not prepared to agree to Mary's *INSTALMENT PLAN.* He didn't see why *they should postpone the wedding for the sake of* a licentious beast like HANDS.

"And what about my TROUSERS? And my keys. You owe me for those as well."

"I'll drop the keys round tomorrow," said *Roy*, "but I wouldn't bank on seeing THOSE TROUSERS again. They were disgusting; only fit for the bin."

"Well, you're going to have to PAY FOR a new pair then, aren't you?"

Roy didn't see it that way. The way he figured it, it was a fair exchange: one pair of trousers for one **skirt**. Except that it wasn't quite, of course, since Hands no longer had the **skirt**, but *either* he hadn't noticed it was missing FROM HIS WARDROBE **OR** he no longer cared about it. In the end, BOTH *GARMENTS* HAD BEEN ELIMINATED FROM THE TOURNAMENT, so at least in that sense it was equal.

"I want my money and I want it now. And give me my keys. **Where are they?"** Hands tried to shove his way past MARY INTO THE HOUSE.

ROY leapt forward and grabbed him by the scruff of the neck, to pull him back. "Get out!" he said tightly. "You've no right to come in here." Luckily, Mary must have recently polished the front step with

Cardinal POLISH

or JOHNSON'S WAX

which gives a full, rich, lustrous shine, but MAKES FOR A slippery surface on which to place a mat. The mat skidded from under him and he went down like a sack of King Edwards. *Roy* yanked him to his feet and pushed him off the STEP INTO THE FRONT GARDEN. His feet caught up in the bushes and he fell backwards, finding himself relegated to the second division.

Hands quickly got to his feet. Humiliated, he straightened his coat. "You can't push me around," he said.

"Shut up!" said Roy. "You're just a liberty-taker, but this time you're on the receiving end and it feels blooming terrible, doesn't it?"

Hands muttered some uncomplimentary phrases, but it seemed Roy had gained the upper hand. He was surprised how good he'd been at throwing his weight about. His chump-chop muscle tone, so hated on dressing-up days, had made light work of the troublemaker. It was much easier, he discovered, to win battles in a pair of trousers than in a SKIRT. How those Scotland the Brave soldiers managed to wield a Claymore at the battle of Culloden wearing a kilt instead of trousers was beyond him. You've only got to bend over a bit quickly and EVERYONE CAN SEE YOUR pants.

"Now stay away from here," advised Roy, tucking THE FRONT Door key back under the mat before Hands caught sight of it.

" Without wishing to be dogmatic on such an intensely personal matter, by way of general advice I would say that your best bet is to let the whole matter drop."

"Oh no. I want my money first," said Hands.

"Well, you're not getting it, so you can shove off!"

"Well, I'll just have to go to the police, then. I'll tell them it was you WHO knocked me out so you could steal my WAGES."

"You can't make that charge, it's ridiculous." said Roy. " You can't make it stick. Anyway, you won't go to THE POLICE. You've got just as much to lose as I have."

Mary said: "Just go AWAY!"

The Gestapo couldn't have phrased it much better than that.

"What about my HEAD?" whined Hands.

Mary showed little sympathy. " GET YOURSELF SOME ASPRO. THEY NOW COME IN TWO SIZES.

It's your own fault for doing what you did. DISGUSTING. I bet THE POLICE would like to hear about the kind of '*Ladies*' you're interested in."

Mary was getting into her stride. "It is ILLEGAL, you know." She was back on Roy's side now. She gave Hands a look of contempt. She knew his sort, or at least had heard about them. "He's probably been had up for it before," she said, mocking him. "He's probably already got a

POLICE RECORD."

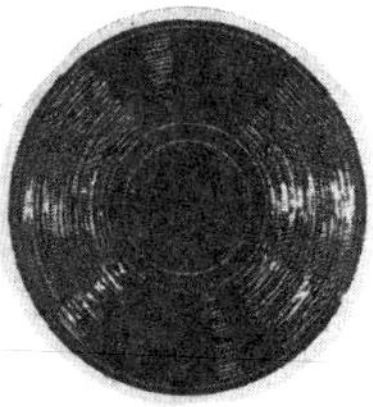

ROY saw Hands's expression change and his heart gave a little flutter. Aha! – he was cracking. Now he wasn't so cocky. Now there was a look of fear. So he *did* have a RECORD. In desperation HANDS retaliated with a few home truths in plain language used mostly by sailors.

"I'll be back," he ADDED. "You haven't heard the last of this."

"Yes we have," said *Roy* firmly. "This is the end of it."

But Hands had one more card up his sleeve. "Really?" he said, his voice thick with sarcasm. "It might not be the end of it as far as your girl-friend is concerned. Oh, sorry, I forgot. 'Fiancée'. They told me the happy news at the LAUNDRY."

NOW that he was back in the land of the living, Hands was a loose cannon, liable to blow a hole in THEIR WEDDING PLANS. Roy began to feel a throbbing in his temples. He longed to possess, for just half an hour,

4.0.6

the power his ancestors had used to solve just such impasses as this.

"You stay away from her." *Roy* clenched a helpless fist.

"Too late, chum. I've already seen her." Hands was laughing at him.

"What did you say to her?"

"Say? I didn't say anything. Didn't need to. *A picture paints a thousand words.*"

"What PICTURE?"

HANDS didn't answer, but let out a large theatrical laugh. It was quite accomplished, as if he had been practising it at home. He was being deliberately provocative. A minute ago he had been sprawled out on the garden path, but now he **had somehow clawed his way to the top of the charts.** If he **had been twenty years younger he might have** climbed up on the garden wall and sung "I'm the king of the castle, and you're the dirty rascal". On his way out of the gate, he wrenched **a big** MAUVE

FLOWER

from the rhododendron bush and threw it over his shoulder on to the path.

24

ONCE ROY had settled MARY down —— she'd been in quite a CHICKEN FRICASSEE about the whole matter —— he raced back to the Post Office to see what damage had been done. He would have DRIVEN and parked the VAN round the corner, but, fearful that Mr. White might happen to pass that way and see it, he decided to leave the van at home and walk there instead. He was in enough trouble already.

"Where's EVE?"

Auntie was busy with a customer.

"She's not here."

"Did a man come in looking for me?

"Yes, he had a photograph HE wanted to give you."

"What PHOTOGRAPH?"

"I don't know; I didn't see it. He gave it to EVE. Asked her to give it to you."

"Where's Eve now?"

"She went out about an hour ago."

"Out where?"

"She didn't say. She was very upset. What's going on? Have you two had a fight?"

IT turned out that HANDS really had had

FILM in the **CAMERA**

that day we had tea at the Excella café. The photograph lying on EVE's bed was in colour too, which would have been nice under normal circumstances. I was squinting against the sun a bit, but otherwise it wasn't a bad picture. *There* I was, posing demurely against the window of ***DOWLING'S PHOTOGRAPHIC STUDIOS***, looking the consummate professional in my specially chosen **INTERVIEW** ensemble. The blue SUITCASE lay open on the floor, spilling its contents on to the **RUG**, and the same items of clothing that I had been wearing that day were now lying out on the bed. **Eve** must have pieced everything together from the PHOTOGRAPH to re-create my INTERVIEW OUTFIT in its entirety. Everything (or nearly everything) was there: my red pixie jacket, the POWDER BLUE, STUD-FASTENED SKIRT BY ALEXON; black satin evening gloves and handbag; even the matching blouse with the **Peter Pan** collar, though this had suffered considerable wear and tear, the legacy of Roy's RAILWAY BRIDGE liason with the police. The ONLY thing missing was the **VIEWS OF LONDON SCARF**, but that was because I'd left it in the waiting room back at the laundry, WHICH IS WHY I wasn't wearing it in the PHOTOGRAPH. And the **red** *shoes* weren't there either, of course — shoes should never be on the BED; it's bad luck — but otherwise she'd put the whole thing together as if she'd been coordinating a day-wear outfit from the autumn collection of a major fashion house. The clothes were arranged on top of the bedcover in much the same way as MARY had taken to doing FOR ME AFTER *Roy* got the job at WHITE's. She'd even topped the whole thing off with *MY* wig like *Mary* used to do.

ON *the* DAY, the ensemble had been the perfect choice, peppy yet professional, with enough vim and verve to turn the gentlemanly head of someone *like* Mr. HANDS. BUT NOW, lying sprawled out on the bed, it lacked some of its original allure. *Every woman* knows nothing *is so ageing, so unattractive, as dull, lifeless* clothing.

ONCE Eve had all the clues in front of her, the family resemblance must have been all too apparent. Or else, HANDS had tipped her off when he called in to the post office earlier. Roy imagined him thrusting the *PHOTOGRAPH* under Eve's nose. "Look familiar does she, love? His sister? No. There *is* no sister. LOOK AGAIN. It's him."

ROY turned the key in the LOCK and lay down next to THE clothes while he tried to think what to do. There was barely enough room for them both on THE BED. Only the day before, it had been Eve lying there beside him, and now she was gone.

There was no point in going after her. Nothing he could say now would make things right again. Perhaps they'd never been right. How could he expect someone as pure and lovely as Eve to want to marry a man with such a

HUGE Wardrobe

full of GUILTY

indiscretions? Especially having seen them STREWN before her like that. She had made it clear that she had no time for immoral people, and Roy had told one GIANT ECONOMY SIZE lie after another, filling her whole heart like blown sand drifting everywhere, making a desert of what might once have been a fair and beautiful garden.

IT WAS HARD TO JUST

IT ALL, to take the needle off the record halfway through the overture. He had been attending to my needs ever since the accident. It had not been an easy time for him at the beginning. Where does a young man go to find out about WOMEN'S PREREQUISITES? **Clothes,** hair, make-up? Men are generally terribly misinformed in these matters. It seems unbelievable that they are almost completely ignorant of the simplest facts. He didn't know any **WOMEN** himself, and an education based on observing his mother seemed somehow wrong.

AS *Roy* GREW UP, and I grew with him, it became necessary for him to find me bigger clothes to fit my blossoming figure. And there was much to learn. Roy had a million questions, and, between them, his friends in the women's weeklies had the answers. Over the years, the **MAGAZINES** had become an invaluable source of advice **as he took me from** little girl through those difficult teenage years into the fulsome splendour of womanhood. Now, though, each one of them, he was sure, would be well and truly stumped by this particular quandary. There was no easy solution and the strain of it all was making his head spin.

ROY must have passed out for two or three minutes. **HE** awoke to find that he was lying with his head on my **wig.** The **wig** somehow seemed to be wet with HAIR DYE or something, which he noticed, **to his horror,** had left a heavily conspicuous stain on one of **EVE**'s *fluffy white pillows.*

HE looked around for some **Omo** or **Daz**, thinking he might soak the **PILLOW-CASE** in the sink. There was a block of ***Fairy soap*** and some **LUX** in one of the kitchen cupboards. He **looked to the back of the packet for guidance.** One cannot be expected to guess how new fabrics should be treated. Reliable manufacturers will usually give clear cleaning or washing instructions, and it goes without saying that these should be followed. He filled **the sink and scattered** **A GENEROUS HELPING** **of soap flakes into the tepid water,** ***swishing*** **them with his hand.** He really envied Mother her electric water heater—the water comes out in a full gush, absolutely piping hot. He **stripped the pillow of its case and submerged it in the soapy solution.** Looking up then, he caught his reflection in the mirror. "Oh, hello," he said, surprised. "I thought you were in Scotland."
But it was not himself **he was talking to, it was** me.

I MUST HAVE come down unexpectedly on the Flying Scotsman **BECAUSE** there I was, in all my glory, a little dishevelled from the journey, I'll admit, but otherwise looking like my old, WONDERFULLY familiar self. Slimmer and fitter than ever! Choosing the right outfit for travelling is vitally important and it is wise to go for fabrics that will not crease—drip-dry cotton poplin or easy-care Tricel, for example. For my big return journey, I wore my pencil-slim ALEXON powder blue skirt with the rayon taffeta lining over leg-flattering S-T-R-E-T-C-H nylons, my Peter Pan collar blouse and RED pixie jacket, accessorising the ensemble with shiny black evening gloves and bag. Darling sweet EVE had thoughtfully laid everything out on the bed ready for me. To go with it, I chose a modest navy easy walking shoe instead of the RED BOULEVARD courts, which for some reason I could not find, and to complete the outfit I wore a rayon satin scarf with views of London on it. The scarf wasn't with the other garments on the bed, but I found it amongst Eve's things in the wardrobe, and IT WAS JUST WHAT WAS NEEDED TO COMPLETE THE LOOK. I knew she wouldn't mind me wearing it.

RUMMAGING IN THE suitcase I was surprised to discover that ONE pair of LACE-LOOK PANTIE-BRIEFS was heavily soiled with something red and WAXy, as if someone had used them to red-brick polish the front doorstep. I couldn't imagine who would do such a thing. Casting them aside, I found my make-up and set about prettying myself in the

mirror.

The lighting here was **BETTER** (though rather less forgiving) than in our bathroom at Afferton Road and I was a little alarmed to notice some **UNWANTED HAIR GROWTH** on my upper lip. *Many women suffer from this embarrassing problem, but it can be easily eradicated with the help of Triste depilatory cream.* I made *a mental note to buy some from* the *chemist's* the **NEXT DAY**. It is pleasant to use, but more surprising is the hairless miracle you see before your eyes within minutes. In a jiffy, the **ugly**, unwanted hair is gone, and your skin is clean and hair-free. **In the meantime,** I took some cream foundation and applied a thick layer to the area in question, hoping to conceal the unsightly emergence.

A sense of calm came over me. I always feel more relaxed when I'm all dolled up and dressed in something nice. I looked around the room. It was ***delightful.*** IT had THAT pretty, FEMININE TOUCH THAT always seems to elude Mary. *I could be happy here. Very happy.* All my clothes hanging up in the wardrobe next to EVE's. Sitting together at the little table discussing MAKE-UP TIPS AND HAIR-

STYLES we'd seen in the magazines. Whole evenings where we'd try on each other's clothes and experiment with JEWELLERY AND ACCESSORIES. Roy wasn't going to be around. EVE had made it perfectly clear that she had no room in her life for dishonesty and deceit. It would be just EVE and me. Girls AT HOME together.

I might even find a job. Something to keep my mind occupied and to help with the household expenses. It was silly of me to apply for the DELIVERY DRIVING job. I was never going to get it. Driving is man's work, and anyway I'm far too feminine AND GLAMOROUS for that sort of thing. I should have been more ambitious, really gone for the career positions I've always wanted. An *Avon lady*; I'd be perfect for that. V*isiting housewives in their homes* and *discussing cosmetics and beauty products with them.* OR a judge on *Come Dancing*? *Yes, please.* EVERY Monday evening millions of women are taken away from their firesides in a brand-new Ford Anglia to a dream world of swirling dresses and gallant escorts at Victor Silvester's Dancing Club. And though few men will admit it, viewing figures show that they, too, enjoy this night out. I could even be one of the dancers, doing the paso doble in a fabulous sequined gown, though I'd probably have to have a few lessons first. Or what about a job as a sales assistant *at Marcia Modes*? I imagined myself surrounded by beautiful clothes and spending

MY day advising women which dress or hat would best suit them. A longish walk, or a shortish bus-ride, and I'd be back home IN OUR COSY LITTLE NEST to discuss the events of the day WITH EVE.

I was getting beyond myself. I knew the symptoms. I sometimes get overexcited like this when I allow my mind to wander off on its own, without a responsible adult to take charge. It was time to see reason and face the facts. *EVE* didn't want to spend her evenings with me; she wanted to SPEND them with *Roy*. From time to time, every marriage goes through THE ROCKY MOUNTAINS, but things invariably sort themselves out, especially if the couple are prepared to sit down and discuss the problem sensibly and maturely. Given time, **EVE** would understand about **THE DECEIT**. Roy *would explain everything clearly and concisely in plain English.* Forgive us our trespasses, and no harm done. With a fresh start, A NEW LEAF, and a brand new promise, that suitcase could be **packed up again** before you could say

FAROUK.

Au revoir, **Norma**; *bonjour*, *Roy*, FULL-TIME HUSBAND.

Someone tried the handle. Then there was a knock at the door. I assumed it was Auntie, **wondering what was going on.**

"Roy? Let me in." It was EVE.
I didn't quite know how to answer her. *She'd never met* me *before,* and in her present state I wasn't sure if this was the best time to
ORGANISE A 'GETTING-TO-KNOW-YOU' PARTY.
"He's not here."
"Roy. Let me in. I want to talk to you."
"I'm afraid he's not here," I reiterated in my **BEST Dora Bryan** sing-song voice.
"Roy? I can hear it's you. Open the door. Let's sit down and discuss this."

What was there to say? I'd already decided what had to be done. For their marriage to succeed, I had to be out of the picture once and for all. No hiding **at the back of the wardrobe,** no *turning up unexpectedly,* like *an uninvited guest.* The problems of young married couples, forced by the housing shortage to live with one or other set of parents, are well documented, so having a SISTER living there with them in the nuptial chamber was clearly a recipe for marital disharmony. I was not prepared to stand in the way of the sacred union. WHEN *two*'s COMPANY, THREE'S a crowd — everyone knows that. If I couldn't stay in Dundee, the least I could do was to go back ***HOME*** **TO** Afferton Road. That would be my WEDDING present to them. Realistically, I wonder how long things would have lasted with EVE and I sharing the same wardrobe. A young bride is only too happy to have her husband's

suits snuggling up against her frilly feminine things, but she does not want ANOTHER

WOMAN'S FROCKS

crushing her *delicates.*

It took a moment to sharpen my resolve, and in the meantime Eve's knocking and calling became more insistent. Her voice had a swelling concern, a panicky tone. I **knew the picture** she **had in the back of her mind:** ROY kneeling in front of the ***GAS OVEN*** with his head nestling on the plate of **HALF-EATEN** treacle pudding **from last night.**

It was ***time to go.***

Eve had said she wanted to sit down and talk things over. **That meant** she was ready to forgive, ready to try and understand. She was such a warm and caring person, and she loved *Roy* so very much, she **would do anything to save their marriage.** Given time, she would learn to accept things the way they are — or the way they had been.

EVE was growing impatient. I turned the key and opened the door. She had obviously expected to see Roy, not me, so it must have taken her by surprise. **The shock was physical.** She reeled back from me as if she had been pushed, groping at the banister to steady herself. She could not have looked more surprised if she had seen **HER MAJESTY QUEEN ELIZABETH EMERGING ON HORSEBACK.** Her mouth hung open **LIKE** a **TRAPDOOR.** Unable to close it, she raised her hand to cover the exposed hole.

"It's all right, my dear. I was just leaving." I manoeuvred the suitcase **OUT ON TO THE LANDING.** "You've been so marvellous to me—but you must understand I couldn't stay in your house in the circumstances. I just couldn't. It wouldn't be fair. I've no wish to ride rough-shod over the emotional needs of others."

"Roy?" **EVE** stared, unable to hide her alarm.

(page 423)

"Don't worry," I said, " Roy will be back shortly. And when he returns you can sit down and have a nice long chat."

Her eyes took in the whole outfit, registered the scarf but said nothing. Perhaps she thought I'd stolen it. It would have taken too long to explain that it was actually mine. She stepped back as I passed her on the stairs, flattening herself against the wall like a **shadow**. She did not know me, but there were tears in her eyes as they searched my face for the **FAMILY LIKENESS** behind the ***make-up***, looking for some resemblance to the man she loved.

I should have taken the back **DOOR**, to spare Auntie the same shock, but '**IN FOR A PENNY, IN FOR A POUND**' I went through the SHOP. She looked vaguely puzzled to see me stepping out from the back, but didn't get herself into a **froth** or CHANGE COLOUR.

Heaven only knows who she thought I was, and what I was doing there.

It was lovely to be out on the street in the cool evening air. The shops were just closing in the little **BLOCK** opposite the LAUNDRY, everyone keen to get home for their tea. THE RSPCA labrador with the coin slot in **the top of his head** was being taken in for the night. Next door, **D. ROSE, Family Butcher,** was cleaning down his window display with a damp cloth while a young lad in an **oversized** APRON dealt with the *awning* outside.

A LITTLE further along I saw Miss HARROW waiting at the bus stop. Her eyes fastened on me as soon as she spotted me, obviously recognising me from the day of my interview. The outfit would have acted as a reminder there. **My red PIXIE** jacket adds a unique note to my look, which tends to lodge itself in people's memory. Unforgettable, that's what I am. As I approached, her eyes almost started from her amiable cream bun face. I saw her mouth the words 'Oh my God', and then she said Roy's name. This was to herself, not to me, but I still got the message loud and clear: the **UNWANTED facial HAIR** was too noticeable. I would have to deal with it first thing in the morning. She didn't seem in the mood for a chat so I kept moving at a brisk pace.

"Good evening, Miss Harrow," I said as I passed. There came no reply. Miss HARROW looked as though

SHE MIGHT NEVER SPEAK AGAIN.

THE outside of your house is all that most people see of it. You want it to do you justice and to add a pleasant note to the street in which you live. With this in the forefront of his mind, *Somebody's* **husband** was in his garden mending the **GATE.**

A faithful companion, he allows no liberties with his home, defending it valiantly. He needs only half a pound of meat at midday, and hot milk and a biscuit at night. If he thinks it inadequate he will forage for more, so have no worry. This LITTLE MAN knows all the tricks.

IT'S quite a walk from CROSS *Street* to Afferton Road, especially for a woman who is carrying LUGGAGE, but now, somehow, the suit case was no longer the heavy burden it had previously been.

STEP BY STEP, THE SENSE OF CONTENTMENT IN ME GREW. LIKE all these OTHER WONDERFUL PEOPLE, *I was going* HOME. HOME. HOME to sitting by the fire with Mary, watching our favourite programmes on TV, with our Ovaltine and SUPPER SANDWICH. ***Ooh, yes***, and today was Friday, so it would be ***Take Your Pick*** with Michael Miles. You didn't nod your head then, did you? No. Bong!

PERHAPS Mary's friend, Betty, was still stricken with flu, so MARY would be spending the evening at home. ***There's a lot to be said for it.*** In towns and cities across the land, housewives would be attending to those little jobs that might have been neglected during the WEEK: sewing a button on a shirt, or ironing a cushion cover. Others might be hanging a pair of stockings over the bath to dry, or PRACTISING FIRST AID by the fireside, while the man of the house sits in his favourite chair contentedly puffing at a pipe full of Erinmore smoking mixture. Pleasantly fulfilled by a nourishing meal of **SARDINE FINGERS**, the more artistic husband might help to clear the table so he can start on a bit of fretwork. **OR** ***he*** might have a go at **PAINTING BY NUMBERS — a Cornish fishing scene** perhaps, **or a lady in a crinoline** *from days of yore* — remembering that with all such activities it is essential to lay newspaper down first to protect the furniture.

For most young ladies such as myself, Friday evenings are traditionally set aside for hair washing and setting, in preparation for Saturday's big dance date with a young man from the office. **IN** my **CASE**, the date would be with DIXON OF DOCK GREEN followed by a sing-song on the '**WAKEY WAKEY!**'

Billy Cotton Band Show,

but I'd still want to look my best. If you're wise like me, you will decide what you're going to wear and make sure that everything is clean and fresh-looking . . . you'll collect the accessories you need and lay them together so that you don't have to rummage round for gloves or a clean blouse at the last minute . . . you'll clear the day's rubbish from your handbag and see that your shoes are spick and span. You'll also go to bed well before

THE WEATHER MAN, so that you can brush your hair and cream your face without encroaching upon your beauty sleep.

CLICK-CLACKING her way along the pavement in a pair of oversized ladies' SHOES was a *little* ***junior madam.*** She couldn't have been more than six years old, yet she was already developing a healthy interest in WOMEN'S **fashion footwear** and was keen to try things out for herself.

THE SHOE *style* WAS ALL TOO FAMILIAR. The Boulevard fashion court is a classic design, and RED is the very latest colour this autumn — frivolous and gay enough for the modern miss, yet smart and practical enough for the stay-at-home housewife. No doubt, at a HOME nearby THE girl's mother would be frantically searching for those same **shoes** intending to give them a quick going-over with a soft brush so that she could be sure of being appropriately and attractively dressed when her husband came home from work. **Dirty, scuffed shoes** men can't abide. But well-polished ones, in good repair, will win her top marks every time.

At a HOUSE near the CORNER the curtains were already drawn but a light in the upstairs **BOX** ROOM suggested someone had the paste-pot and scissors out and was hard at work on their scrapbook. Home recreation can be such fun — rewarding, too.

I really must THINK about starting a SCRAPBOOK. My dressing room is piled high with all the WOMENS magazines I have saved over the years. Wouldn't it be wonderful to collect together my *favourite fashion features, all the hints and tips on glamour and etiquette that* I *have found especially* USEFUL, and keep them together in one big book? It would be my very own edited highlights, as if I had written the articles myself. And through them I could tell my own personal story. If published, it would be *a guide to womanhood, dealing with all the things that matter to the average woman.* ***Something to*** *get into and feel part of. Its scope* would be *wide and varied enough to cover every feminine interest, her beauty care,* her *wardrobe, her home arrangements. Tips on how to make even the most simple dress look elegant. A step-by-step guide to walking in heels* ***for the very young.*** *There'd be wonderful complete stories and* *serials, heart-to-heart features,* **and** *help and advice for those who need it. For the woman alone, the family woman—for 'everywoman'.* ***It was a marvellous idea.*** I'd get MARY to buy me a **SCRAPBOOK** tomorrow, so that I could start straight away. I used to think I had nothing — nothing, that is, except that strange female quality that no one has ever really been able to define. But now I realised I was a veritable fountain, ready to spout.

M A R Y would be so pleased to see me. If only she had known I was coming, there would have been one of my favourite meals on the table—roast chicken followed by peaches and cream— to welcome me home, but as far as SHE KNEW I was still in Scotland. *(Actually, she thought I was* buried six feet under in a field somewhere in the countryside. I've never been to Dundee, but I imagine it's much the same thing.) So, of course, I'd be the last person she'd be expecting to see.

I cut the corner through Mr. VALENTINE'S garden into **Afferton Road.** There, viewed through eyes bleary with emotion, was the old homestead, looking as warm and as welcoming as ever, the lights inside giving off their familiar ***TANGY ORANGE-FLAVOUR***ed glow. It could not have been more inviting if Mary had hung a flag out of the window saying 'Welcome home, *Norma*' and given the garden path a light dusting with icing sugar.

I stood on the pavement, soaking in the atmosphere like a cardigan in the bath, imagining the emotional scene as I walked through the door. THE RETURN OF THE PRODIGAL daughter. Mary, tearful and devoted, would break up a bar of Fruit and Nut in my honour, or she might even **slip** on her coat and pop down to the ***OFF LICENCE*** to fetch *a box of Milk Tray*. She sometimes did this for special occasions (Christmas and the like) and we'd sit with the **BOX** between us, taking it in turns to pick our favourites. Whoever ended up with the **MARZIPAN** would suck the **CHOCOLATE** off it and **SPIT** the soft centre out on to the fire. Yes, it was a good life, and I was glad to be returning to it, not only for myself, but also for *Roy* and **EVE** as well. Things had not worked out quite as I had expected in the outside world. I was better off at **HOME**.

IT WAS getting darker now, and the night sky was falling gently into place behind our **HOUSE**. Silhouetted against it, the heavy chimney sat astride the rooftop LIKE A squat old man in a black coat, smoking his entire cigarette ration in one go. THIS MEANT the fire

INSIDE

was aglow and the FRONT room would be warm and cosy.

True to her twilight REGIME, there was Mary at the window, drawing the curtains SO *that* none should witness any of the homely activities within. But why, I wondered, was Mary wearing a HAT indoors? THIS she never did. Mary's never really been one for hats. She'll sometimes wear a headscarf if there's a sharp wind, and she keeps a little plastic Rainmate in her handbag, which comes out if it starts to rain, but that's about it. It wasn't a hat that particularly suited her, either. It was brown, with a *little* RED FEATHER in it.

OF COURSE, as I got closer, I realised it wasn't Mary standing at the window; it was HANDS. And now, with a final snatch at THE FABRIC, the curtains were fully drawn and the last glimmer of light was shut out. IN a frantic panic I took to my heels and made for *the* HOUSE, *fearful of what he might be doing there.*

AS I STEPPED OUT on to the road, there was the sound of a horn, and I turned too late to see the VAN coming towards me at breakneck speed.

A GREAT soft blanket of calm swathed me, letting me know that I had made the right decision. The cool BLACK TARMAC felt good under my body. MY EARS bubbled with something warm and sticky, MUFFLING THE SOUNDS AROUND ME.

THE back of my head had come to rest in A POTHOLE IN THE SURFACE OF THE ROAD, which was extremely fortunate. An airless wind brought the musty smell of asphalt to my nostrils. There was something wet, and I was aware that my WIG must have been leaking HAIR DYE, but THE ROAD was dark, so I hoped that the stain would not show. In a few days, a WORKMAN would come along and fill up the hole with fresh, black tarmac, patting it flat with the back of his spade.

I WAS LYING IN A FIELD *with that floating-on-air feeling,* eyes closed to the bright sunlight. SomeONE came near to take the suitcase away; I felt the handle slide from my LAZY grasp.

For a second, I thought I saw Mrs. Price looking down at me, but when I looked again, she'd gone. It was the queerest sensation, as if I were slipping, slipping away under something dark and smooth, slipping easily, like a thin dinner plate sliding to the bottom of the washing-up bowl.

JUST AS the darkness was closing in around *me* a kind and reassuring hand touched my brow. Though I was too tired at that moment to open my eyes, I knew for certain that it was Mary and that she had come to ***MAKE EVERYTHING BETTER.*** It's what any girl wants when she finds herself in a predicament such as this.
"I didn't see it coming, *Mum*. It's my own fault."
"It's nobody's fault, love. It was an accident. No one is to blame."
She hadn't *called me* 'love' since I was little.

Cooking, cleaning, dressmaking, decorating. In a busy workaday world, every woman needs to yield to the forces of nature and take a few minutes to escape the daily grind. Proper rest is vital for nerve-restoring nourishment. With the right kind of sleep, she will awake refreshed, invigorated and fully prepared for the day ahead.

There would be a period of convalescence, of course—it's to be expected after an upset of this kind — but I knew that this time everything would be all right. And, of course, it would be the perfect opportunity to work on my SCRAPBOOK. *Mary*

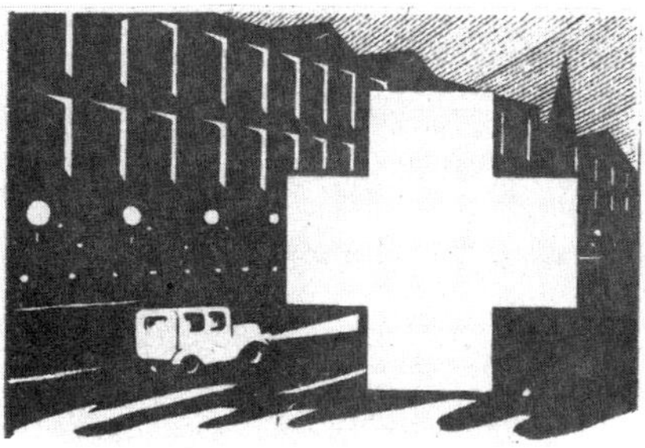

would take care of things.

NO

AMBULANCE

— *simply* carried **HOME**
in the arms of **forgiveness**
and laid to rest in my room.

BACK at the little flat above the *POST OFFICE*, **EVE** would be waiting eagerly for her beloved Roy, brimming over with compassion and forgiveness, and wearing her attention-winning negligee set, frivolous and bridal, with a wide, cherry-coloured ribbon to tie at the throat and float in long streamers to her toes.

ROY, fully recovered from the re-recent mishap, and having reached the final chapter of the **SCRAPBOOK** story, would come bounding up the stairs, two at a time, free from responsibility, free from worry, ready now to give himself to her completely.

He'd take her in his arms, with tenderness and worship shining in his very blue eyes. And the words his beloved would speak would **run up and down the keyboard** of his spine, like beautiful chords of music.

"Dear Roy, I love you. I never knew how much until I thought I had lost you. I could not have gone on living without you."

"Can you ever forgive me, dearest?"

"There's nothing to forgive. I understand."

"Do you, my darling?"

She would give a yearning sigh and wind her slender arms tightly about his neck, drawing his dark head down to hers.

" I understand so much . . . so much," she'd say.

AND then he was there — right there in the beautiful moment. **HE** pulled her closer to him, his cheek pressed against hers. She went on in the same soft, vibrant tones : " 'I'm so *happy*. I never dreamt there could be such happiness. That's another thing I've learnt. It's not ideals that make you happy, nor romantic dreams. Real happiness within the marriage union is achieved through tiny sacrifices and ***the soft*** ACQUIESCENCE ***of*** compromise."

THE warmth, compassion, and extraordinary love in her **deep-filled** eyes swept away any residual pain, and the memory of that COMFORTING look would stay with him for the rest of his life.

All at once, their lips were joined together in holy matrimony. **The** kiss was a poem, and the poem was bordered with dainty crayon flowers in pastel shades and headed by a blue angel, complete with hovering wings and bare celestial feet.

Lost in the depth of her sweet embrace, Roy felt himself slipping into a heavenly reverie where the future seemed to stretch before them like a rosy dream. In that moment of mutual surrender, bliss touched them with a sweet and gentle hand as they learned from one another the unselfishness of true love.

THE END

The making of the book

Woman's World has been collaged from individual fragments of text (around 40,000 in all) found in women's magazines published in the early 1960s. It has taken five years to produce.

In my previous book, *Diary of an Amateur Photographer*, I used scraps of found text from photography manuals and cheap pulp thrillers to tell parts of the story. I began to wonder if it would be possible to create a whole novel using nothing but words cut out of magazines...

I started writing this book in the usual way. When I had completed a rough draft, I then searched through hundreds of women's magazines, cutting out anything that seemed relevant to the scenes I'd written – sentences and phrases that, when joined together, could be rearranged to approximate what I wanted to say. These cuttings were then filed and from them I began to reassemble my story. Little by little, my original words were discarded and replaced by those I'd found. Once the transition was complete, I could start pasting up the pages as artwork.

The method was primitive: scissors and glue. Apart from a little tweaking here and there to enlarge very small type to a readable size, everything was done by hand. The artwork alone took two years.

Working from the library of collected material meant surrendering my writing to the element of chance and forced me to be inventive with the words that were available. The language of women's magazines from that time is distinctive and although I have taken their words out of context to tell an entirely new story, the voice of the original 1960s woman's world remains.

Graham Rawle,
London, 2005.

Acknowledgements

I would like to thank my brilliant editor, Clara Farmer. Thanks also to Toby Mundy and everyone at Atlantic Books for their passion and commitment.

I am grateful to Margaret Huber, Camilla Nicholls, and Carlo Gébler for story feedback, and to Elizabeth Bond and Mathew Clayton for advice. Thanks to my mum, Jessie, for access to her rich memory bank of all things 1962. For helping to scan the artwork and tweak the final commas and full-stops, I am obliged to James Dawe and Emily Constantinidi.

Special thanks to my lovely wife, M, for her unfailing support and invaluable gift for knowing how to mend faults and rectify weaknesses in other people's work.